Elliot Sweeney is a community psychiatric nurse from London. He was awarded the Fisher Scholarship to attend the Curtis Brown Creative novel writing course, and he's also been supported by Spread the Word through their London Writers Awards Scheme. The Literary Consultancy has showcased him as a Spotlight Author, and he's written for *Alfred Hitchcock's Mystery Magazine* and *Switchblade*, amongst others.

Praise for *The Next to Die:*

'A promising and hard-hitting debut'
Sunday Times

'*The Next to Die* is a remarkably assured debut. It oozes the sour tang of authenticity, mingling psychiatry and crime with the mean streets of London. Kasper has the hallmark of the classic crime fiction protagonist, brutal but with an underlying compassion.'
Andrew Taylor, bestselling author of *The American Boy* and *The Ashes of London*

'With pitch-perfect tone and quality to the writing, *The Next to Die* is a great new piece of London noir and a terrific debut.'
Amer Anwar, author of CWA Debut Dagger-wimming *Brothers in Blood*

'A superb, heart-thumping thriller that sucks you in with its breathless action, The Next To Die is, without doubt, my favourite read of the year.'
Carol Wyer, bestselling author of the DI Kate Young and Detective Natalie Ward series

'*The Next to Die* hooked me immediately with its formidable pace and fluid style. Kasper is a fascinatingly flawed but honourable character very much in the Chandler mould. A wonderfully assured debut, perfect for fans of dark and gritty thrillers.'
James Oswald, bestselling author of the Inspector McLean series

'An outstanding read. Gritty and compelling with a cast of richly-drawn characters, this is an exceptional book. A collection of menacing bad guys cause a whole heap of trouble for Kasper, the damaged hero, and that ending - wow!'
D. S. Butler, bestselling author of the
Detective Karen Hart series

'A terrific debut featuring the dark and dangerous Dylan Kasper, a protagonist who seems to have stepped straight out of a Chandler novel into the present day. Brilliant modern noir.'
Trevor Wood, author of *The Man on the Street*

'A stylish noir thriller with shades of Chandler that also manages to be bang up to date with big modern themes. This is a dark, gritty and compelling debut from a writer to watch.'
Lisa Gray, author of the Jessica Shaw series

'Gritty, gripping and heartbreaking. Elliot Sweeney hasn't just added a vital new dimension to the city thriller, he's also created a brilliantly broken and utterly unique hero in Dylan Kasper. *The Next to Die* is authentic, compelling, and I couldn't put it down.'
Tim Glister, author of the Richard Knox series

'An addictive and emotional roller-coaster of a read. Fast-paced yet beautifully written, with quirky characters that draw you in, this is a outstanding first novel.'
Lisa Ballantyne, bestselling author of *Once Upon a Lie*

'I read *The Next To Die* in one delicious feast, turning page after page, absorbing twist after twist to the very end. Elliot has a seemingly bottomless bag of characters you can't help caring about - and a masterful way with the telling adjective.'
Her Honour Wendy Joseph QC, author of *Unlawful Killings*

'Sweeney manages to break your heart, turn your stomach and lead you by the nose through a sickeningly believable tale of excruciating loss, unflinching violence and bloody redemption.'
Sam Tobin, author of the Manchester Underworld series

THE NEXT TO DIE

Elliot Sweeney

WILDFIRE

First published in 2023 by
WILDFIRE
an imprint of HEADLINE PUBLISHING GROUP

First published in paperback in 2023 by
WILDFIRE
an imprint of HEADLINE PUBLISHING GROUP

2

Cataloguing in Publication Data is available from the British Library

ISBN 978 1 4722 9262 9

Printed and bound in Great Britain by Clays Ltd, Elcograf S.p.A.

Headline's policy is to use papers that are natural, renewable and recyclable
products and made from wood grown in well-managed forests and other
controlled sources. The logging and manufacturing processes are expected
to conform to the environmental regulations of the country of origin.

HEADLINE PUBLISHING GROUP
an Hachette UK Company
Carmelite House
50 Victoria Embankment
London
EC4Y 0DZ

www.headline.co.uk
www.hachette.co.uk

For Clare

Prologue

It was a black day.

I'd had a good run of late, but got them sometimes. Still do.

After skulking round my loft room for most of the morning, I put on some joggers and cycled to Savages Boxing Club. I was bludgeoning the heavy bag, and had a decent sweat going on when my phone pinged – a voicemail from Tommy Berkowitz.

The thwacks of punches and clangs of barbells were deafening, so I stepped outside. My nape prickled when Tommy's voice came through.

He sounded calm. Too calm.

'Kasper, I've messed up. There's only one way to fix this. I found out what happened to you. Christ, I'm sorry it has to be this way. You'll know what to do, OK?'

I heard muffled movement, and the message ended.

Shit.

I tried calling back, but it went straight to voicemail. Three more attempts, and on the final one I said, 'Tommy. It's Kasper. Cut the crap and ring me when you get this.'

Twice more, I listened in case I'd missed anything. I hadn't though.

I paced in a circle, my thoughts rattling without focus.

Eventually, I called Diane. Skipping awkward hellos, I jumped to it.

'This kid I linked up with – Tommy Berkowitz. Ring a bell?'

'Oh yeah,' she said, 'the one with the nutty professor dad, right?'

'That's him. Tommy's involved in vice, Diane. Has a history of trying to jump off bridges, too. Now he's left me a garbled message, like he was about to do something really dumb. You hear anything?'

'No. And telling you would be a breach of confidentiality, Kas. You're not police anymore, remember?'

'I know.'

A pause. 'I'll make a few calls. If I get a hit, I'll bell you.'

'I owe you,' I said, and hung up.

I started walking, my sweat turning cold. Twelve long minutes later, my phone went:

'Me again,' Diane said, the sound of a car engine in the background. 'I'm calling from a police car, Kas, driving to a train station.'

My throat grew tight. 'Why?'

'Listen. It's a fatality.'

I leaned a palm on a wall, suddenly weak, struggling to focus. Five years evaporated, and I was back in the hallway of my old house, my ex-wife staring at me from the kitchen. I was in my dressing gown, a phone to my ear, listening to words from a police operator that made no sense.

'Kas, I—'

'What train station, Diane?'

'Upper Holloway.'

A hole blew open in my chest, and expanded with each kick of my heart.

'Kas!' she said. 'You there?'

'It's happening again,' I managed. 'Isn't it?'

Chapter 1

OK, let's rewind a few days.

My landlady, Dr Steiner, had gone to visit an on–off girlfriend in Brighton. Before she left, she gave me some guest passes for this fancy health club in Hoxton, a place called the Equilibrium. The passes were gifts from a former colleague of hers who hoped to quash her aversion to anything exercise-related. Bemused, a lit Dunhill in hand, she offered them to me as an alternative to the bin.

Within minutes, I clocked the kind of place the Equilibrium was – City boys, gym-bunnies and lechy men with money to burn made up the clientele. I stuck out like a hobo who'd stumbled into Fortnum & Mason. Mirrors were everywhere – in the reception, around the gym, even head-to-foot in the juice bar – allowing members a three-sixty view of themselves wherever they went.

To be fair, there was quite a bit to look at here, whatever your predilection, and it made a change from the macho brawn of Savages, my usual training spot. It was also here that a troubled young man called Tommy Berkowitz introduced himself to me.

I'd been to the club a couple of times by then, and this Friday afternoon had blitzed my shoulders and back with the free weights before hitting the treadmill. *London Calling* by The Clash filled my headphones, an alternative to the saccharine pop bleating from the speakers. Afterwards, I decided to head upstairs and treat myself to a coffee at the juice bar.

Coffee here came in handle-less bowls and cost four pounds a pop, more if you chose a fancy milk – there was soy, almond, cashew, coconut, oat or lactose-free. I played safe, ordered black, and took a bar stool.

The bar was oval-shaped, with high ceilings and glass walls partitioning the space from the rest of the club. Lean, well-groomed men and women sat at the tables, most sipping protein shakes and nibbling quinoa salads. Sweaty Betty and Lululemon were the labels of choice, and there were tattoos and tans aplenty.

There was a wide fitness studio to the right of the bar, where a dozen or so healthy young women were doing yoga things on mats. Most were scantily dressed, their faces lacquered with full make-up, which bemused me.

At the rear of the studio, I spotted the sole male in the class. He was young, late teens or early twenties, tall and doughy, with spotty cheeks, large eyes and honey-coloured hair that flopped over his brow in a comma when he changed position. His fingernails were painted red and he wore a silver hoop in his left nostril. A scuzzy grey tee, navy tracksuit bottoms and pink socks made up his workout gear. For completely different reasons, he seemed about as out of place here as I did.

I was on my second coffee when his gaze flitted up. He had rich, dark brown eyes, the colour of tree bark in spring, and they held mine fully. He grinned.

As the rest of the class moved seamlessly into a downward dog, he stood, grabbed a pair of All-Stars and a jumper from the floor, and pushed through the studio doors. I watched as he headed across the foyer, came into the bar and stopped a couple of feet from me, still grinning.

'Buy me a drink?' he said, in a light, husky voice.

'No, thanks,' I replied.

'Aw, come on.'

I tried looking past his shoulder at the class, but he was blocking my view.

'You're in my way,' I said.

He flicked his fringe, placed a hand on the bar and stayed as he was.

'You don't need to be shy. I saw you checking me out. It's OK. I won't tell.'

It occurred to me I was being propositioned.

By a boy.

Well, this was a first.

'Look, mate,' I said, 'I think you've got the wrong end of—'

'Tommy,' he said.

'Huh?'

'My name's Tommy. Not mate. What's yours?'

I told him.

'Kasper? So cute.'

'Thanks. I think.'

This, he took for an invitation to take the stool beside me.

'Tommy,' I said, 'I wasn't looking for company.'

'Give me a chance. You haven't even got to know me yet.' He was close enough for me to catch the cigarettes on his breath, and a sickly perfume that made me think of strawberries.

'Maybe I don't want to know you,' I said, a bit harder than needed.

As I spoke, two ripped, well-tanned young men entered the club and began peering at us from the foyer. I've trained with steroid-heads over the years, and recognised the signs.

'Why not talk to them?' I said, pointing at the pair. 'They might be more your cup of tea.'

Tommy looked over, the movement stretching his neck – briefly, a thin curve of indents became visible around the right clavicle, riding up to the side of his chin. The scarring could've been caused by anything, but I'd seen similar, and my gut told me it came from a ligature.

He turned back, scowling.

'Oh, please. They're meathead pill-poppers. Not my scene.'

'Silly me,' I said.

'Tell you what. How about I buy *you* a drink?'

That should've been my cue to leave with a curt, 'No, thanks.' I'd finished my coffee, was due to work a shift at McGovern's pub in a few hours, and had no reason to stay.

But truth be told, I had nothing much to do till then. Plus this kid was starting to intrigue me, just a little.

'All right,' I said. 'Coffee. Black.'

He gave the order, along with a request for something called a Detox Green Machine, to a sultry barman with a Hercule Poirot moustache. The Detox Green Machine involved a lot of spinach and kale shoved tightly into a blender.

As Tommy's drink got pulverised, he looked me up and down.

'You stick out here, don't you, Kasper?'

'Yes.'

'Are you rich?'

'No.'

'What do you do?'

'I used to be a policeman.'

'Wow.'

'Now I work in a pub.'

'Pulling pints?'

'Yup.'

He seemed disappointed. 'I thought you might be rich. There's some guys who come here, they've got so much money they can afford to dress down like you.'

I looked at my faded tracksuit and scuffed Gazelles. These days, this was dressing *up*.

'So, why are you here?' he said.

I shrugged. 'The club's letting in oddballs and misfits. It's part of this new community inclusion scheme. I'm from the latest batch. But don't tell anyone, will you?' I tapped a nostril conspiratorially.

He blinked several times. I stayed straight-faced.

Then his mouth widened and he let out a high-pitched laugh.

'Oh, you're funny,' he said, pushing my shoulder.

'Gee, thanks,' I said.

I probably should've asked Tommy the same question – why was *he* here? My guess, he was looking for something more than a six-pack. He was awkward-looking, with smoker's teeth and doleful eyes that hadn't quite had the sleep they needed. At least six feet tall, he carried his height uncomfortably, his head bowed, knees knocking, his legs bandying inwards like a pair of golf putters. He reminded me of an adolescent giraffe I'd seen on a David Attenborough documentary recently – long and clumsy, kind of vulnerable too.

'Ooh, our drinks,' he said, as the barman served us.

Tommy's was radioactive green and came in a tall glass with half a dozen straws sticking out. As he manoeuvred around the straws, I noticed more scars on his forearm, a thin ladder of smooth translucent marks the size of razor cuts. His fingertips were marred too, the cuticles picked and raw; there was a small tattoo on his right wrist showing a day, month and year – I couldn't see which – and beside it, a bruise the size of a thumbprint that looked recent.

'Yummy,' he said, gulping some and licking his lips.

'Cheers,' I said, and drank more coffee.

'I've seen you here before,' he said. 'You were pushing weights down in the gym. You're pretty buff.'

I thought about flashing a bit of bicep; instead, I had another sip.

'Don't get smug, though,' he added. 'You're no Tom Hardy. You could use a shave. You should cut your hair, too. You're at risk of looking like one of those mid-life hippies. No offence.'

'None taken.'

'Tell you what. Why don't you and me go for milkshakes after? I know this great place near my house. The chocolate malts are yum-tastic.'

'Yum-tastic?'

The grin returned.

'Nice of you to ask, Tommy, but I'm more of a pub man.' I finished my coffee. Three drinks down, I was aware of a mounting pressure in my bladder. 'Where's the gents?'

'That way.' He pointed to the rear corridor past the yoga studio. 'I'll wait for you here. Make sure you come back, Kasper.'

I took my phone and wallet off the bar and left my hoody on the back of my stool. As I pushed through the juice bar doors, I glanced back. Tommy was sipping his drink, his eyes fixed on me.

Patronising the Equilibrium toilets was an absolute pleasure. The hand soaps were Molton Brown and the whole enclosure was subsumed in musk and minimalism.

After attending to essentials, I splashed water on my cheeks and considered my reflection. Whatever my thoughts about my new-found acquaintance, he was right about one thing – I definitely needed a shave.

Tommy was still at the bar, but he wasn't alone. The stool where I'd left my hoody was now claimed by one of the lumps I'd seen earlier. His friend was standing in front of Tommy, pointing a finger in his face and saying something I assumed wasn't complimentary. As I wandered back in, I caught the tail end:

'...I told you, don't come here anymore. You're not welcome.' His voice was all east London, and he snarled as he spoke. 'Now piss off.'

'Ah, Jazz,' Tommy said, his eyes looking between the pair, seeking mine. 'I'm just having a drink with a friend.'

'Friend?'

I stopped behind them, my hands loose at my sides.

'This is Kasper,' Tommy said, gesturing at me. 'Say hi.'

The one called Jazz turned to me and tried to look hard. I just stared back.

'Kasper?' he said. 'That really your name?'

'I just came for my hoody,' I said.

'Your mum named you after Casper the ghost?'

'Yeah,' I said. 'Spooky, right?'

He looked me up, then down. 'He's not your usual office-type, Tommy. You're lowering your standards a bit.'

His mate on the stool began to laugh. I didn't say anything.

Up close, the side effects of steroid use were pretty unpleasant. They'd both tried hiding the greasy skin and pimples under their tats and sunbed tans, but hadn't done a great job.

Languidly, Jazz stretched across the bar and took a gulp of Tommy's drink.

'Nasty,' he said, and spat it back into the glass.

'That was his,' I said.

'Get lost, Kasper.' He returned the drink to the bar and dismissed me with a hand-flick.

'Jazz, please . . .' Tommy said.

'Maybe you should leave,' I said, a little stronger.

'Gonna make me?' He still wasn't looking my way.

The other one laughed again.

A beat started in my head, like the patter of faraway drums. This wasn't going to end well.

'Yeah,' I said. 'I am.'

That's when he made a move. He was fast, turning a pivot, grabbing my chest and pushing me, not hard enough to make me stumble, but with enough force to get a reaction.

Well, an *over*reaction. I blame the coffees.

I took his wrist and twisted it back, up, and around his body in a single move. He growled and tried to flex and pull away, so I rammed his arm behind him, hard enough to make it hurt.

That got a yell.

The chatter ceased around us. I shoved Jazz forwards and released him. His frame made him top-heavy, and he tripped over a stool and landed chest-first on the floor. Shaking, he sat on his knees, clutched his wrist and breathed hard through his teeth.

I looked at the other one. He was still on the stool, mouth agape.

'Stay seated,' I said, grabbing my hoody. 'Try anything and I'll put you down, too.'

He stayed seated.

Tommy's eyes were feral. I thought for a moment he was about to freak out. Instead, he reached for his green drink and inverted the sludge over Jazz's head.

'Ugh,' someone said from one of the tables.

'Mess with me,' Tommy said, 'and you mess with my friends. Understand?'

Jazz gave a whimper as the gloop ran down his brow.

'What the hell's going on?' A rather thin and surly receptionist from the front desk had appeared. In her most assertive voice, which wasn't very assertive, she repeated the question.

'Nothing,' I said. 'Just been showing my friend Jazz a dorsal extension. He overdid it and spilled a drink. Right, Jazz?'

Jazz remained on his knees, clutching his wrist. He'd be OK. He'd need a shower and might want to skip the bench presses for a day or two.

Without waiting for a response, I walked past the woman and made towards the exit, sensing eyes following me. I pushed through the turnstiles and stepped outside, welcoming the cool spring air that hit my face.

My heart was beating fast. I'd not had a scuffle like that in a while, and the adrenalin was pumping.

Keen to leave, I headed to the rear car park, where I'd chained my bike to the railing. I was halfway gone when I heard my name called out.

I looked back at the Equilibrium entrance. Tommy was standing there.

'Kasper, wait!' he said, and cantered over, stopping a few feet from me with his hands locked together in front of him. 'Look, I'm sorry about what happened there. We were having a nice time until that idiot rocked up and spoiled things.'

'Don't sweat it,' I said. 'Too bad you lost your drink.' I turned, about to push off.

'Hold on.' He came round, gripping my handlebars and depressing the brakes so I couldn't move. 'Don't go just yet.'

'What is it, Tommy?' I was a little exasperated now.

He flicked back his fringe. 'Let's meet for that milkshake.'

'Why?'

'I just want to thank you for helping me.'

'You're thanking me now.'

'All right. I want to *show* you I'm grateful.'

'You know I'm straight, right?'

'Course.' He nodded. Again, I caught sight of the scars around his neck. It tightened something in me.

'I don't get this,' I said. 'What's your interest?'

A shrug. 'I like you, I guess.'

'But you don't know anything about me.'

'Not true. I know you're a bit nutty. Like me.'

No arguments there.

'So will you?'

'Maybe.'

'Maybe yes or no?'

'Just maybe.'

'Mystery man. OK, let me add you on WhatsApp. I'll message you later and you can decide.'

'Don't do WhatsApp.'

'Facebook?'

'Nope.'

'God, you're old-fashioned. I'll text you then. Give me your mobile.'

It'd been a long time since anyone asked for my number.

He punched my digits into an iPhone sheathed in pink bunny ears.

'Well, OK, Kasper,' he said, looking up, grinning that grin. 'See you soon, hopefully.'

I pedalled off.

Chapter 2

A little before eight the following morning, I was roused by my phone vibrating on the bedside table.

'Mr Kasperick?' A man's voice.

'Yeah?'

'This is Professor Saul Berkowitz.' He said the name as if he were waiting for me to start clapping.

'Have we met?'

'No.'

'Then what can I do for you?'

'I'm Tommy's father.' A pause. 'He's the young man you encountered yesterday. Surely you remember. I overheard him talking about the altercation. I want to meet with you to discuss the matter. Immediately.'

I squinted against the sunlight coming through the blinds of my loft, and sat up in bed. My head was a little fuzzy from the drinks I'd put away during and after last night's shift at McGovern's.

'I'm kind of tied up today,' I said.

'It's the weekend.'

'I was thinking of having a shave on your son's advice.'

I heard a sniff of disdain. 'I think what I have in mind will interest you more.'

'How so?'

'You used to be a policeman. Correct? I might have a job for someone with your set of skills.'

'This job involve money?'

'It does.'

'Why not tell me over the phone?'

He paused. 'I'd prefer to talk in person. I'm at my office. We could meet here any time you like.'

'Does Tommy know you've called me?'

'How else do you think I got your number?'

I waited a few seconds, weighing it up. I had about thirty quid until I got my next pub wages, so a bit of cash would help. Today was also my day off, and as usual, I had nowhere to be.

'How much were you thinking of paying me?' I said.

'Enough to make it worth your time.' He suggested a number.

I asked for more, not expecting it.

He agreed.

'Fine,' I said, swinging my legs out of bed, avoiding the clothes and pizza boxes strewn on the floor. 'Let's have your address.'

The postcode he gave took me to a black and white four-storey townhouse in the academic hub of Bloomsbury, adjacent to the university union and a vast Waterstones bookshop. Students were milling about in twos and threes, clutching textbooks and coffee cups, most managing to look studious and hip at the same time.

Inside, a sign told me I'd entered the Department of Psychosocial, Psychosexual and Pacifistic Studies. A shaven-headed, gender-ambiguous receptionist gave me my guest pass, followed by a querulous stare when I asked them whether the department's hefty name ever got abbreviated to 'Pee-Pee-Pee'.

Saul Berkowitz's office was on the top floor. It was a square room, surprisingly big, with grey walls and a high ceiling. A looming bookcase stood to the left, perpendicular to a sash window, which was partially curtained. Tiananmen Square, MLK and other peace and love posters dominated what little wall space remained. Central to the room was a large mahogany desk atop a red Persian rug.

After inviting me in, my host sat behind this desk and began tapping a marble paperweight, scrutinising me. I took the chair opposite.

'I appreciate you giving up your time, Mr Kasperick,' he said, in a deep, mellifluous voice.

'You're welcome.'

'Tommy did say you carry an imposing presence. "Big, tough and butch" were his exact words. I see what he means.'

'Thank you,' I said. 'As a sideline I work as a lion-tamer.'

I saw the flicker of a smile. 'And may I say what an interesting surname you have.'

'You may.'

'Polish, I assume?'

'Yes.'

'Where from?'

'Warsaw. When the Nazis started rounding up Catholics as well as Jews, my grandparents took flight with my dad and uncles and ended up in north London.'

'Well then, we have something in common. My family

were Austrian Jews. Granddad had the foresight to flee before the persecution began.'

As he spoke, his finger began drawing invisible circles on the paperweight. I looked at it. Engraved in the marble were the words: *Live simply, so others can simply live.*

Noticing my interest, he smiled more broadly. 'A Quaker friend gave this to me. The message speaks to my values.'

'Praise the Lord,' I said.

The smile thinned. 'You want to know why you're here?'

I nodded.

'I'm sure you've guessed it concerns my son?'

I nodded again.

'Tommy seems to have taken a shine to you. To be frank, he's enamoured. Yesterday afternoon I heard him rabbiting on to his sister about this man who came to his rescue. Straight away, I knew we had to meet. You understand why, don't you, Mr Kasperick?'

I leaned back, my chair creaking arthritically, and considered Professor Saul Berkowitz more fully. His name and voice had rung a bell when he'd called, but it was only now that I realised why. A year or so back, he'd hosted a hippy-dippy debating programme on Radio 4 that my landlady used to mock. From memory, it had him jousting with militant fundamentalists, right-wingers and other undesirables on the merits of non-violence and spiritual harmony. I don't recall a second series.

Like his son, the professor was tall, my height, but unlike me, he carried a lean and lanky frame, with wrists like pipes jutting from his tartan shirtsleeves. Grey hair was scrunched like sink scourers above his ears; his nose was dotted with liver spots, and his clear blue eyes sparkled with intelligence from behind his horn-rimmed glasses.

I figured he was one of those socks-and-sandals intellectuals you see at CND and climate change marches. There'd be a decent supply of herbal teas somewhere in the office, but I thought it best not to enquire.

Instead, I said, 'It's Kasper. Not Kasperick.'

'I beg your pardon?'

'My name. The only person who went by Kasperick was my dad. He's dead.'

He opened his mouth, closed it, and nodded.

'Right then. Kasper it is. Please, call me Saul.'

'OK, Saul, we're acquainted. Let's cut to it. Tommy told you I clumped someone, and you want to pay me to back off. Right?'

'On the contrary.'

I tilted my head. 'Huh?'

He looked over at the bookcase, removed his glasses, gave them a clean with a hanky and returned them to his face.

'You've completely misunderstood the purpose of this visit. I want your *help*.'

Now I was interested. 'Go on.'

'I'm scared I'm losing Tommy. And I don't know what to do about it.' He looked at me squarely, his eyes suddenly glazed with emotion.

I folded my arms across my chest.

After a moment, he said, 'Tommy's nineteen. This all began around the time his mother Judith became ill. She passed two years back. Liver cancer. There we are in San Jose when Tommy was one.'

He swivelled a photo next to the paperweight. It looked like a professional family shot, and showed a younger, hairier Saul sitting beside a pale, sharp-featured little girl of about six and a slim woman with rich brown eyes. A puffy baby was in the woman's lap.

'My son has always been sensitive. But since Judith's death, he's changed.'

'How?'

'First, he dropped out of drama school, and started moping about. Then he began acting out. Screaming. Crying. Scratching and burning his arms with cigarettes. All totally out of character. I put it down to grief, or discomfort around his sexuality. Not having his mum to confide in was a great loss. Tommy and Judith were very close, you see.' A distant look came over him. He blinked several times and went on. 'Harriet is his older sister.' He pointed at the girl in the photo. 'Tommy dotes on her. But she's busy with work. And I have my commitments here. As a result, things have become so much worse.'

'Worse?'

He nodded. 'Yes. He's started carrying out self-destructive . . . risk-taking behaviours. You know what I'm getting at, don't you?'

I shook my head.

Something seemed to be clogging Saul's throat.

'Tell it like it is,' I said.

'Someone is coercing my son to do . . . *things* against his will. And it needs to stop.' The lilt to his voice had gone. He almost spat the words.

'OK,' I said. 'I'm guessing you don't know who's doing the coercing?'

'Correct. He won't tell me. That's the point of this conversation.'

My memory returned to the kid I'd met at the Equilibrium – his paper-thin confidence when he approached me, the seductive look he wore; I remembered the bruise on his wrist, those scars mapping his neck and arms, and the crazed look to his eyes when he tipped his drink over the meathead I'd shoved.

Yeah, I could believe something was amiss.

'You've met Tommy,' Saul said, seeming to read me. 'You've seen how he acts. What do your instincts tell you?'

I shrugged. 'He's wilful. A little over-friendly. But that could be caused by anything. Have you tried talking?'

'Yes.'

'And what does he say?'

'He tells me he's perfectly fine. He's an adult, and knows what he's doing.'

I gave a *so-what-can-you-do?* shrug.

'But that doesn't mean a thing.' He took a deep breath. 'At first, I thought he'd met someone, what with the late nights, posh perfumes, flashy clothes and expensive gym membership. He said he was going out, mingling. I was happy for him. Until the behaviour changed further. He stopped being my shy Tommy. Do you understand?'

I indicated that I did. 'But that's not proof of anything.'

'There've been several incidents,' Saul said, sharply. 'A few months back, he got beaten up outside a club. He insisted he didn't want the police involved and that it was just a random mugging. But I know my son. He was lying.'

'OK,' I said. 'What else?'

'In February, he got sectioned in a psychiatric hospital. Police found him over London Bridge with a noose around his neck, trying to jump. They had to restrain him. He's still got a rope scar.'

'I've seen it.'

'Well, it gets worse. Six weeks back, another attempt: this time an overdose in a public toilet. I thought we'd reached rock bottom. They gave him antidepressants. Things quietened. But then the week before last, the police found him again, bawling in a Shoreditch backstreet. Earlier that night, he'd been seen approaching men and propositioning them, like some kind of . . . of rent boy. He had a razor in his pocket, and fresh scars on his arms.'

Reflexively, I rubbed my own forearm.

Saul lifted his glasses to wipe his wet eyes.

This was getting uncomfortable. I'd known the man all of ten minutes; already, he'd pulled out some of his family's dirty laundry.

'How about this Jazz?' I said. 'You think he knows something?'

'I don't know,' Saul said wearily. 'That's why I wanted to talk to you. You see, I need a man who can find these things out. This world is alien to me.' He leaned across the desk and stared. 'What do you think?'

For the second time in as many days, it dawned on me that I was being propositioned by a Berkowitz.

'I think you should get Tommy a decent therapist,' I said. 'My landlady used to be one. If you like, I could ask her advice?'

He shook his head. 'Oh, please. I've emptied my bank account paying thousands for London's top quacks to contradict each other and then turn their backs. Borderline Personality Disorder is the label they tag on Tommy. Frankly, the whole thing is quite useless.'

'I see,' I said, not really getting it. 'So what did you want me to do?'

He sighed again, and went back to rubbing the paperweight. I wondered if a genie might pop out.

'First, I'd like you to meet Tommy again. He's dying to see you.'

'And then what?'

'Try to earn his trust.'

'Why?'

'So you can protect him, of course. Like you did yesterday.'

'Protect him?' I puffed air from my cheeks. 'Look, Saul, I'm no bodyguard. Besides, you don't know anything about me.'

'That's not strictly true.'

'Really?'

He smiled. 'Tommy told me you were a policeman. I have contacts in the Met. I made a few calls. It wasn't hard. Eventually, I spoke with a Detective Sergeant Diane McAteer. I believe you two were acquainted?'

I stifled a laugh. 'You could say that. What did Diane have to say?'

'She told me that before your resignation from the force a few years back, you had quite the aptitude for helping people out of ruts. She said in certain instances, you were known to go beyond the call of duty.'

'Did she?'

'Forgive my probing.'

'You're forgiven. But I still think you have the wrong man sitting in your office for this kind of gig.'

'Perhaps I do. But even if you're not a bodyguard *per se*, you certainly look the part. Hopefully that will be enough. You know how to handle yourself, judging by yesterday's display.'

I could see I wasn't going to deter him. 'Yeah,' I said. 'I do.'

'And you work in a public house?'

'Uh-huh. At my local.'

24

'No plans to return to the police then?'

'None.'

'Why?'

'I don't like being told what to do anymore.'

'I can imagine.' He smiled. 'You're a straight-talker. It's refreshing.'

'Thank you.'

'I get the sense you're a bachelor?'

'Divorced.'

'Children?'

A thud landed in my chest. I waited for it to pass.

'No,' I said. 'No kids.'

He nodded, looking satisfied. 'The question is, will you agree to my request and see Tommy again?'

Already, something sounded off-key about this whole situation. Maybe if I'd asked a few more questions and tried probing a little deeper, I could've saved myself a world of pain.

But I didn't.

'All right,' I said. 'I'll meet your son. We'll go for milkshakes and have another chat if that's what you want. But don't expect me to turn Sigmund Freud on him, Saul.'

'I'd find that hard to imagine.' He smiled again. 'Thank you, Kasper,' he said. 'Now, let's sort out your fee.' He straightened his glasses, reached into his drawer and retrieved a chequebook and fountain pen. 'Accept this as a retainer. I believe they call it that in the films.' In old-fashioned cursive handwriting, he wrote out a cheque and slid it across to me.

'All right,' I said, checking the details before folding it into my wallet. 'But let's be clear, I'm not your employee. I reserve the right to pull out at any point if things go weird.'

'Understood.'

I got to my feet. There didn't seem much else to say. We shook hands over the desk. His grip was strong.

I walked to the door and reached for the handle, then paused. A thought had crossed my mind. I looked over my shoulder and said, 'I still don't get it. Why me? Why not hire a proper bodyguard to do all this?'

Saul hesitated. 'It was something else Detective McAteer told me that clinched it.'

'What was that?'

He leaned back in his chair and looked at me intently, rubbing the paperweight again.

'She said you're a *decent* man.'

I swung by a pawnshop to cash Saul's cheque, and then headed home.

As soon as I unlocked the front door, I was greeted by Marmite, my landlady's jet-black tom. Dr Steiner wasn't due back from her trip to the south coast for a few days, and I had her vast Georgian semi to myself. She'd owned the house for thirty-two years, and for the last five of those, I'd rented its loft space for a nominal fee.

After capping my first Magners, I spooned out some food for Marmite and we spent a little time chatting in the kitchen before I made an omelette with mushrooms and cheese.

I tried watching the news as I ate but it was all too depressing, so I switched to a nature documentary about the snow leopards of central Asia. Marmite studied me from the windowsill, and when I'd finished my tea, he came and licked the plate. As the end credits rolled, I poured my first inch of Bushmills to accompany the cider, sat beside him on the couch and considered my newly acquired job.

I suspected Jazz could be eliminated from my enquiries as Tommy's pimp. The guy was brawny, but there wasn't much backing it up.

That meant someone else was responsible, if it was happening at all.

Maybe Tommy was just confused and acting out for a bit of attention?

If so, Saul should start treating him like the young man he was rather than hovering around with kid gloves and employing someone like me to snoop.

I gave this idea some thought, and binned it.

There was more going on here. Already, I could sense it.

Around eight, my phone vibrated – a text from Tommy:

Hey Mr K! Sorry if Dad grilled you. He means well. Wanna meet me for that shake? Mwah.

He signed off with one of those smiley-face things.

I typed back:

OK

It was late by the time I went to bed. Sleep rarely comes easily, and the alcohol I drink only dampens the voices I hear when the past has the inclination to return, but never drowns them.

I played one of my dad's old Bob Dylan LPs and lay down on the mattress with my eyes open in the dark. Before long, the music ended; I let my eyelids close, and listened to the hiss and crackle of the stylus on the turntable, and the creaks and sighs of the empty house.

Chapter 3

Tommy was right about one thing – the chocolate malts *were* yum-tastic.

We exchanged a few more texts and I met him in person again on Sunday afternoon at a mock-American diner called Sally-Anne's Milkshake Shack. The place was in a particularly boujee part of Clerkenwell plotted a few minutes from his house.

He rocked up wearing a lavender jersey, oversized and frayed at the cuffs, matched with black skinny jeans and a different pair of All-Stars. His acne seemed worse, with a cluster of new pimples sprouting around his chin, and his eyes were hidden behind his floppy fringe.

Three-thirty was perhaps not the best time to come to Sally-Anne's – the place was choc-a-bloc with teenagers and hipsters, most staring at me as if I were a wrestler who'd stumbled into a nursery. 'Walk the Line' by Johnny Cash strummed from the speakers, though, so I could just about cope.

At the bar, a woman with a tea-cosy thing on her head brought us our milkshakes. I reached for my wallet, but Tommy beat me to it.

'Put your money away, Kasper,' he said, pulling out a gnarled cardholder. 'This is on me, to say thanks.' That distinctive strawberry scent wafted from him.

'Fair enough.' I took a stool.

He put a credit card on the waitress's reader. It declined payment.

'Dammit,' he said, trying again, getting the same result.

He patted his pockets and looked up at me, blushing a little. 'Have you got any cash? I must've left my other cards at home.'

He was lying, I could tell, but I didn't want to press it.

'Don't sweat.' I gave the woman a tenner. 'Your father's paying me to be here, remember.'

'How much has he given you?'

I told him.

'Wow. For that amount, I bet he's asked you to be my personal bodyguard or something, right?'

'More or less.'

He started laughing, the same laugh as before, high and loud. A few heads turned.

'I was telling my sister Harry how you sorted Jazz out. Dad overheard. Straight away, he was like, "Tommy! I demand you give me this Kasper man's number!" What a drama queen.'

I was impressed – it was a pretty good impersonation of Saul.

'He's an interesting man,' I said.

'Funny. He said the same thing about you.'

I took a gulp of shake and smacked my lips. 'Boom,' I said.

'Told you they were good.' He took the spoon from his glass and licked the chocolate ice cream. 'Just so you know, Jazz is fuming. He reckons he's going to beat you up next time he sees you at the gym. Be warned.'

'Yikes.'

'You're not bothered, are you?'

'No.'

'Are you an SAS man or something?'

'I box. Jazz wasn't to know.'

Tommy nodded, and flicked his fringe. 'Most men are wimps. You're different.'

I took another hit of shake. 'How about you? What's your story?'

'Didn't Dad tell you? Going crazy's my big talent.'

'Come on. Name something you're good at?'

'Aw, Kasper, I hate this game. When I was sectioned at that mental hospital, they made us sit in a circle each morning and say three positives about ourselves. I was useless at it.'

'I only want one thing.'

He pulled a face. 'OK, OK. Horses. Before Mum got ill, we used to go riding. Oh, and acting. I went to drama school for a bit, till she died. I was all right at that too, I guess.'

'That's two things,' I said. 'Show-off.'

He began to laugh again.

Outside, traffic was passing. At random, I focused on a pair of double-decker bus drivers leaning out their windows, exchanging words before heading their separate ways. I could sense Tommy's eyes on me.

'You've got a sadness in you,' he eventually said.

'How can you tell?'

'I just can. Takes one to know one.'

I looked over. 'If you say so.'

'You're also weird, Kasper. Anyone ever tell you that?'

'Yes.'

He grinned. 'Don't take that the wrong way. I'm weird too. It's just, some people are weirder than others. You get it?'

'I get it.'

'Knew you would.'

Not a lot more was said. We drank the rest of our shakes and left the diner.

Outside, Tommy said he'd had a 'sick' time, and I told him likewise, not entirely sure what that meant. And I expected that to be that.

It wasn't.

The following morning, another text pinged through from Tommy, asking to see me. This time, I suggested a stroll, somewhere a little less enclosed than Sally-Anne's, and he suggested the canal near his house. We met mid-afternoon.

He seemed tired that day, with bags beneath his brown eyes and a general skittishness to his demeanour. He was wearing a billowy jersey that said *Eat Me!* across its front. Through the strawberry perfume, he smelled strongly of cigarette smoke, and beneath that, sweat.

At first the conversation was stilted, and I found it hard to think of things to say. What do young adults talk about? I had no idea, and standing there, twenty-odd years Tommy's senior, I felt clunky, awkward, acutely aware of my *un*-wokeness.

Surprisingly, though, Tommy didn't seem to mind. Before long, he was steering us into a quieter residential road of looming Edwardian houses. He stayed a few feet ahead, smoking Marlboro Golds, looking back over his shoulder every now and then, as if to make sure I was paying attention.

As we crossed a road, his phone started ringing. He pulled the bunny-eared mobile from his back pocket, looked at the screen, gave a whoop, and answered.

'Harry!'

Straight away, he was talking animatedly. 'I'm with him now, sis.' He looked over his shoulder again. 'That's right.

Kasper's his name. The guy from the gym I told you about. Dad's asked him to take care of me.' More laughing, and he tipped his head back and said, 'See you tonight. We'll talk more about it then. Love you.'

He hung up and looked at me. 'That was my big sister, Harriet. Hey, maybe the three of us can meet up?'

'Maybe.'

'What if—' he said, but his phone went again.

This time he looked at the screen and frowned. He hit answer, held the device to his mouth.

'Fuck off, DT,' he said and hit the cancel button, shaking his head.

'Friend?' I said.

'As if.'

'Secret admirer?'

He sighed. 'Just some loser who needs to get over me.'

'DT's an odd name?'

'Don't spoil our energy, Kasper.' Tommy sped on ahead, sparking another cigarette as he walked.

The Berkowitz family lived in an end-of-terrace property. The kind of place an estate agent would say was 'in need of modernisation'.

The exterior walls were cracked plaster and pebble-dash, all of it marred brown and yellow by decades of weathering; the sills were peeling, the shingled roof disjointed, and the porch tiles and paving uneven; moss had overgrown much of the lower exterior, and the guttering downpipe hung precariously from the wall like a loose bone.

Tommy strolled to the front door and removed a set of keys from his pocket.

I lingered by the gate, ready to make my excuses. I'd done

as asked – meeting Tommy on two occasions, building some rapport, albeit fragile, and making sure he didn't jump off any more bridges while in my company. True, I still hadn't a clue what was going on in his life, but a start had been made.

So when I said, 'I think I'll go now,' I didn't anticipate the sorrowful look he gave me in response.

'Come in, Kasper. *Please*. Harry and Dad are out all day. I'm always alone. There's a beer in the cupboard I can give you.'

I could see I wasn't getting out of this one.

'Ten minutes,' I said, and his face lit up.

In we went, and straight away Tommy disappeared towards a galley kitchen at the head of the hallway. I heard him humming, cupboards opening and closing, and had a mooch around to pass the time.

There seemed to be an organised clutter to the home. The hall was festooned with papers on every surface – bank statements, handwritten notes, utility bills, books and folders, envelopes and loose papers, all stacked on nearly every flat space, with others piled on the faded parquet floor. A grandfather clock stood by the staircase, ticking; to its right hung a large family photo showing Saul, his late wife Judith, a dark-eyed, sharp-featured girl I assumed was Harriet, aged about ten, and Tommy as a toddler.

'Happy families,' I heard behind me, and turned.

Tommy was looking at the photo and holding a can of Red Stripe. 'Here's your drink.'

'Cheers,' I said, and took it. 'You not having one?'

'I don't drink, Kasper,' he said, as if I'd asked a weird question. 'Come in, come in. Let's relax in the lounge.'

I followed him into an L-shaped room that overlooked a garden, the floor creaking under my boots. There were two scuffed velvet sofas, a large Persian rug like the one in Saul's office, and, further back, a chipped oak dining table and chairs.

Ceramic objects adorned the mantelpiece, along with framed family photos, more of which were fastened to the walls. Although everything looked ornate in that *Antiques Roadshow* kind of way, the place had a dated, shabby feel — the ceiling was clouded with damp, and wallpaper curled around the crevices, like dry skin. There was a lingering smell, a bit like mothballs, and dust motes distilled the remnant sunlight of the afternoon.

Tommy slumped on one of the sofas and swung his legs over its arm. I sat on the other and cracked the can. Lager frothed up, spilling over the rim and on to my shirt. I took a big swig to avoid spillage, then placed the can on the floor and rolled up my sleeve where it had got soggy.

Tommy was giggling. 'Oops,' he said.

'Yeah, oops,' I said, but with a grin. 'You've got a nice pad.'

'Don't lie. The whole house is knackered.'

'How come your dad doesn't spruce the place up?'

'Because of Mum. She passed away here, up in the attic room. Dad says the house is all he has left of her. He's so sentimental. He really should sell it. It must be worth a fortune.'

'Your sister lives here too?'

'Yup.' He pointed to a small photo on the mantel showing a thin young woman in a graduation gown, holding a degree certificate. 'That's Harry. She got the brains *and* the looks, lucky thing. She's pretty, right?'

I tried to think of a diplomatic answer. 'Depends on your point of view.'

He sat up, feigning affront. 'You don't fancy her?'

'I'm old enough to be her father.'

'Fair point,' he said, smiling, but the smile faded as he took the photo and rested it on his lap. Looking at it, he said, 'I owe her so much, you know.'

'How come?'

'When we were little, she helped me. And when Mum got sick, she was there for me again. I wouldn't have made it without her.'

'You loved your mum a lot, didn't you?'

'Course I did. Didn't you love yours?'

'Never knew her. She died when I was a baby. I was raised by my dad.'

'I'm sorry. Poor you.' He turned his wrist, showing the tattoo I'd first seen at the Equilibrium: the number 16-02-67 written in thin cursive letters. 'Mum's birthday.'

'That's nice, Tommy.' I drank some lager. It tasted warm and tinny.

'How old are you, Kasper?' he said.

'Forty-three. Hard to believe, right?'

'Any brothers or sisters?'

'Nope.'

'Girlfriend?'

'Nope.'

'Boyfriend?'

'I thought we'd covered that.'

'Can't blame a kid for trying.' He giggled. 'I guessed you were single. You've got that single-guy look.' He flicked away his fringe. 'And you don't take any shit, do you?'

I found myself smiling at his choice of words. 'No,' I said. 'I suppose I don't.'

'Those marks on your arms. Did you do them?'

I considered him for a moment, then placed the beer on the floor and followed his eyes. Pale scars were visible below the hairs on my forearms where I'd rolled up my sleeve, laddering up like train tracks. They'd faded over the years, but to the discerning eye there was no doubting what they were. I'd no idea Tommy had noticed.

'I saw them the other day in the milkshake place, and just now when your beer exploded. Do you mind me asking?'

'Ask away. If it gets uncomfortable, I'll tell you.'

'When did you start?'

'A few years ago.'

'How come?'

'It was a bad time. I lost someone close.'

'Who?'

'My daughter. Rosie.'

'Oh.' He looked away, then back. 'Dad said you didn't have kids?'

'I don't. Anymore.'

He nodded slowly, taking this in.

'Want to talk about your daughter?'

'No.'

'OK. One more question. Do you still do it?'

'Same answer,' I said, the words heavy in my mouth, 'and I'm sure this isn't the kind of stuff your dad wanted us talking about.'

'Yeah,' Tommy said, 'you're probably right.'

As we'd been speaking, I'd noticed his demeanour had changed, the voice less theatrical, mannerisms less flappy. Perhaps I was starting to see the real him?

'Mum used to put cigarettes out on her arms,' he said, returning the photo to its spot. He leaned forward on the sofa, rested his elbows on his knees and his chin in his hands. 'I remember watching her. I never understood why she did it. Then after she died, I started doing it too. Mad, right?' He smiled, picked at a fingernail. 'People think if the parents are screwed up, then their kids are going to be too.'

'That what you think?'

'I think the world's a messed-up place. I think people who *don't* have problems are the real nut-jobs.'

'I'm inclined to agree.' I stood, walked to the windows. The garden was a tangle of grass, weeds and a cracked patio. A huge eucalyptus at the head of the lawn was overshadowing the paving, its branches clawing over the fence into the neighbour's garden. 'But there's got to be better ways to cope than slicing up your arms or using them as ashtrays, Tommy.'

'Do you think I'm crazy?'

'Why do you ask?'

'Stop answering a question with another one.'

'Fair enough. I *don't* think you're crazy. Better?'

'So what *do* you think? About me?'

I turned. His eyes were hooded beneath his fringe.

'Like you said the other day, we've both got a sadness. And yours is taking you to some pretty dark places. Maybe you're doing stuff you don't want to, and you'd like a way out, but don't know how to find it. And that's why you're drawn to me.'

He nodded slowly. 'Mum would've been so ashamed if she knew what I was up to.'

'Then stop it.'

'It's not that easy.' He lowered his head, hair flopping forwards again. 'This isn't such a good idea, us talking. Maybe you should go now.'

'Look at me, Tommy,' I said.

He flicked the hair away. The gesture revealed wet, milky-brown eyes. He was crying.

'Look how big I am,' I said, starting to feel a bit helpless. 'Is someone scaring you? Forcing you to come on to blokes and do stuff you don't want to? Let me scare them back. I'm good at it.'

We shared another silence. There seemed to be a lot of silence between us.

He kept looking at me, his eyes leaking. It became hard to watch and I turned back to the window.

Eventually, I heard him get to his feet. We stood there, side by side, not speaking. Outside, the sky was a thin magenta, petering out as clouds crept in. A robin landed on the lawn and paused, as if in contemplation, before jumping away.

'So, Tommy,' I said. 'You want to take a chance and tell me what's going on?'

His reflection nodded in the glass. 'I made a mistake and got myself into something ugly. I thought I was doing the right thing. But now I'm trapped. It makes me feel like shit. And I don't like feeling that way.'

'I'm pleased to hear that.'

'I want to tell you about it. But not here, in this house.'

'Why?'

'Dad and Harry will be back soon, and I'm meant to go out later. This needs time. I've never told anyone all this from the beginning. Let's go somewhere private.'

'OK. When?'

'Can you meet me? Tomorrow night?'

'Fine.'

'Kasper,' he said, his voice barely a whisper, 'are you really my friend?'

I looked at him. 'Yeah,' I said. 'I'm your friend, Tommy.'

He nodded again, slowly, and then returned to looking out the window.

I left it at that. I guess I could've pushed deeper, but didn't. How I wished I had.

Twenty-four hours later, I was on my bike, pedalling away from Savages Boxing Club, uphill towards Archway Road, my breathing harsh, the taste of iron coating my mouth.

I reached Upper Holloway station in fifteen minutes, and was met by flashing blue lights, a huddle of bystanders, London Underground staff, police, an unmarked mortuary van and an ambulance. The sky was blotched with clouds, darkening and unsteady, and a sharp wind dried my eyes.

Saul was already there, talking frantically to a paramedic, his hands gesticulating. The paramedic shrugged and pointed at the station. Flapping yellow tape cordoned its entrance; the shutters were down, train staff in clusters nearby, talking covertly, several smoking.

I saw Diane by a police Fiat, a Met badge pinned to her coat. A thin-shouldered woman was with her, mid-twenties, with a jet-black bob and a matching blazer. Tinted aviators hid her eyes, but I recognised her from the graduation photo Tommy had shown me. Harriet Berkowitz, his sister.

A moment later, she walked briskly to Saul. I watched the two hug, say something I couldn't make out, then look at the station in unison.

Two teenage girls to my right were sharing a box of chips. The tail end of their conversation caught me. One said, 'Boy went splat,' before bringing her hands together with a clap. I swallowed down a sick taste, dismounted my bike and approached Diane.

Five years had passed since we'd stood this close. She'd changed her look, dropping the jeans and jumpers for a neat black combo, and straightening out the frizzy afro. It was a far more formal look than the Diane I remembered, but she pulled it off effortlessly.

She tried a smile. I rested on the Fiat and tried one back.

'I'm sorry, Kas,' she said. 'I don't know what to say.'

'Nothing you can say,' I said. 'But, thanks. You're sure it's him?'

She shrugged. 'The sister gave me a description. It sounds like a match.'

'He jumped?'

'No question.'

'Where's he now?'

'Down there. CID ruled out foul play. Mortuary staff are doing their thing.'

To the right of the station entrance there was a kebab shop. A middle-aged man stood outside, wearing a navy TfL jumper, smoking. His dark skin had turned ashen, and his eyes stared into the distance.

'Who's he?'

'The train driver. He's pretty shook up.' She paused. 'So are you, by the looks of it. You sure you should be here?'

I shrugged. 'Where else am I going to be?'

She nodded.

'Thanks, Diane,' I said, and began wandering towards the driver.

He spotted me a few feet away and took a step back. 'Who're you?' he said through a cloud of smoke. 'I already talked to the police.'

'I'm not police.' I stopped in front of him.

Up close, his lips were dry, nostrils flared.

'I'm sorry,' he said. 'I couldn't stop in time. Believe me.'

'I do. It's not your fault.'

'I can see him—'

'I know.'

'It don't make sense. Why'd a young man do something like this?'

No answer.

'You a relative?'

'No,' I said. 'I was a . . . friend.'

I breathed out slowly, and offered the train driver my hand. He shook it. Sweat stuck our palms together.

Both of us started at the clang of the station shutters. Two men in charcoal mortuary uniforms appeared. They were pulling a narrow stretcher sealed with shiny black tarpaulin. The police and paramedics stood aside, allowing them to move their cargo towards the van.

Stutters came from Saul, high and staccato, as if his throat was blocked. Harriet was next to him. Her lips were tight, and her head slowly shook.

No one spoke. There was no fanfare, no screams. Just a body getting carried out on a Tuesday afternoon.

A third man wearing jeans and a Henley shirt emerged from the station. He was plain-clothes police, you could tell from his movements. A see-through evidence bag was in his hand. As he passed us, I made out the contents. A bunch of keys. A plastic cardholder. And an iPhone, sheathed with pink bunny ears.

The mortuary men opened the van doors and slid the stretcher in. Behind me, Saul's stutters became sobs, which rose with the turning wind.

The van doors closed, the motor started. Then it was pulling away, becoming immersed within the traffic before disappearing from sight.

'Some friend,' I said.

Chapter 4

While Tommy's body was taken to the mortuary, a couple of Met officers drove Saul and Harriet further north, where they were to be interviewed at a police station. Not knowing what to do, I tagged along.

Within a square, stifling interview room, a pair of plain-clothes, coffee-breathed officers asked them the same questions in a barrage of ways:

Any idea why Tommy did it?

Was there a suicide note?

What about previous attempts?

After learning he had a history of self-harm and had recently tried hanging himself from London Bridge, the change in their expressions was subtle but unmistakable. Both scribbled down what Saul told them, nodding intermittently, an implicit under-standing now shared between them – Tommy was a crazy. Crazies put themselves in front of trains. There was nothing to investigate here.

Halfway through, Harriet removed her aviators and stared at the table. Her eyes were deep-set and dark, jarring with the bone china of her skin. She had that pale, chiselled look some men go for; but to me she looked like someone who lived on caffeine, nicotine and hard angst.

Saul asked the police if they knew anything about Tommy's last movements.

He'd been spotted on CCTV, one said, pacing the platform for half an hour; prior to that, witnesses saw him walking around the surrounding area, crying.

'Crying?' Saul's voice was clipped. 'And no one stopped to ask him if he was OK?'

'No, sir,' the other one said, itching the back of his neck. 'It appears not.'

Shortly before the interview finished, the officers asked what my connection with Tommy was. After a pause, I said I was a family friend, which seemed to satisfy them. It didn't me.

I considered playing them the voicemail message Tommy left me, but held back. What help would it be? Saul and Harriet would have to endure the pain of hearing him.

And he'd still be dead.

Around two in the morning, they were both shown to a family room. I went to the reception area of the police station and planted myself on a narrow corrugated bench. I dozed a little, but mainly just sat there with my eyes closed, listening to a dull thud in my head.

Seven o'clock, and a flurry of day-shift officers came on duty. Immediately after, the night crew began shuffling out in ones and twos. Someone stuck on a radio, and tinny pop music corroded the air.

A stooped, lowly old boy wearing a soiled blazer and flat cap shuffled in and plonked himself on to the bench opposite me. Most stations have one or two of these oddballs who hang around, striking up conversation with whoever will listen.

'Hi,' he said, smiling, his teeth like spilled rubble.

I noticed he had a badge on his lapel that said: *What doesn't kill you makes you stronger!*

'Christ,' I said, rising stiffly, stretching my arms to the sound of my spine clicking.

I hadn't eaten since all this kicked off, so darted out, found a convenience shop round the corner, bought a Kit Kat and Coke and shovelled them down on my walk back.

Inside the station, Saul and Harriet had reappeared. The old boy was trying to talk with them now, but was meeting a brick wall. One look told me neither of them had got any more rest than me. And when Saul spoke, I knew sleep would be the last thing on his mind.

'They need me to identify Tommy's body, Kasper.'

I tried telling him he didn't have to do this, that a recent photo, dental records, even a description of the tattoo on his wrist would suffice.

But Saul insisted. 'He's my son. I have to see him. Do you understand?'

Of course I did.

An unmarked car took us through the morning traffic of Tufnell Park, Kentish Town, then further up towards Kings Cross. Our driver was a rotund liaison officer called Jenny. Flatly, as if reading from an autocue, she informed us Tommy's death certificate had been completed by a duty doctor, and that in due course, there would be an inquest. None of us replied.

The mortuary was accessed through St Pancras Park, also home to a coroner's court that stood adjacent. Jenny parked and we followed her across a small green towards the entrance.

It was a bold April morning, a boldness that made the purpose of our visit surreal. Tall oaks loomed above our heads, their leaves blossoming into a vibrant green. Ahead, a trio of tourists had dismounted from their Boris bikes to take a few photos. A straggly male was slumped on a bench, drinking from a can of strong lager and muttering between sips.

I'd been wearing the same tracksuit since yesterday, and was starting to smell gamey. A shower sounded good. To be frank, not being here sounded good, too. I didn't know what I was doing hanging around, or where it would lead.

But I couldn't leave. Tommy had seen to that.

As Saul and the officer walked ahead, I found myself side by side with Harriet. Her eyes were hidden behind her aviators again, and she had a cigarette on the go.

'I'm Kasper,' I said. 'We've not properly met.'

'I know who you are.'

'If there's anything I can do—'

'There's nothing.'

'I'm sorry, Harriet.'

'Yeah,' she said. 'It's a bit late for that, isn't it?'

Mortuary interiors are all much of a muchness, and this one followed suit — white walls, metal chairs, colourless lighting, clinical smells, pamphlets giving information on bereavement groups and support lines; the implicit certainty of death clung to the place.

We walked up a short hallway towards the reception area. A thin, equine woman was behind a desk. Jenny flashed her ID. 'I'm with Thomas Berkowitz's next of kin,' she said.

The woman nodded and looked at her computer. The only sound was her nails on the keyboard.

Harriet and I took seats. Saul remained standing. A moment later, the receptionist said it would be twenty minutes before Tommy was ready to be seen.

Seen? He sounded like an exhibit.

Immediately, Harriet was on her feet, heading outside with a deck of Marlboros. Jenny took a seat a few along from me. After a minute, she withdrew a phone and started tapping.

Saul was still on his feet, motionless. His eyes were red and narrow behind his glasses, and his chest moved in slow, rhythmic breaths.

Now was the time to talk to him, or at least to try. I could tell him about my daughter, how a child's suicide is a pain beyond measure, or some crap like that.

But nothing came.

Perhaps Rosie's death was still too raw for me to find the words.

Or perhaps, more simply, I was afraid of Saul's response. He'd be enraged that I'd put ideas into Tommy's head; he'd think I'd let his son down, just like I'd let my little girl down five years ago. And, probably, he'd be right.

So I remained as I was, mute, slumped on a hard plastic chair, staring at a wall.

Time passed, finally pierced by the receptionist's voice. We all looked over.

'The mortician is ready,' she said.

Without a word, Saul ducked out to retrieve Harriet. When they returned, she smelled of fresh cigarette smoke.

'OK, Harry,' Saul said. 'Let's go.'

She shook her head. 'I can't, Dad. I'm sorry . . .' Her lips drew together in a flat line.

Saul paused, and looked at her gravely. For a moment, I thought he was about to snap. Instead, he nodded.

'I understand,' he said, putting a hand on her shoulder. 'I'll go alone.'

'Do you want me to come?' I said.

For the first time that morning, he looked at me squarely. 'Do *you* want to come, Kasper?'

My hands were shaking. I buried them in my tracksuit and held his stare. 'Yeah,' I said. 'I want to.'

Another small, square room, the ceiling low, the space minimally furnished.

My nose pricked at a distinctive, chemical aroma sharpening the air. It made me think of apples: not sweet, fresh apples but mushy ones beginning to rot. I breathed through my mouth to avoid it.

This room wasn't like the mortuaries portrayed in films where there are saws and scalpels and specimen jugs containing organs. We could've been anywhere, were it not for the metal gurney centre stage.

A body lay supine upon it, entirely covered with a pale green sheet that outlined the contours of limbs, a torso and a head. A wan, overweight mortician wearing pastel blue scrubs was standing at the end, waiting.

Saul approached the gurney and I stepped back until I was against the wall. Liaison officer Jenny was somewhere to my right.

Swiftly, the mortician pulled back the top of the sheet. I breathed out audibly.

'The impact was to the young man's midriff,' he said absently. 'Death would have been instantaneous.'

There were Tommy's head and shoulders. Until that second, a part of me hadn't quite believed it would be him.

Saul said nothing. He made a fist and brought the knuckle beneath his nose.

The mortician had done a good job, I suppose. Tommy looked crystalline, his eyes closed, mouth closed, skin as smooth and white as a cod steak. The ring had been removed from his nostril. His floppy hair was parted neatly to one side. The rope scar around his neck was barely visible. He was a child.

The only sign of injury was a brownish patch to the side of his temple, a darkening that stretched to his ear like an islet on a map. It could've been a birthmark. But it wasn't.

Slowly, Saul lowered his hand and took off his glasses. He leaned over his son. It was as if he was examining him forensically.

Then the first crack showed. He put his mouth to Tommy's forehead and kissed his brow. 'I'm sorry,' he said.

What can be said about the next chunk of time? It passed without meaning. Seconds, minutes – I can't say how long I was there, watching a father, a man like me, inspect his dead child. No words could actualise what Saul was experiencing, but it would tarnish everything for the rest of his days, an indelible tear.

He whispered things to Tommy I couldn't hear and stroked his hair. Finally, he stepped back. He turned and looked at us all with firm, wet eyes.

'This is my son,' he said. 'Thomas Saul Berkowitz. I can confirm it.'

'Understood, professor,' said Jenny.

'Now, I'd appreciate it if you took my daughter and me home. We're very tired.'

Chapter 5

I should've showered and gone straight to bed, but instead did little else but drink for the rest of that day. Ploughing through the Bushmills, I tried thinking things through, but before long the drinking overtook the thinking, and I woke the next morning with the hangover I deserved.

At the dawn's first light, I headed for Savages Boxing Club to seek solace in violence. A couple of Irish bare-knucklers first opened the place on the site of a disused abattoir, where it remains to this day, situated between a Chinese chip shop and an abandoned ironmonger's, in a part of northeast London the hipsters are yet to reach.

I spent thirty minutes clumping the heavy bag and another twenty skipping until I felt ready to start chucking punches at someone. That someone was Ricky, an eighteen-year-old ex-gang runner whose jailbird dad Neville was residing in Wandsworth Prison at Her Majesty's pleasure for his involvement in a spate of armed robberies.

Normally, Ricky and I were a pretty even match, but normally my head wasn't pinging about on tangents as it was today: sleep-deprived, groggy, and fixating on cracked iPhone screens and bloody train tracks.

'C'mon, Kas,' he said after a dismal second round. 'Making this too easy for me.'

He was right. I was slow and heavy-handed, sweating out booze, and he was taking advantage of it.

Over-compensating, I stepped in hard and caught a trio of body blows. Heat and pain riled me, fuzzing my focus. More followed.

I called it quits not long after. Leaning on the ropes, I unstrapped my headguard and spat into a bucket.

Ricky's brown skin glowed under the fluorescent lights above the ring. He came to my corner, sniggering.

'Losing your touch, old man. You OK?'

I grunted something, headed for the locker room, had a scalding shower and left.

Walking east, I bought a black coffee from an Italian pop-up, found a bench in Victoria Park, topped up the coffee with a glug of Bushmills from my hipflask, and listened to Tommy's voice message again.

When I'd done enough of that, I scoured the internet for news about a tube station suicide the day before last. A barrage of stories attacked me, all saying pretty much the same thing – there'd been a fatality, a young man hit by a train; he was nineteen, known to have mental health problems; police weren't treating the death as suspicious . . .

Bollocks.

There were three missed calls from Diane, but I wasn't in the mood to talk just then. Instead, I switched the phone off, leaned back and shook my head.

This wasn't my fault – that's what I tried telling myself. I'd met Tommy three times, and his problems had been with him long before I rocked up.

But it didn't quite wash. Like with Rosie, I could've done more. Maybe if I'd badgered him to tell me about this secret he had, he'd have spilled. And maybe then he'd still be here.

And what I couldn't displace from my mind was the *way* he chose to die, the violence of it, the harshness, and how he'd done it only a matter of hours after I'd told him about my daughter. It was a big *fuck you*, a final scream at the world. And he knew I wouldn't be able to ignore it.

'*I'm sorry it has to be this way,*' he'd said on the voicemail. '*You'll know what to do.*'

The booze and coffee swirled in my empty stomach. I closed my eyes and pictured Rosie and Tommy together, heaped across dismal rat-infested train tracks, enmeshed in blood. An impulse to join them whispered in my ear like a tired friend until a sip of coffee burned my lip, the pain bringing me back.

Looking around for a distraction, anything to keep me from this plughole, I focused on the grassy banks. Trees were spilling petals that rained like confetti, the breeze lifting them towards the lake, where a red pagoda stood. The tulips, magnolias and daffodils in Victoria Park are spectacular in early spring, and today they were a swarm of yellows, creamy pinks and purples. Normally, I'd sit and soak it up, but right then their brightness seemed lurid, their scents sickly, and I pulled out my Wayfarers to block them.

As I finished my drink, I watched people, waiting for answers to come.

None came.

A young couple were strolling hand in hand, sharing an ice cream.

Behind them, a small boy sat upon a three-wheeled cart being pulled by a thin woman smoking with her free hand.

Further back, a heavily bearded man walked his heavily bearded dog.

Life was sauntering by.

Yet a mile or so west of here, Tommy Berkowitz lay cold on a slab.

I could hear John Coltrane's *A Love Supreme* playing on the stereo as I unlocked the front door. Dr Steiner was in the lounge, sitting in her armchair with Marmite resting on her lap. She had a lit Dunhill on the go, the filter sheathed in one of several ivory holders she kept.

'Ah, Kasper,' she said, her face obscured within the smoke.

'Hello, Dr Steiner,' I said, walking in. 'Welcome home.'

I became her tenant after responding to an ad in a launderette window, six or so months following Rosie's death, and in the years since, I'd never dropped the formality of her title; tellingly, Dr Steiner never objected to this.

She was a retired psychiatrist, revered by many in the field for her intellect and insights, and shunned by others for a candour that bordered on rudeness. Early into our co-habitation, after I learned of her profession, I made it known that I was her tenant, not her patient, and had no interests in being therapised. In turn, she made it abundantly clear that she was my landlord, and had no desire to analyse me. Yet over the years, she'd become something of a confidante, and I to her, and in spite of our differences, I now considered her the closest thing I had to a friend.

'Did you enjoy Brighton?' I said.

'I did,' she said, lowering the music with a remote, 'but I missed my home comforts and present company.' She gestured at Marmite. 'What have you been feeding my cat? He's thin as a rake.'

Rather than answer, I leaned down and gave her a hug, reciprocated with hard twiggy fingers across my back. Marmite stared imperiously.

Today, Dr Steiner wore an oversized T-shirt, embroidered with sequined letters that read *Too Glam to Give a Damn!* On her thin legs were plain black tights, on her small feet, eight-hole Dr Martens. Her skin was dark, like cracked hide, and what mousy hair she still had was cropped short and thin.

'How was the train journey back?' I said.

'Dire. I was trapped next to a medical student wanting to talk about the decline of the NHS, as if I cared anymore. I had to flash Mildred and say I was having a bit of trouble *down there* before he finally shut up.'

Mildred was the name Dr Steiner had given the stoma bag she wore around her midriff. Now sixty-seven, she'd survived two bouts of bowel cancer, the second leading to the removal of a section of her intestine and the fitting of the bag, which prompted her retirement. She'd picked the name Mildred in memory of a former girlfriend with whom her relationship had ended sourly. Apparently the two shared much in common – both were full of shit.

'Sit, Kasper, let's talk,' she said, reclining. 'You're looking some-what bedraggled today, even by your standards. Is there a reason?'

On the coffee table was a pot of tea and two cups. I poured some, adding milk and sugar. Then I took the armchair opposite and told her all about Tommy Berkowitz.

As she listened, Dr Steiner's eyes grew narrow and their pupils reduced to pinpoints, but the rest of her stayed entirely still. None of what I said seemed to shock her, but then very little did. I've never known someone as impervious to life's indignities as she.

When I'd finished, she said, 'I'm sorry. How awful. He copied your daughter's death.'

'Yes.'

'April really is the cruellest month.'

I looked at the floor.

'This isn't your fault. You know that, don't you?'

I didn't answer.

She reached for her cigarette. It crackled as she drew in fresh smoke. 'What a mess. I leave you for a week, and look what happens.'

I managed a smile, but it faded quickly.

'This kid had a secret,' I said. 'Something burning him up. There's a reason he did what he did, and in this particular way.'

'Perhaps,' she said. 'But if he did have a secret, he took it with him.'

I shrugged. 'We were supposed to meet. To talk about it. He asked me if I was his friend.' It sounded limp.

I could feel the doctor's eyes staring intently, and knew what was coming next. 'I don't think you're up to this, my dear,' she said.

'Up to what?'

'Whatever it is you're planning.'

'I'm pissed off.'

She waited.

'I could've done more. This . . . it shouldn't have happened, Dr Steiner.'

'What shouldn't? Your daughter's suicide? Or this Tommy's? Because it sounds to me like you're confusing the two.'

I flinched, spilling tea into my saucer. Over the years, I'd grown mostly accustomed to Dr Steiner's directness. Mostly. But there were times, such as now, when her remarks made my muscles recoil like an archer's bow.

A long silence followed, time for her to finish one cigarette and light another.

'So, what will you do?' she finally said.

I put down my tea and looked at my hands. Rough, worker's hands, scabbed and calloused. I turned them over and made fists. The skin drew taut, stretched white around the knuckles.

I think the answer had been with me all day. It just needed saying.

'I'm going to find out why he did it.'

Chapter 6

Straight away, I called Saul Berkowitz and said I'd like to come over.

'Why?' he said, his voice gravelly.

'To talk about Tommy.'

A long pause. Then, with a sigh, he said that I could.

Next, I called Diane. 'Sorry for the radio silence. It's been a weird couple of days.'

'No doubt. I've been worried. This thing with the Berkowitz boy must've stirred up quite a bit.'

'It has. I'm just figuring out my next move.'

'You know the dad called me last week? He was checking up on you, asking if you were likely to do anything loopy to his son.'

'He mentioned that. Thanks for vouching for me.'

'I'm kind of wishing I hadn't now.'

I hesitated. Her voice sounded good.

Before I knew it, I said, 'Do you want to meet up? You know, go for a walk or something. It was good seeing you the other day, in spite of the circumstances.'

'Five years of nothing and you want to go for a walk. Why?'

'For a chat, I guess.'

'You and me, like a couple of old mates?' She didn't try to mask the incredulity.

'Forget it,' I said.

'Wait a sec,' she said through a laugh. 'Don't be so sensitive. Early next week I'm off. Let's do something then.'

'You sure?'

'Why not.'

'Cool.'

'Meantime, you're not planning anything nuts around this Tommy, are you?'

'Me?'

Another laugh, this time with a little uncertainty. 'Stay in touch, big man,' she said, and hung up.

Before heading out, I showered, shaved, changed into a black shirt and Levi's, and uprooted a bunch of lilies from Dr Steiner's garden. Then I packed the flowers and the remaining cash Saul had paid me into my backpack, and cycled east.

Parked in the Berkowitz drive was a dinted navy Skoda. Judging by the crumpled Marlboro carton on the dash, I guessed it belonged to Harriet. I was halfway up the path when the front door to the house opened.

Saul hadn't changed out of the tartan shirt and chinos he'd been wearing two days back. The clothes were creased and grubby now, hanging loose; his hair was matted, and without glasses, his face looked jowly and frail.

He studied the lilies. 'Thank you,' he eventually said, taking them with both hands.

'I owe you this too,' I said, handing over the cash. 'It's a few quid short. I'll get you the rest when I can.'

'I never asked for this money back.'

'I know,' I said. 'But I didn't earn it.'

He took the twenties and looked at them, as if unsure what they were. 'Come in,' he finally said.

I followed him into the lounge, passing the heaps of paper, the ticking grandfather clock, avoiding the family photo showing Tommy as a baby that seemed to glare from the wall.

Harriet was sitting on the sofa. She wore a charcoal blazer, grey chinos and soft-heeled loafers. The sound of my boots made her look up. Her skin was pale, and her small, deep-set eyes were quite unlike her brother's, hard and piercing.

'Why's he here, Dad?' she said, her voice curt.

'He brought these . . .' Saul was still looking at the lilies. 'And this.' He sat beside her, gave her the cash, placed the flowers on a cushion and the cushion on his knees.

Harriet looked at the money and counted it; she counted it again and returned to me.

I sat on the armrest of the adjacent sofa and said, 'I'm so sorry about your brother, Harriet.'

'So you said at the mortuary. What do you want with us now, *Mr* Kasper?'

I looked to Saul, as if the question came from him. 'I want to find out what happened.'

The two glanced at each other.

Harriet was the first to speak: 'We *know* what happened.'

'No,' I said. 'We know Tommy did what he did. But there's lots missing. I'm going to put the pieces together.'

'Dad?'

I carried on looking at Saul.

'Kasper,' he said, rubbing his eyes, 'if there's anything to investigate, the police will take care of it, surely.'

Not a chance, Saul, I felt like saying. In the Met's eyes, this was a clear-cut suicide. And judging by Diane's tone earlier, they were stepping back.

'The police won't look into this in the way I plan to,' I said instead.

'I don't understand,' Saul said. 'Why won't they?'

'Tommy had problems. The inquest will bring back a verdict of suicide. There was no actual crime committed.'

'Well,' Harriet said, enunciating slowly, 'if there's *no* crime, there's *nothing* to find out. So go away.'

'No,' I said. 'With the greatest respect, I didn't come here to ask for permission.'

'What if I insist you leave this alone?' Saul said.

'I'll ignore you.'

He nodded.

'This is outrageous!' Harriet pushed herself off the couch and began waving a finger in my face as if it were a conductor's wand. I resisted the urge to shove it away. 'You come here and start laying down the law. How dare you! I should call the police. Who do you work for?'

'I don't work for anyone. Call the police if you like. It won't make a difference.'

I held her stare.

Saul sighed. 'Is that it?'

I returned to him. 'No. I also want to see Tommy's bedroom and look through his things.'

'Certainly not!' Harriet said. 'Now, I'm warning you—'

'Shh, Harriet!' Saul said firmly, holding up his hand. 'Be quiet. Please.'

Startled, she sat back down and glared at me.

'Come on, Kasper,' he said. 'I'll take you to his room.'

As we reached the upstairs landing, I heard the front door slam, followed swiftly by the growl of an engine. I caught sight of Harriet's Skoda zipping away from the drive.

'I'm sorry about Harry,' Saul said, behind me. 'She's not taking this well.'

'No need to apologise.'

I turned. He lingered at the foot of a winding staircase.

'First, my wife died up in this attic,' he said, indicating towards the stairs, 'now Tommy's gone too. This house is full of ghosts.'

He looked down at a see-through evidence bag he'd retrieved from the kitchen. It contained Tommy's belongings.

'They gave me this.'

I waited.

He peered up. 'The liaison officer left us leaflets for support groups and bereavement counselling. She said talking can help bring closure. But can you ever find closure, after something like *this*?'

'Perhaps,' I lied.

He reached into the bag and fished out the keys. 'I'll unlock his bedroom for you.'

'Did Tommy always keep his room locked?'

'Yes.'

'Why?'

'I don't know.' He held up a silver key from the bunch. 'It's this one. Come on.'

The smell of strawberry perfume was the first thing to strike me as I stepped into Tommy's bedroom. It was a small rectangular space, kept surprisingly nondescript. To my right was a white slatted wardrobe dotted with heart-shaped stickers; beside it, a desk and a chair. Pens, notebooks, sweet wrappers, biros, aftershave and scrap paper lay scattered across the surface of the table, along with an ashtray and a pile of lime green papers that looked like medicine prescriptions.

There weren't any posters or pictures on the walls, just three framed photos like the ones downstairs, showing the Berkowitz family at different ages, always looking happy and united. It didn't feel like a young man's room. It was sterile, cold, like a jigsaw puzzle missing a load of pieces.

By the window was an armchair partially covered with a red knit blanket. Beneath it, shoes and clothes, jeans and joggers, all folded up. To the right of the chair was a bed, its duvet pulled back. The indentation of a body was vague but discernible in the mattress.

Saul was hovering behind me.

'Are you sure you want to be here?' I said, not turning to him.

'Yes.'

'OK. I'll be as careful as I can.'

I began with the wardrobe. As I opened the door, the bed springs squeaked. Saul had sat down on the mattress.

Tommy's clothes were arranged neatly, a mixture of casual and glammed-up evening wear. It was all colourful stuff, with pinks, reds and purples his colours of choice; the shelves held shirts, pants and socks, folded in piles and colour-coded.

I rooted around, checking corners and crevices, and the base, floor and surfaces of the wardrobe in case anything had been concealed. Nothing had.

Next, I turned to the desk. The prescriptions were for venlafaxine, an antidepressant. There were six in total, each for twenty-eight days' worth. It appeared that Tommy hadn't taken any of them to the chemist to get the pills.

The strawberry perfume came in a light red bottle and was called Joop, a pricey brand I'd seen in Boots. The scraps of paper were receipts and dog-ends, and told me nothing.

The drawer was unlocked. Inside were empty cigarette packets, hairbands, some euros, nicotine patches, an unopened pack of condoms, an address book with nothing written inside and an A5 leather-bound diary.

I flicked through the diary pages – *Yoga class at 11, GP at 2* – nothing personal. In the back, there was a folded Barclaycard statement from February. I learned from this that Tommy owed in the region of seven and a half grand, and had been amassing a hefty dollop of interest each month. I considered asking Saul about this, but refrained when I looked at him. His eyes were distant. He was somewhere else.

Instead, I returned the credit card statement to the diary, the diary to the drawer, slid the drawer shut and got down on my knees. Under the wardrobe were shoeboxes, cigarette butts, a lighter and a ceramic ashtray; further back, a voting registration, an invitation to a sexual health screening, more shoeboxes and another credit card bill, this one for over nine grand.

One by one, I pulled the shoeboxes out. Inside the first was a stack of family photos. Most showed Tommy as a toddler with his family and various other people. The back of each photo had the date it was taken, the people it showed and the location. The handwriting was Tommy's, recognisable from his diary. I read a few of these inscriptions at random:

Me and Mum, California, 12-02-07
Mum Dad Harriet and me, Christmas, California style, 25-12-08
Mum's fiftieth, California 16-02-17

I stayed with this final photo the longest. It showed Judith Berkowitz with her hand resting on Tommy's shoulder. She looked gaunt; her skin was shrivelled, her eyes grey. Yet she was smiling, as was Tommy. His cheeks were puppyish, and he'd grown his hair into the same floppy fringe he'd had when I knew him. On a table in front of them was a birthday cake. The word *MUM* was embossed on its icing.

I returned the photo to the box and leafed through a few more snaps, just to see if anything stood out.

But nothing did. And I felt like an intruder. Tommy and his mother were both dead, and this was their private world I was prodding into, uninvited. I rushed through the rest.

More snaps were stacked haphazardly inside a different shoebox marked *Work party for Daddy*; several were torn or cut up, as if they'd been remnants meant for the bin. Most featured the Berkowitz kids over the years, as babies, toddlers, school kids. Several had an infant Tommy dancing in a play. He was standing on his tiptoes like Billy Elliot, wearing a peach leotard and matching tee, his cheeks plump and rosy.

I recognised Saul and Judith among a mix of adults. They both looked younger and fresher, smartly dressed, with departmental lanyards round their necks.

Another man caught my attention. The image was a little blurry, but I could see that he was stocky and tall, with pale skin, deep, intense eyes and a bushy, Burt Reynolds moustache. He was standing next to Saul and behind a young Tommy and Harriet, a hand on each of the children's shoulders. For no particular reason, I stared at the man's hand, then turned the photo over and looked for his name on the list. It wasn't there.

I turned to Saul. He was gazing ahead. I couldn't tell if he was aware of me or not.

'Do you know who this man is?' I said, and held up the picture.

He looked over. His eyes narrowed. 'May I?' he said.

I leaned over, handed it to him.

He stared at it. 'No,' he said. 'It's an old photo. I don't remember who that is.'

He returned to staring into space, the photo still in his hand but forgotten, and I placed the others back in the box and returned the box to its place under the wardrobe, along with everything else I'd pulled out. I stood in the centre of the bedroom and looked at the bare walls, thinking about what I'd just learned.

Not much.

Tommy owed a lot on credit cards. So? Lots of kids are feckless with money.

He was prescribed happy pills but didn't take them, had a heap of old photos stashed away, and kept his bedroom locked, even though there was nothing much to steal.

Where was I going with this?

Saul's presence in the bedroom was a distraction. I peered round. He remained on the bed. The plastic bag containing Tommy's belongings was at his feet. The photo had disappeared.

'I thought he might've left a note,' he said, dimly. 'I gather a lot of them leave notes.'

'Some,' I said. 'Not all.'

He nodded. 'Have you found anything, Kasper?'

I looked at the bag. 'Can I see what's in there?'

He handed it to me.

Inside was the plastic cardholder Tommy was carrying in Sally-Anne's Milkshake Shack and his bunny-eared iPhone. I turned the phone over and jolted back. The screen bore a thick fracture across the glass, the kind that comes from a hard impact. It spider-webbed into small white fissures, leaving the surface jagged to the touch.

The cardholder contained a fiver, a bankcard, a gym card for the Equilibrium and some loyalty cards for food outlets and coffee places. I tapped it on the desktop to make sure no small pieces of paper were lodged or hidden there, then put the cards back as I'd found them and took up Tommy's iPhone.

It made a strange rattling sound. I figured it for dead, but wanted to be sure. By the desk leg there was a charger. I plugged the phone in. To my surprise, the Apple insignia appeared beneath the cracks, asking for a six-digit code.

'Any idea of the password, Saul?'

He shook his head. 'Afraid not.'

I thought back to my conversations with Tommy. He'd shown me the tattoo on his wrist of his mother's birthdate. That had six digits.

I put the phone on the desk, then knelt to retrieve one of the shoeboxes from beneath the wardrobe. Picking out the photo of Judith Berkowitz's birthday, I read from its reverse again:

Mum's fiftieth, California 16-02-17

A subtraction in my head, then I typed 1 6 0 2 6 7 into the phone – Judith's date of birth. Straight away, I was in.

I spent the next twenty minutes trying to disentangle the apps and downloads Tommy had installed. Facebook and WhatsApp I could get my head round; Instagram and Snapchat were alien. Regardless, it seemed he deviated from most young adults by leading a comparatively quiet online life. Emails were benign, mainly spam and ads; his Facebook had seventy-six friends, largely girls his age. His profile picture was a recent headshot. It showed a smiling Tommy, a certainty in his expression – just another nineteen-year-old enjoying life.

The WhatsApp messages gave little away. The last dozen text messages were from Saul on the day he died:

Where are you, Tommy?
Getting worried now, Tommy

And the final one:

Please call. Dad x.

I went to the phone activity section and scanned through recent calls. Like a boot to the chest, I saw the last thing he did was send me his parting message.

There were six voicemails that hadn't been listened to: one came from me after I'd heard the voicemail he'd left, one from an Irish-accented Barclaycard employee enquiring about unpaid fines, and four from an increasingly fraught Saul, pleading for a call back.

After listening to these, I laboriously jotted down all of Tommy's contacts, which included the number for someone called Jazz – presumably that lump I floored at the Equilibrium.

Several contacts seemed to have nicknames, like AJ, Brasso, Bear and DT.

I paused at the last of these.

DT.

My mind went back to the afternoon Tommy and I had strolled near the canal. He'd hung up on someone called DT.

I took down the number and circled it.

Lastly, I checked his Safari browsing. I already knew what I'd see.

Sure enough, my daughter's name was on the most recent

tab – local newspaper articles from five years back, recounting Rosie's death, how she'd done it, even the name of the station: Upper Holloway.

He'd copied her.

It felt like I'd been kicked in the gut. I tried to hide the surge of emotion, turning my back on Saul, breathing slowly through my mouth to ride it out. Air came out in a shudder. I waited.

When I was ready, I switched the phone off, waited another moment, then put the things back in the plastic bag and handed it back to Saul. He seemed oblivious to the change in me.

'Have you learned anything?' he said. 'Whatever you find out, please tell me.'

Again, I came close to telling him about Rosie. The man had a right to know where Tommy had got the idea to kill himself.

But I held back. Saul was liable to flare up, lose his rag, and any hope of getting information from him would be lost.

And there was more than that. I guessed I was ashamed to tell him the truth.

'I don't know anything,' I said, 'yet.'

I wanted to go, but there was a question I had to put to him: I decided to do it squarely. 'Saul. Listen. I know you've been asked this already, but I need you to have another go. Can you think of any reason why Tommy did this? Take a moment before answering.'

He shook his head.

'OK.'

Neither of us had anything more to say. The silence did the talking.

When enough time had passed, I said, 'I'll see myself out.'

Chapter 7

It took three hours to ring all the numbers on Tommy's phone. Young-sounding women answered the majority of these calls, and told me they either knew him from school, the gym, a performing arts place he'd dropped out of or the psych hospital where he'd been sectioned last year. Only three knew of his death.

By call ten, I'd grown accustomed to the stilted silence that followed this news; by call twenty, I was numb to it.

Jazz, the meathead I'd bounced at the gym, was a little less hospitable. Politely, I told him who I was and offered to buy him a coffee in exchange for a chat. He suggested I perform an impossible sex act on myself and hung up before I could respond.

Fair enough.

I rang the nicknamed numbers last, and reached a few well-spoken men who all denied knowing a Tommy Berkowitz before making excuses. The rest of the calls diverted me to voicemails, DT's among them. A lively voice told me I'd reached Dominic Tyrell, Deputy Exec for Whelan & Smyth Financial Services, whoever they were.

I hung up and found Dominic on LinkedIn. The headshot showed a financier with wavy brown hair and a pukka smile.

Now I had a place to start snooping.

I went to bed around eleven. Talking with Saul, searching Tommy's room, then telling umpteen of his friends that he'd killed himself had flattened me; yet my thoughts were restless, pinging around my skull and depriving me of the sleep I needed.

That liaison officer talked to Saul about closure, as if there was such a thing.

Poor bastard. He had no idea what he was in for.

Nothing can prepare you for the slicing effect a death like this has. I should know. Aged fourteen, Rosie was suddenly gone. I became rudderless. Lost.

Those first few days after it happened are like a gap. I tried keeping things together, more for Carol than for me; where I was numbed, she was wrought with anguish, and the sound of her grief filled the house. Rather than help, my lumbering presence seemed to wrangle her further, and we ended up sitting in the lounge, the curtains drawn, unable to even look at each other.

I ate and drank, lay down and got back up, dressed and undressed, and none of it meant a thing. I knew I inhabited my body and was capable of doing the things I had to – planning the funeral, paying for the casket, collecting the ashes afterwards – but I was encased in a block of ice.

It was only later – six months perhaps, after the anger had kicked in, and I'd walked out on the house, the job, Diane, my ex-wife and everything that defined me, and all the tears and condolence cards and phone calls had stopped coming in – that the realisation hit home. I was here. Rosie was gone. My princess.

I must have drifted off at some point and dreamed a dream of tracks and blood and trains screeching. When I woke, it was pitch dark. My body shook and I was soaked in sweat. For a few seconds, I had no idea where I was.

I drank water from a glass on the bedside table and splashed the rest on my face. Then I got up, stripped off my wet clothes, pulled down the sheets and stood naked by the dormer window. Slowly, my breath started to temper, my clammy skin to cool.

It was half three. I put on a dressing gown and went barefoot downstairs. With the kitchen lights off, I stood in the conservatory in front of the bay windows, looking out at the night.

The thought occurred to me to go out, maybe pay for some company to see me through till morning. Visiting prostitutes had become a bit of a habit, and not one I was entirely comfortable with, but these last few years it'd been all the intimacy I could handle.

I came close, and had my phone out. Then I caught my reflection in the window and the idea crumbled. There stood a man who should be alone.

Marmite snaked between my legs.

'Hello, mate,' I said, and gave him my hand to sniff. He purred approvingly.

I scooped out some food from the fridge and fed him an early breakfast. Then I took a teacup from the sink, poured out an inch of Bushmills from a bottle on the counter and drank it in a single tasteless hit.

A few hours later, I was running five miles under a purple sky with the emerging sun hot on my face and the breeze cool on my back. Once home, I showered, percolated coffee and left a cup, along with some toast and a copy of the *Guardian*, for Dr Steiner.

Before setting off to find Dominic Tyrell, I considered my appearance in the hallway mirror. My eyes were puffy from a crap night's sleep, my hair greasy and unkempt, and the salt-and-pepper stubble on my chin looked sharp enough to strike a match on. I'd put on newish Levi's, a black tee, a North Face fleece and scuffed Caterpillars. When venturing into the City, a shirt and tie would be preferable, but I reminded myself that a man like me would always stick out in London's financial centre, no matter how spruced up he looked. I left as I was.

A little after eight, I was chaining my bike to a rail near Bank underground station. A wave of suited men and women were marching from the station, most clutching coffees and smartphones. All seemed to share the same expensive tastes in tailoring, and none seemed happy to be heading to their respective offices for the working day.

Whelan & Smyth Financial Services was based within a glass-fronted monolithic building, and was easy enough to find. A turnstile entrance was inside the foyer, manned by an elderly concierge dressed in a navy suit and cap. As financial people tapped through the turnstile, he mouthed 'Good morning' to each of them and smiled amiably. Few reciprocated.

Opposite the building was a narrow coffee shop with a clear view of the entrance. I positioned myself in a window seat, ordered black coffee and a sticky bun from a desolate waitress, and began staring at Whelan & Smyth, waiting for Dominic to rock up.

Surveillance work requires patience and concentration, qualities that have never come naturally to me. I sipped my coffee and chewed my bun, studied faces, admired figures, disliked others, and didn't spot Dominic. Everyone coming and going into Whelan & Smyth moved perfunctorily, and all ignored the concierge, who kept mouthing 'Good morning' nonetheless.

I'd counted four hundred and forty-one suited professionals, thirty-five buses, two pregnant women, a wheelchair, a milk float, a fire engine and a guide dog; and I'd drunk three coffees, eaten a second bun and discovered new realms of boredom by the time Dominic finally appeared at five to ten.

Superficially, he matched his LinkedIn profile, but he looked a little more haggard and quite a bit older. His face was blotchy and sagged; he had blow-dried hair worn in a side parting, with a shiny bald patch at the crown. Maybe five-ten, and a couple of stones overweight, he was wearing a black pinstripe suit and carrying a black briefcase. Within five seconds, he was inside the belly of the building and I was none the wiser as to who he was.

But I knew *where* he was.

I left the waitress a decent tip that failed to stir her and headed out of the café. Figuring Dominic would finish work around five, I had some time to kill.

The morning was like spring mornings are supposed to be: blue, bold and balmy. Ten minutes of walking and St Paul's Cathedral appeared; to my right was the Millennium Bridge, leading to the former power station that now housed the Tate Modern. A flock of teens were ahead, vaping and checking phones. To the left stood a pair of beggars, both stooped under sleeping bags worn like capes.

I lay on a grass bank and snoozed a little to make up for last night's lost sleep. Half two I was walking the scenic route around Mansion House, cantilevering up side roads, eventually heading back to the same window seat in the same café to catch Dominic leaving his offices.

Quarter to five, he reappeared. I darted across the road. The spill of rush-hour bodies was adding a buffer that could've made him easy to lose, but his wavy hair and the general cut of his jib helped keep him in sight. He looked preoccupied, like he was following a trail of string, his brow down, brief-case knocking against his thigh.

I stopped dead when I saw he was headed for the under-ground. Since Rosie, trains have had pretty bad associations, and I make a point of finding other means of transport. But on this occasion, I couldn't see an alternative – unless I was willing to lose Dominic, which I wasn't.

Deep breath, head down, I followed, and through the turnstiles and down the escalators we went, towards a Central Line platform where a jammed westbound train was just pulling in. Dominic squeezed into a packed carriage. I entered the next set of doors of the same carriage, wedging myself between a suited woman reading *War and Peace*, and a stocky bloke munching from a packet of beef McCoy's.

As soon as a seat became available, Dominic slumped into it. He rested his briefcase on his lap and began massaging his head, as if he had a migraine.

Each time the train accelerated, there was a screech that cut through me. I wanted to close my eyes, try shutting it out, but I couldn't risk losing sight of Dominic. Then, halfway to Oxford Circus, the train began stopping and starting, gaining speed, shuffling to a halt. Sweat was beading on my forehead by now, and I was starting to get some funny looks, no doubt for the grizzly expression I wore.

Fortunately, as we were pulling into Notting Hill Gate, Dominic stood and manoeuvred from the carriage. I pushed out too, and we headed for the escalators that took us to ground level.

A moment later, I was back out in the open, taking lungfuls of delightfully polluted city air. I'd have liked to cool down and ground myself a little, but I couldn't amble – Dominic was already away from the main drag of shops. I fished out my Wayfarers, kept him in sight and carried on.

Each corner of the capital has a different smell, a unique energy, and this patch was unfamiliar. There was the usual array of EEs and Costas, Boots and Prets, but these were nestled beside retro music shops, fashion boutiques and posh second-hand bazaars with Chanel handbags and Gucci heels on display.

After a few minutes, Dominic went into a bustling pub and emerged with a glass of spirit. Ever the cool sleuth, I ducked by an estate agency and watched.

He took a seat at an outside table and became immersed in his phone, his attention only wavering when a couple of buff young men, Tommy's age or thereabouts, sauntered past. He licked his lips and his eyes flitted round, seeming to follow their every move.

With his drink finished, he left. I pursued.

Another few minutes, and Dominic arrived at an ostentatious house situated on a wide road of other ostentatious houses. Marble steps led up to a pillared entrance and a wide white door bearing a brass knocker.

I walked leisurely by. Dominic seemed woefully unaware of my existence. He pulled out some keys, dropped them, picked them up and opened the door. Briefly, I heard a child call 'Daddy!' before the door clicked shut.

I did a U-turn and wandered back. A chiffon curtain parted in a neighbouring house, and an old woman's face appeared, staring at me balefully. I smiled. She didn't.

Suddenly, the Tyrell front door opened. A tall, overweight woman in an ill-fitting floral dress came on to the porch, followed by a girl of maybe ten wearing a school uniform. The woman had a cluster of empty wine bottles and was holding them away from her body, as if they were infectious.

I lifted my phone and pretended I was taking a call. She stomped to a wheelie bin and began depositing the bottles into it. A moment later, Dominic appeared in the doorway. He'd removed his shoes and tie; his expression was like a deflated balloon.

Turning to him, the woman said shrilly, 'Honestly, Dominic, I ask you to do one job!' before clunking in the last bottle, ushering the girl and him back into the house and slamming the door behind them.

And who said money can't buy happiness?

I finished my pretend call, made a mental note of the address, not that it would be easy to forget, gave the curtain-twitcher a second smile and began walking back the way we'd come, on the lookout for a bus headed north of town.

Chapter 8

Thirteen hours later, I was standing behind a different maple and watching the same woman who'd lambasted Dominic as she left the Tyrell house. A night's sleep hadn't done much for her: she looked ready to pick a fight with someone she knew she could beat. Two primary-age girls were with her, one of whom I'd seen yesterday, both dressed in leotards. Together, the trio trotted in the direction of the high street, leaving Dominic home alone.

This time, I'd come wearing a cunning disguise – shorts, trainers, a hoody and a baseball cap, plus my trusty Wayfarers. With luck, Dominic's prying neighbours would assume I was a minor celeb out on a morning jog and not call the police on me. Resting my palms on the maple trunk, I began stretching my quads and hamstrings while watching the Tyrell front door.

I was extending my right glute when Dominic appeared. He was wearing a cord dressing gown, pyjama bottoms and slippers. In one hand was another wine bottle for the recycling; in his mouth, an unlit cigarette.

I wanted the next bit to be quick, so crossed the street at a canter. He was sparking the smoke when I reached the porch gate. The sound of my footsteps made him look up. Uncertainty tightened his face.

'Can I help you?'

I climbed the steps, pulled down my hood and looked hard at him. 'Hello, DT,' I said.

I wanted him rattled – and he was. His eyes widened and his nostrils suckered in.

'You must be mistaking me for someone else,' he said, a slight lisp on the 's'.

'Don't think so, mate. We need to talk. Now.'

'I'd rather not, thank you. I'm expecting an important call and—'

'Dominic, we can do this one of two ways.'

'I'll call the police.' His voice was wobbling. 'I mean it—'

'Not if I don't let you.'

The lit cigarette dangled precariously from his mouth. I pulled it away. His bottom lip stuck to the filter.

'I'm not here to hurt you,' I said, stubbing out the cigarette on the bottom of my trainer, 'but we *are* going to talk.'

'Why?'

'Tommy.'

He gulped, and the wine bottle clanked to the ground. Perspiration was already glistening on his forehead and pooling in his philtrum. 'Who?'

'Give me your phone,' I said.

'What?'

'You keep saying who, why and what to me, Dom, I'm going to get angry. Now hand me your phone.'

His mouth opened, and stayed that way. With his left hand, he pulled a smartphone from his pocket.

'Unlock it.'

He did.

I took the phone, punched in Tommy's number, hit call and waited. A couple of seconds later, the name CC appeared on the screen. I held it up.

'CC? What's that stand for?'

He breathed out heavily, expelling smoky air. 'Cupcakes. That's the nickname he said I should call him. He's sent you, right? Wanting to scare me off? That little shit.'

I pocketed his phone and took his collar with my right hand. He stuttered something unintelligible.

'Don't call him that again,' I said. 'His name was Tommy. He's dead.'

'Dead? He can't be!'

I studied Dominic's face. Unless he was a shrewd actor, he hadn't known Tommy was dead.

'He jumped in front of a train,' I said. 'You didn't know?'

'No. This is all wrong. I can't help you—'

'Dom,' I said, 'you're making this harder than it needs to be. I'm not leaving without information.'

'I don't know anything!'

'Perhaps. But if you don't talk to me and let me decide that for myself, you'll leave me no choice.'

'Meaning?'

'I'll be forced to have a chat with the woman I saw leaving this house with those two pretty girls.'

'She'd think you were a crackpot,' he said weakly.

'Really? My experience, most spouses know when the other half's playing away. I'm guessing Tommy wasn't your first bit on the side. Right, Dom? Or should I call you *DT*?'

He looked like he needed to hawk something up. I was aware we were standing on his porch, I still had him by his collar, and to a neighbour or passer-by, it might look like I was trying to extort information through force and intimidation. Which I guess I was.

I let go of his collar and took a step back. Immediately, he slumped against the front door and grabbed his neck as if I'd strangled him.

'Dominic?' I said. 'What do you say?'

'Oh God.'

'Oh God, what?'

'OK, OK.'

'OK, what?'

He reached into his dressing gown pocket and fished out a set of door keys. Attached to them was a circular framed photo. It showed the two little girls I'd seen earlier.

'You'd better come in,' he groaned.

Dominic led me along a quarry-tiled hallway and into a large living space dominated by a marble fireplace with a raised hearth. To the room's rear was a sky-lit open-plan kitchen-conservatory that looked as if it'd been lifted from the pages of *Ideal Home*. Everything here was so new and clean and immaculate that it seemed forbidding – were the circumstances of my visit different, I'd have removed my shoes.

'My wife has taken the girls to ballet,' he said. 'They'll be back by eleven.'

'Well, we'd better not dawdle,' I said back.

The conservatory window overlooked one of the most exquisite gardens I've ever seen. The lawn was vast, trimmed like a military crew-cut, encircled by hydrangeas, rhododendrons, magnolias and azaleas; beyond was an oval pond, weeping willows, conifers and what appeared to be an American redwood tree.

'Nice pad,' I said, and turned to him.

Dominic grunted, opened an oak cabinet and removed a decanter of spirit. Everything about him seemed tired; his face, movements, even the way he breathed.

'Brandy?' he said.

I hesitated. A man I'd just accosted was offering me a drink at a quarter to nine in the morning.

'Why not?' I said.

With his back to me, he poured an inch into two tumblers. Fat creased at the rear of his scalp, turning a carbuncle red.

I took a glass and drank some. It was the good stuff. My mouth filled with a warm cherry taste that coursed down like honey.

With a drink in one hand, Dominic unlocked the conservatory door and we stepped on to the patio. He put his brandy on a ledge and lit a cigarette.

I came and stood beside him. 'My name's Kasper,' I said. 'Sorry I had to scare you.'

'How did you find me?' he said, blowing smoke at the sky.

'Your number was on Tommy's phone.'

'You're his pimp?'

'No.'

'Boyfriend?'

'No.'

He looked at me, expecting more.

I drank my brandy and said, 'I need you to tell me everything you can think of about Tommy and why he might've killed himself. Everything, Dominic. Understand?'

'I don't know, I swear. I didn't even know he was dead until you told me just now.'

'If you're lying, I'll find out and come back. It'll be a lot easier to tell me the truth now.'

'I don't know anything!'

His voice was puny, a rent in the quietness of the morning. It bugged me. It also suggested he was telling the truth, which bugged me even more.

'All right,' I said. 'You called Tommy a little shit. Why?'

He sighed.

'Let me guess,' I continued. 'He was blackmailing you? Some kind of honeytrap. Right?'

He sighed again. Sighing seemed to be a defining feature with Dominic. To pass the time while he geared himself up to speak, I took another sip of his exquisite booze.

'Yes,' he finally said. 'Yes, you're right.'

'OK. Don't leave anything out.'

Over the next ten minutes, Dominic told me the story of how he first encountered Tommy. It was six months back, at a place in Shoreditch called Mick's Bar. Apparently, Tommy strolled up to him and asked for a drink. The story sounded eerily familiar to when Tommy had approached me.

'We had a good time. He seemed so . . . *innocent*. Christ, it's embarrassing, talking about this with a stranger.'

'You're doing fine,' I said.

'At first I thought he was on the game. That's the kind of bar Mick's is, and that's what I'm used to. Lots of attractive boys looking for men like me, older, curious, and with cash. But instead, he took me to an apartment nearby. Not your typical knocking shop. This place was expensive. When we were alone, he seemed nervous, more nervous than I was. And after, he never asked for money.'

I felt a tingle in my belly. Pieces, ideas, new sides to Tommy were coming together, taking shape. 'So you didn't pay for sex?'

He shook his head. 'Tommy told me . . .' He stopped and sucked deeply on his cigarette. 'He said he was attracted to me. I believed him. You must understand, my marriage . . . it's not satisfying. I've tried to keep this side of myself hidden. My wife and I . . . well, our relationship isn't close. I've slept in a spare room since our youngest arrived.' He looked at the patio, rested his tumbler on a ledge and lit a second smoke. 'I thought Tommy was gorgeous. I fell for him.'

'Until he dumped you?'

He nodded. 'Like a sack of bricks.'

'Then what? Did he threaten to chat to your understanding wife the same way I just did?'

'No, no.' Sigh. 'It was crueller, more premeditated.' He looked at me unsteadily. 'He started sending me videos.'

'Videos?'

'Of us, together. Showing . . . you know . . . *everything*.'

Now we were getting somewhere. 'Where were the cameras?'

'I don't know. He must've had them hidden.'

'And then he showed you these videos?'

'No, they got sent.'

'Sent how?'

Dominic inhaled again, held the smoke and let it spray from his nostrils. 'First they came by SMS from withheld numbers, and then anonymous emails sent through Tor – the browser. Untraceable.'

This was all sounding pretty high-spec to me, more than I figured Tommy capable of single-handed. 'And then came the demands for money?'

'Yes.'

'How much?'

'The first time? Five hundred pounds. Cash.' He stubbed his cigarette on the patio and pocketed the butt.

'After that?'

'Tommy kept asking for more. Six hundred. Seven. Eight. A grand. Always cash. Otherwise the videos would get sent to my wife.'

'Didn't she suspect anything? That's a lot of money.'

He gave a weak chuckle. 'We're not poor. I have several bank accounts. Private money, spread around. It's not difficult to keep expenses hidden. What I can't control is those bloody videos.'

'Oh,' I said.

'My wife's from a powerful family. Years ago, she found out I'd had a fling. She was appalled and had me sign over everything in case I cheated again. All this – the house, the car – she'd get the lot. I didn't know what else to do but pay.' He lit up again, now on his third smoke.

'OK,' I said. 'Let's talk about these payments. Exactly how it works. You gave the cash to Tommy?'

'No, no, it's this strange routine. I put the cash in a brown envelope and take the envelope to some place in the middle of nowhere. I place it in a public bin at a specific time, then leave.'

'So you never actually saw Tommy with the money?'

'Correct.'

'When was your last payment?'

'Two weeks back.'

'How much?'

'A grand and a half.'

'So the amounts kept going up?'

'Yes. And I had nothing to bargain with. I wanted Tommy

to give me a guarantee. If I paid a fixed amount, the videos would be destroyed and that would be it.'

'You asked him for this?'

'Well, I tried to.'

'What did he say?'

'He wouldn't answer my calls. When I saw him at Mick's Bar, usually with a new victim on his arm, there were always minders about, stopping me.'

'Minders?'

He nodded. 'I heard they actually beat up some poor sod like me who got heavy with him.'

'Were there others?'

'Oh yes. He snared plenty more, I'm sure of it.'

'Tell me about these minders. Names? What do they look like?'

'I haven't a clue. You'll find them at the bar. They're like you. Big lumps, watching, always ready to step in. There's one particular thug. He's terrifying. Has a tattoo on his neck. I thought he was Tommy's pimp until you appeared.'

Minders. Pimps. This all sounded quite lucrative, and more than a little dodgy.

But things were still unclear. I drained my brandy and put the glass on the ledge.

'Let me see them.'

'What?'

'These videos. You need to show them to me. Now.'

I wasn't sure if it was a gasp, a squeal or a mix of both I heard.

'Why?'

'Because I say so.'

'Now listen, Kasper,' he said, the brandy giving him some

balls. 'You're not police. What right have you got to snoop into my life like this?'

'I've not got any right. But I'm telling you how it is.'

'No! I won't be—' he started. I turned and stared at him, and something in my expression made him stop cold.

'Behave, Dom. So far I've heard you piss and moan and not show any regret for a dead kid. He was a nice person. Nicer than you. Try and dick me about, I'll get angry. Understand?'

His cheeks puffed out like a trombonist's. 'I don't have the videos anymore,' he said quietly. 'They're all deleted.'

'Come on. City boys like you know all about tech. Find them. I don't mind waiting. We've got till eleven, unless you'd like to introduce me to your wife and kids? We could all watch them together, if you'd prefer.'

His complexion seemed to darken. He breathed in and shook his head. He was stuck, and knew it.

'Wait here,' he said. 'I'll get my laptop.'

'Bring the brandy too.'

Ten minutes later, I was on a bench in the shade of the Tyrell patio, scrolling through a bunch of sordid videos of Tommy with Dominic. All the short films were taken from a waist-height camera, probably concealed in a wall or a mantelpiece. The sound was muffled, the picture grainy, but overall, the quality was clear enough.

Naked, Dominic's body was pasty, his droopy chest laden with curly brown hairs. He had skinny arms, a spotty behind; his stomach was large and bulbous, like a hard-boiled egg.

Although taller than Dominic, Tommy looked impish and very young. He was soft, pale, hairless apart from the flop of fringe he kept flicking from his eyes. He made all the right sounds and smiled appropriately to whet Dominic's desire, but there was something lacking in this Tommy. I was watching a performance.

One close-up section showed the pair in full view. They were finished, standing in their pants, giggling, smoking cigarettes. Tommy's brown eyes were staring directly into the lens.

'He knew about the camera,' I said. 'You can tell from the way he's positioned you both.'

'Of course he knew,' Dominic said. 'It was a set-up.' He poured more brandy. 'And now you know, too. You must think I'm despicable.'

I closed the laptop and didn't respond.

'I love my children, Kasper.'

'Good.'

He looked at me expectantly.

'One thing I don't understand,' I said. 'When I told you Tommy was dead, you said he can't be. Explain.'

'Isn't it obvious?'

'No.'

'I've had another demand for money.'

That explained why he looked so cranky. 'When?'

'Huh?'

'When was the demand?'

'Two days ago. I'm to deliver the cash next Monday. Tommy must've sent it before he killed himself. Perhaps guilt finally got the better of him.'

A tuning fork pinged in my ears.

'Tommy couldn't have sent this latest demand,' I said.

'How do you know?'

'Because he was already dead two days ago.'

I paused, let things settle. As I did, Tommy's words returned to me:

'*I thought I was doing the right thing . . .*'

The right thing – this wasn't a straight-up monetary gain scheme.

'How much is this new cash drop meant to be?' I said.

'What?'

'The money, Dom. How much have you been told to bring?'

'Two thousand, cash. But why? You told me he's dead. Surely that means it's over and—'

'Dom,' I butted in, 'I'm not sure if you're a mug or just plain stupid. Tommy wasn't doing the blackmailing. You were both being used.'

His eyes darted left to right as he took this in. 'By who?'

'I have my suspicions. But I need proof.'

'Proof? How will you get it?'

I stood.

As the realisation sunk in, Dominic's mouth sagged and he began to tremble. He took the final cigarette from his pack. He was having trouble catching the flame, so I cupped my hand around it. If there'd been a sharp gust of wind at that moment, I think it would've toppled him.

'You're going to help me,' I said.

Chapter 9

So, I'd learned something new about Tommy, and had a rough idea of what I was going to do next. But I couldn't put the rest of my meagre life on hold. That afternoon and evening, I was down to work at McGovern's.

A little after noon, I was back north of the city, cycling past the thrusting blocks of the Paradise Towers Estate where I grew up. The spring sun was illuminating the waste kept hidden by the night – unidentifiable rubbish spilling from the bins, broken bottles, drugs paraphernalia, a stained mattress fly-tipped by the football cage. A trio of women in hijabs power-walked laps around the football cage; behind them, Vietnamese pensioners held t'ai chi poses on the yellowing grass. A few rough-sleepers were slumped on benches: drunks, addicts, the displaced and forgotten; some sleeping, the rest staring vacantly.

McGovern's was one of the few ramshackle boozers that remained from my childhood. It was pitted against the wave of frilly vegan cafés, craft ale cocktail bars and namby-pamby bistros popping up at an exponential rate in northeast London. I'd pulled pints here the last few years, and considered the job a stepping stone back into gainful employment, if you could call it that.

There was little that was frilly here. Two hanging lamps cast bars of dusty columnar light on to the faded pine floor. Old Spurs and Irish Stout posters were tacked to three of the walls; from the fourth hung a gnarly dartboard.

Paddy the landlord was doing a beer-pipe clean when I arrived, and had slosh buckets beneath the draft taps to pump steriliser into. Sweat patches darkened his grey tee, and his face was wet and ruddy.

A Donegal man, Paddy was a sober alcoholic, and had been the only person willing to employ a down-on-his-luck ex-plod when I came looking for work. My job interview went something like this:

'Know how to pour a Guinness?'

'Yup.'

'Reckon you can handle yerself if the drinkers get tasty?'

'Yup.'

I worked my first shift that night.

Rumour had it that Paddy used to be a proper tearaway in his day. Drink took him to jails, institutions, homelessness and the brink of death. He dried out in a Thai monastery, hooked up with a woman he met there, fathered a baby, split from the woman when she relapsed, came to London with his daughter Suzanna and took up as a publican in one of northeast London's mankiest boozers, an unusual vocation given his past, but one that kept him on the frontline of life's inequities, and aware of how much he had to lose.

I think Paddy's work ethic was the main reason McGovern's didn't go under. He was at the pub seven days a week, cleaning, stocktaking, or sharing the craic with his countrymen well into the small hours. Whatever the weather, he was always hot and clammy, and carried a permanent wheeze from the roll-ups and fried breakfasts he favoured.

Our daytime patrons tended to be the have-nots, weirdos, widowers, crackpots and one or two bona fide crazies; all came alone and nursed their pints and brandies. A little later came a sprinkling of flat-capped old geezers and functioning alcoholics drawn to Paddy's rock-bottom prices and reliable banter.

I percolated some coffee and drank three cups behind the bar as I chatted with a bricklayer from Tipperary, also called Paddy. He had the rubbery complexion certain habitual drinkers wear in midlife, plus a scatological sense of humour that rarely failed to amuse me. To be honest, it was good to chat, for it took my head somewhere other than Tommy Berkowitz, dead for nearly a week.

Around four, Landlord Paddy nipped out and returned with two bacon and egg butties. We ate at the bar, and I asked him about Suzanna, now sixteen. Last time I saw her, she'd tried to hoodwink me into popping vodka into her lemonade, much to Paddy's disapproval.

'She's not good, Kas,' he said, shaking his head. 'That girl's out late each night, fraternisin' with the boys, so.'

He wedged a doorstop of bread, meat and yolk into his mouth and chewed. Unable to find a napkin, he wiped his hands on the thighs of his jeans.

'She's just a kid, Pad,' I said, recalling the headache I used to give Rosie when she spent evenings out with mates. 'Let her have some fun.'

'Fun? Out there's a dangerous place. Men only want one thing. Say it ain't so?'

I shrugged.

'Speakin' of which,' he said, leaning in with a grin, 'when're you finding yourself a lady-friend, young Kasper? Have your own wee family. Settle down.'

I smiled. Paddy was one of the many acquaintances I'd made over the past five years who knew little of my past, other than that I had one and preferred not to talk about it. 'Think I missed that boat,' I said.

'Have you, fuck. You could take your pick if you just smiled a bit more.' He chuckled and began rolling a fag.

I finished my food and collected our plates. The ping of the old-fashioned register sounded as Paddy began totting up cash.

'Go on, Kas,' he said, handing me a week's pay, close to a couple of tons in total. 'Have a wee break, and I'll see you later for the night crowd.'

I trousered my wages and we shook hands across the bar.

Outside the pub, I called the Equilibrium.

'My personal trainer Jazz borrowed my phone charger,' I said in my most affable voice. 'You know when he's in next? My battery's dead and I really need to check my Insta.'

The woman on the other end of the line seemed to understand my dilemma, which was more than I did, and told me Jazz liked to train mornings, normally around ten. I thanked her and hung up. *See you tomorrow, Jazz.*

Paddy's suggestion that I should try connecting with someone of the opposite sex was not entirely without foresight. Following an exchange of text messages yesterday evening, I'd arranged to meet Diane McAteer that afternoon for a stroll.

She and I had first met when I was a uniform. The scene was a bungled Post Office robbery that I'd stumbled upon by chance. I'd apprehended one of the thieves as he tried a Houdini escape trick through the back window, and was holding him in an armlock and waiting for backup.

Diane was the first copper to respond to my call. She slammed him over a ledge, stuck the cuffs on and kneed his crown jewels when he tried to bite her. I think I fell in love there and then.

My family life was not so good at the time. Carol and I had tried reconciliations and couples counselling for the sake of twelve-year-old Rosie, but we both knew the marriage was finished in all but name.

Diane was a working-class Caribbean girl already on her way up the Met ladder; she had a sharp head, strong values and a clear goal. I, on the other hand, was a die-hard bobby whose aversion to authority and tendency to favour rough justice always scuppered my chances of a promotion.

In spite of these differences, it didn't take long for our mutual attraction to show. For a good couple of years, we had an arrangement – we weren't living in each other's pockets, but we were together. Carol knew, Rosie knew. The plan was I'd leave the marriage and we'd set up.

But that's *not* what happened.

Instead, Rosie died.

The whole lot blew apart, and I walked out on everything.

Today, I nipped home, showered, changed into fresh Levi's and a blue linen shirt and headed back out, my heart beating unusually fast at the prospect of seeing Diane. I was nervous. Wherever this went today, it had to go slow.

She'd suggested a walk, and I'd suggested a disused railway line running through the back-end of the borough, now a rugged path popular with joggers and walkers.

I passed the tube exit a few minutes early and spotted her over the road by the entrance. With her was Murphy, her indomitable pooch. I gave the pair a whistle. Diane waved back.

Murphy was a light brown lurcher crossed with a Great Dane. Diane had adopted her from an Alzheimer's-suffering uncle who'd christened the dog thinking she was a he. By the time the error came to light, the name had stuck. Last time I'd seen her, Murphy was little more than a pup; now she was the shape of an elongated donkey, and carried a heavy protrusion around her belly that could mean only one thing.

'Big doggy,' I said as I wandered up.

'That how you always greet an old flame?' Diane said.

'Not you. *Her*.' I pointed at Murphy and her swollen gut. 'She's in the family way, by the looks of things?'

'My girl got knocked up,' Diane said, and laughed. 'She's due next month, aren't you, Murph?'

'Who's the dad?'

'Some stud she met in the park. I let her off the lead for five minutes and look what happens.'

Murphy strained to sniff me and I cupped her jaw, kneading her coat. Diane manoeuvred around the dog's lumbering frame and we shared a hug.

Being in her late thirties had in no way diminished Diane's features. Her brown cheeks had lost some of their fullness, perhaps, replaced with a firm bone structure that accentuated her olive-green eyes. She still had a distinctive gap between her front two teeth, a feature she always used to threaten to have fixed, and a scattering of freckles above her nose that would blanch whenever she was angry or we made love. Seniority on the Met demanded she shed the pumps and jeans for shoes and blazers, but I could still hear the patois twang in her accent and the rasp in her laugh.

We started walking, veering along the grassy banks that ascended to the entrance of the path. 'So, Kas,' Diane said, 'how you been these last five years? Fill me in.'

'Fair-to-middling.'

'Diplomatic answer.'

'That's me. The soul of diplomacy.'

She smiled. 'This Tommy Berkowitz thing must've brought up a whole heap of stuff?'

'It has,' I said.

'Let me ask you something. You see his death coming?'

'If I had, he wouldn't be dead.' My voice carried an edge I hadn't intended. 'Sorry. That came out wrong.'

'It's all right. Poor choice of words from me. But I take it from that you're not letting all this lie?'

'I've been making some enquiries.'

'In an unofficial capacity?'

'There's nothing official about me anymore, Diane.'

We crossed through a brick underpass that angled right. This took us on to the gravelled walk where the rail tracks once lay. Green shrubs and scrubland were on either side of us; ahead, a dusty pathway of parched earth.

'So, what've you found out?' she said.

I summarised my morning, what I'd learned from Dominic Tyrell about Tommy's honeytrap scheme, and my plan to follow Dom's money for his final drop.

When I'd finished, she said, 'Yep. I thought so. You're still a fucking fruitcake. Tell me, why get into this mess?'

'It's hard to explain.'

'Try.'

I did my best to find a decent answer, one that wouldn't set me up for Diane's rebuke.

I couldn't. The truth was, I wasn't entirely sure why I was doing this. I just knew I had to.

'Tommy was a nice kid,' I said.

'And?'

'He asked me to be his friend.'

'His *friend*? Are you for real?'

For a moment, I thought she was about to weigh in on me or thunder off.

Instead, she laughed. It threw me.

'What's funny?'

'You're endearing. You're also stubborn, and pretty blink-ered not to realise this is about your daughter.'

That stung, but I kept it down and didn't say anything. Maybe she had a point.

'But it's rare to know a man with a set of values,' she added, 'even if they are half-baked.'

I found myself smiling at this. 'So you think I'm chivalrous?'

'A little. Crazy too. But in a charming way.'

'I'll take that.'

'If I asked you to pull the plug, would you?'

'Nope.'

'Thought so.' She shrugged. 'So, you have any suspects yet?'

'This bar Tommy went to sounds the obvious spot to start looking. Plus his sister seems a bit frosty with me. We'll see what comes up.'

'Yeah, we will,' Diane said, and slowed a little. 'But ser-iously, Kas, promise me something.'

'What?'

'You get into hot water or need any help, call me.'

'Deal,' I said. 'Anyway, that's enough about me. I want to hear about you, Detective Sergeant. How've you been?'

'How'd you think? Mad busy keeping bad guys off the streets.'

'What's seniority like in the Met?'

She rolled her eyes. 'I'm working specialist financial ops mostly. As long as management keep off my back, it's not too bad. Cuts aren't helping much.'

'You living by yourself?'

'Bought a flat in Finchley, big man. Check me out. Home owner.'

'Good for you.'

'I heard you're shacked up with some retired psychiatrist?'

'Uh-huh. She's a chain-smoking lesbian Jew. We've got loads in common.'

That earned a decent laugh.

'So what're you doing for work?' she said.

'I tend bar at McGovern's. Remember the place?'

'The rough old boozer off Tottenham High Road?'

'The very same. I'm back there tonight.'

'Man, you pick your spots.'

'I like it there. It's enough for now. Drop by.'

'Maybe. I've cut back on my alcohol since we split, though. I went teetotal for the whole of March.'

'How come?'

'This guy I was seeing, some life-coach I met on Tinder, he asked me to do a detox thing with him. No booze, no caffeine, no white flour, no nothing but brown rice, juices and fruits.'

'Sounds empowering.'

'Nah. It was torture. I was bored out my skull.'

'What happened?'

'I ended it. He was getting on my nerves. I couldn't wait to get back on the steak and wine just to get rid of him.'

I laughed again, louder this time. Murphy started wagging her tail and heaved Diane on the lead towards a clod of earth.

Not long after, we were sloping away from the walk and up towards the northern exit of Archway Road.

'Buy you a shandy?' Diane said. 'There's a dog-friendly pub up that way.'

I hesitated for a moment and said, 'Not right now. But thanks for asking.'

She nodded, said, 'You look well. I like the hair and stubble. It kind of suits you. I did wonder if I'd ever see you again, you know?'

Cars, buses and bikes swished by on the main road. At random, I stared at a red Audi.

'After Rosie,' I said, 'I needed to be alone. I had nothing to give.' I looked at Diane, then away again. 'That's no excuse, though. I treated you badly.'

'You did,' she said.

'But all this stuff with Tommy, it's forced me out of myself. I feel like I'm coming back to how I was.'

'Yeah, I can tell. But where's it going to lead?'

I paused a moment, and took a chance. 'Maybe we'll do this again sometime?'

'Yeah, maybe.'

We went back to looking at each other, neither of us speaking.

'Well,' she eventually said, 'I'll be getting my bus, then.'

We hugged, a little harder, a little longer. Diane's chin moved up my neck and I breathed the coconut in her hair.

My hand glanced over her shoulder, and for a moment it was like before, until I pulled away.

As we parted, she said, 'Oh, I almost forgot. Someone's been calling round the police stations, trying to get hold of you. He came through to me yesterday.'

'Who's that?'

'His name's Emmanuel Meads. He drove the train that hit the Berkowitz kid. He was asking if I knew the big fellow he spoke to outside the station. I told him I might.'

'What's he want?'

'To talk, I guess.'

'About?'

'Haven't a clue.'

I thought. 'Sure. Give him my number.'

'Don't be a stranger, big man.'

Chapter 10

Reconnecting with Diane left me surprisingly chipper. The following morning, I thought I'd capitalise on my good mood by cycling to the Equilibrium to make friends with steroid-chomping Jazz and find out what he knew.

A strawberry-blonde receptionist was at the desk, engrossed in her phone. As I passed through the turnstile and said hi, she glanced up, gave a limp smile and immediately returned to her screen.

Back in the juice bar, I ordered a coffee and a muffin and positioned myself on the same stool where I'd been sitting the day Tommy approached me. It was strange being back, and I couldn't help wonder what would've happened if I'd told him thanks but no thanks to his offer of a drink.

There wasn't time to ponder. Jazz rocked up a few minutes before ten. He was clad in compression tights and a hoody, the sleeves cut short to accentuate his vast biceps and deltoids. A brunette girl wearing a tiger-print sports bra and leggings was hanging on to one of his arms; over his shoulder hung a Nike training bag and boxing gloves.

I hid my face behind a copy of *Men's Health* magazine and watched him chat to the girl before patting her rear and descending the stairs to the changing rooms. A moment later I followed him down.

The changing rooms smelled of lemony soap and room diffusers. Hair-straighteners, blow-dryers and various toiletries had been tastefully arranged in front of the wall-sized mirrors, and dreamy ambient music circulated from ceiling-mounted speakers.

Maybe a dozen semi-naked males were standing by lockers, changing or unchanging. All these guys were ripped and buff, and talked intermittently as they moisturised, towelled and waxed various appendages. I couldn't help but notice a distinct lack of body hair. A few glanced at me as I wandered past. Clothed as I was, I felt strangely exposed.

The rooms were built in a kind of T-shape, with showers and the steam room to the left and lockers curving round to the right.

Jazz was by a locker at the furthest end, his back to me. Wireless headphones were wrapped over his ears, and his head was bobbing to a rhythm. He was bare-chested, removing kit from his bag. The muscles in his back rippled like bricks sheathed in latex.

I considered my next move. Going in too fast would startle him and maybe provoke another fight, which I was keen to avoid. A slow, open-handed approach sounded better – I'd stop a few feet away, wait for him to peer up, then I'd make peace.

That's what I did.

Sensing my presence, Jazz tensed and looked round. His eyes grew wide. I gave a smile. He flinched as recognition kicked in.

Holding up my hands, I mouthed, 'Hey, Jazz,' so he could understand me over his music. 'Good seeing you, mate.'

He flinched again, putting distance between us, and I saw my error. I turned my shoulder when his fists came up, swung back as he loaded a punch and ducked. He missed my face and hit a locker behind me, maybe breaking a knuckle in the process.

No chance for bridge-building, then.

The impact made a clang, and pain grappled his face. Moving fast, I struck an open-handed slice to his neck: not hard enough to do anything lasting, but with enough oomph for him to feel like he'd eaten his tongue. It was a trick I'd learned as a teenager – nothing's damaged permanently, but it pretty much guarantees your man's going down.

And down he went.

He grasped his windpipe, slid against the locker and sprawled on to the bench at its foot. His face turned terracotta, veins bulging to the surface of the skin. I removed the headphones and lay them by his head.

'Easy,' I said, sitting next to him. 'Just breathe.'

He made a hacking noise.

'What was that racket?'

A chiselled man with a towel around his midriff had appeared. He put his hands on his hips and looked at me about as sternly as someone in his attire could.

'We're all good, mate,' I said, giving the thumbs-up. 'Jazz just choked on some protein shake. Right, Jazz?'

Jazz kept hacking.

I shrugged nonchalantly at the man, as if to say, *what can you do?*

He frowned, waited a moment and then wandered off, looking over his shoulder.

I waited for Jazz's breathing to steady. It sounded like the back-end of an asthma attack.

After a minute or so, he was able to sit up himself. He massaged his neck and stared at the floor. Dribble hung from his lip.

'What do you want?' he croaked.

'I came to say sorry.' I tried for another handshake. 'Let's be friends.'

His pallor was now a curious mix of beetroot red and baby-shit brown. He shoved my hand away.

'Caught me by surprise,' he said. 'I could beat you.'

'No, you couldn't, Jazz. There're things I'm good at. Fighting's one of them. But that's OK. I'm sure you've got other qualities.'

'Piss off.'

'I need to talk to you about Tommy.'

'What about him?'

'He's dead. Jumped in front of a train last week. You hear about that?'

He looked up. 'What?'

I repeated it.

'You're sure?'

'Yeah,' I said. 'I'm sure.'

Suddenly, through all the muscles and machismo, he looked very young.

I gave him some time to process it, then said, 'Before our first scuffle, you said something to Tommy about me not being his usual type. Tell me what you meant?'

'Why?'

Good question. 'Because I'm going to find out why he did it,' I said.

104

He blew air through his mouth and wetted his lips.

'I'm not talking to you,' he said. 'I don't believe a word you're saying.'

'Ah, come on Jazz—'

'You're scum.'

I was beginning to warm to him. 'I'll do you a deal,' I said. 'Talk to me, and I promise to disappear like a nasty smell. Poosh. But if you don't, I'll be forced to tell the friendly staff upstairs and the police about that tidy stash of anabolic steroids you've got in your locker. That's criminal possession, mate, plus intent to supply. You could go to prison. They'd like you inside.'

He blinked rapidly, and kept licking his lips. The bottom one started to tremble.

'How'd you know about the 'roids?'

'I didn't. You just told me. But now that I *do* know, I'll use it if you don't give me what I want.' I gave him time to mull it over.

'All right,' he said. 'Upstairs.'

I bought Jazz an orange juice and myself another black coffee. I was beginning to get used to the sour stares from the Equilibrium staff. The latest came from the pink-haired girl serving our drinks. Palming my change from the counter, she ignored my smile entirely.

'Are employees here always so friendly?' I said when she was out of earshot.

Jazz shrugged. 'You stick out.'

'How so?'

'You're not the usual sort who comes here. You're a bit . . . *rough*.'

I smiled to myself and sipped my coffee. Roughly.

'What's your real name?' I said.

'Jasper.'

'Nice. I'm Kasper.' I took another sip. 'Jasper and Kasper.'

Ignoring my repartee, he leaned in and said quietly, 'How'd you know I take pills?'

'I've been around gyms. Before long, you get a smell for them.'

He shook his head, clearly dismayed. 'Tommy used to have a go at me for using them.'

'Did he?' I said. 'You and him used to talk a bit then, did you?'

Jazz's eyes filmed with tears.

'You had feelings for Tommy. Right?'

He said nothing, just took his glass and began rotating it.

'Did you ever tell him?' I asked.

'Yeah.'

'What happened?'

'He told me I was too young, too much of a gym bro for him. He said he went for older guys with money. That's why I said you weren't his usual type.'

'What makes you think I don't have money?'

'I didn't—'

'Forget it, Jazz. I'm messing with you.' I winked at him. 'Is that why you picked a fight with me? Because you saw I was with Tommy?'

He shook his head. 'Tommy asked me to start on you. It was a set-up.'

My drive to get to the bottom of this was suddenly flattened by a sense of shock.

'A set-up?'

Jazz nodded. 'You never realised?'

'No,' I said. 'I guess not.'

'Tommy was into things like that. Manipulating people. Making them do what he wanted. When you went to the gents, he called me over and said if I made you think I was bullying him, he'd go out with me. He told me you were a pussy, and I should square up to you. You know what happened after that.'

'Yeah,' I said. 'Sorry.' I was still taking this in. 'Why do you think he asked you to do all that?'

'Isn't it obvious?'

'Not really.'

'He was testing you. He wanted to see if you'd come to his rescue. And you did.'

I nodded slowly.

Jazz drank some juice, frowning as he moved his swelling knuckle. He looked me up and down, and said, 'So you're not with the police?'

'No.'

'Who asked you to do this? Tommy's family?'

'No.'

'But you're sure he's dead?'

'I'm sure.'

'I still don't get it. Why dig into his life?'

This time, I decided to opt for the same answer I'd given Diane. 'He asked me to be his friend.'

But being there in the bar, the spot where I'd first met Tommy, it dawned on me that maybe Dr Steiner and Diane had a point: this was as much about Rosie as it was Tommy – and I couldn't let the same thing happen again.

Tears were forming again in Jazz's eyes. 'I think that's what Tommy was really looking for. A friend. Someone he could trust.'

107

'He ever mention money to you?' I said.

'Just that he never had any.'

'You knew about his credit card debts?'

'No. But I'm not surprised to hear it. He was always getting men here to buy him stuff.'

'And these men, you think he slept with many of them?'

'What do you think?'

'I think he did.'

'There you go.' Jazz looked back at his hands. 'You know, I'd never told anyone I liked guys until I met Tommy. I get a lot of attention, but it's mainly from the girls. That's cool, but it's not who I really am. I know Tommy was crazy, but he was so open about who he was. I thought maybe we could help each other. Now it's too late.'

Watching Jazz, I felt for him. Behind that brawn, he was just another mixed-up kid trying to make sense of the world and his place in it.

'You and Tommy ever hook up outside the gym?' I said.

He nodded. 'Just the once.'

'Only once?'

He rubbed the back of his neck. 'About six months back, I asked him out. He said fine, as long as he could pick the place. Well, let's just say that place wasn't my scene.'

'How come?'

'It's this scuzzy gay club not far from here. A pick-up bar, you know? Full of slime-bag businessmen and rough trade boys.'

I nodded. *Slime-bags like Dominic Tyrell.*

'Remember the name of this bar?'

He tapped his brow, thinking.

'Was it Mick's?'

'That's the one. Mick's Bar.'

'So why did Tommy want you two to go there?'

He shrugged. 'God knows. Maybe for the attention. He was getting loads of it, but it was the worst kind, all these creeps eyeing him up. Tommy said he liked it. He even introduced me to the owner of the bar, this weird little guy with gold teeth who kept feeling my arms, paying me compliments, telling me how much money I could earn with my looks. Part of me knew Tommy didn't want to be there. But when I tried telling him, he brushed me off, told me to get a life. It hurt.'

He paused, took a deep breath, held it for several seconds and let it flow from his mouth slowly. 'I know Tommy was nutty. But I can't believe he's actually . . . gone.' He looked at me through red eyes. 'Is this my fault?'

'No, Jazz,' I said. 'Something else made Tommy snap.'

'What was it?'

'I'm not sure yet. But I'm going to find out.' I paused. 'Now I want you to tell me everything else you can about Tommy. Whatever you have, it might help. That OK?'

He nodded, and for the next ten minutes I said nothing, just listened. There wasn't a lot he said that I didn't already know or suspect, and some of it was clearly irrelevant; but when digging, I've found it's a good idea to wait until someone finishes talking, and to pay attention to every detail and mannerism, however minor it may seem.

By the time he'd told me all he knew about Tommy, Jazz looked close to really cracking. 'I'm sorry,' he said. He took a serviette and began dabbing his eyes. 'I don't know what else to tell you.'

'You've done good,' I said.

'Suicide. I never thought *this* would happen. Poor Tommy, I can't imagine it . . .'

'Don't try to,' I said. 'It's not worth it, mate.'

We both looked at our drinks.

Before leaving, I told Jazz a few of the names from Tommy's phone contacts, asked if any rang bells. The only one to chime was Harriet.

'She's Tommy's sister, right?' he said.

'Yeah. She seems pretty uptight.'

'I don't know about that. I mean, when he told me about her, they sounded close. After their mum died, they stuck together, the two of them. He thought the world of her.'

I nodded. 'He ever mention his dad?'

'The professor?'

'That's him.'

'Not really. Just that he'd been on the radio, and travelled a lot with his work.'

I wasn't going to get any more out of Jazz. The kid had just had a shock and needed time to process it. I finished my coffee, made to stand.

'Wait,' he said. 'What if I remember something? How will I reach you?'

I wrote my mobile number on the corner of *Men's Health* and tore it off. 'Here. You think of anything, call me.'

Jazz pocketed it and turned to me. His lips rose into a tremulous smile.

'Take it easy,' I said. 'What you told me today, it was helpful.'

A firm handshake, and I left.

★

I tried calling Saul Berkowitz that evening. The thought of giving him a progress report didn't fill me with joy, but he'd asked to be kept up-to-date, and he might be able to shed a bit of light on the things I'd learned.

Harriet answered the phone.

'Sorry to disturb you,' I said. 'I was wondering if I could speak to your father?'

'Why?' Her tone was curt and decidedly offish.

'I've got a few questions and—'

'About Tommy?'

'Yeah. About Tommy.'

'Well, you can ask me.'

I cleared my throat. 'OK. I've learned he was going to various bars. One in particular, a place called Mick's. You ever hear him mention it?'

'No. Anything else?'

'How about a man called Tyrell? Dominic Tyrell?'

'Never heard of him.'

'What about men Tommy met at the gym? Any names stick in your mind?'

'I have no idea what Tommy got up to at the gym. Exercising, I'd presume. Where're you going with this, *Mr* Kasper?'

'Harriet,' I said, 'I know this is hard, but—'

'How dare you!' she said. 'You don't know anything about my family! This stops now. If you don't leave me and my father alone, I will call the police. Please, just buzz off and let us grieve in peace.'

She hung up.

I looked at the handset.

Buzz off?

What should I do? Call back and pump her for more?

No. She'd only hang up again. And behind her anger, I sensed fear. My guess, it was somehow linked up with the stuff Dominic Tyrell spilled to me about.

But to find out what it was, I needed a hook, a way in. Hopefully Dominic's money would give me one. And if that failed, I'd have to think of something else.

But truth be told, I hadn't a clue what I was about to walk into.

Chapter 11

It was mid-morning on Monday, the day of Dominic Tyrell's final cash drop, and I'd still not heard from him about the time and place.

I was starting to think he'd been rumbled or had bailed on me, until he finally rang at lunchtime. I was at McGovern's, sipping a shandy. In a shrill, slightly hysterical voice, he said he'd been instructed to go to a housing estate in north London at 4 p.m. and leave the cash in a sealed brown envelope in a bin by a climbing frame.

I hung up, looked at the estate's address on Google Maps and did a quick recce of the area. It was in the back-end of Tottenham, my stomping ground.

I called Dominic back, told him to take the cash to the designated spot and not to blow my cover, as I'd be following, then put the phone down on his stuttering objections.

At half three, I was chaining my bike to a lamp post a stone's throw from Seven Sisters tube. There was a Turkish café opposite. I took a window seat with a clear view and waited for Dominic.

The place smelled of shisha and mint tea. Tinny dub played from a PA, and the sounds of sizzling meat and a heated conversation in Arabic permeated from the kitchen. The only other customer was an orthodox Jewish woman on a neighbouring table. She was chewing chicken drumsticks with one hand and tapping an iPhone with the other.

I sipped a Turkish coffee the texture of tarmac and watched the comings and goings on the busy high street. A one-eyed male was begging by the station railings, his face marred with nicks and scabs, telltale signs of crack picking. A few feet to his right were two women, one white, one black African, both holding copies of *The Watchtower* and smiling at whoever walked past.

At ten to four, Dominic emerged from the station. He stood out horrendously, and looked like he knew it. His eyes were fevered, flitting left and right. He swerved around the beggar and nearly stumbled into the two women, who kept smiling. Over his right shoulder there was a tan Gucci man-bag. I figured it contained the cash.

His face tightened when he spotted me through the window of the café. I put a finger to my lips. He nodded, turned and began walking north.

I left a few quid on the table and headed out, then unchained my bike and started after Dominic. I didn't rush, just stayed on the pavement, pushing the bike by the handlebars and keeping the rear of his head visible twenty or so yards ahead.

We passed a vast Tesco, a bus depot, a fried chicken shop, a bookie shop, ethnic travel agents, ethnic food shops, Cash Converters and more chicken shops and bookies before the road opened into bland residential streets of boxy flats and run-down houses.

Ten minutes later, we were entering a grim industrial site characterised by gruel-coloured duplexes, iron railings, orange cladding and heaps of rubble. By now, Dominic was looking decidedly on edge. He kept stopping to light cigarettes, check his phone, or glance over his shoulder to see where I was. This was annoying. If he were being watched, it would've been clear he had a shadow. But by then, I was pretty sure he wasn't.

After passing through the industrial site, we turned right into a residential street and took a left through an underpass. Our destination lay on the other side. I stopped and watched Dominic emerge from the shadows.

A cluster of liver-coloured council flats stood opposite him, bunched together. To their left was a kids' playground, and beside its climbing frame was a bin. Dominic sloped over to it.

Reaching into his man-bag, he removed a brown envelope. After looking both ways, he placed it into the bin. Quickly, he turned and started walking fast, away from the playground, not looking back.

He scurried through the underpass, retracing his steps. Briefly, our eyes met. He looked shaken, but he'd done what I'd asked, and was a grand and a half the poorer for it. I gave him a nod of thanks. The last thing I heard was the flick of his lighter as he fired another smoke.

I checked my watch. Four-ten.

My location was good, and gave a clear view of the bin, but I wasn't an easy spot. I rested my bike against the underpass, folded my arms and watched. I had a fair idea of what would happen next. It was just a case of waiting it out.

Sure enough, Harriet Berkowitz appeared at quarter to five.

After parking her Skoda in a resident's bay, she hurried into the playground towards the bin. She was wearing a black blazer and pencil skirt. Her face was hidden behind aviators.

She didn't bother locking the car or turning off the engine. I guessed she didn't plan on staying long.

A fast scan around and she removed Dominic's envelope from the bin. Without checking its contents, she returned to her car, put the money in the boot and headed for the driver's side. There came the rumble of the engine as she slipped into first.

I had a few seconds to decide my next move.

The policeman in me said to do nothing – go home, take stock and decide my next move in a considered way.

Another urge was to ram the Skoda and wallop the window, scare the crap out of Harriet and drag her and the cash to Saul, leaving him to figure out why she was pimping Tommy.

But I wasn't a policeman anymore. And smashing cars and scaring people wasn't the best ploy either. I needed to keep my cool, and use my head.

I'd figured out who was involved in all this. Now, I wanted to know why.

So, as Harriet's Skoda pulled away, I pedalled hard in pursuit, the setting sun harsh on my face and a hot fuzziness rising in my chest.

Following a car on a bike without being seen isn't easy, and keeping up with a driver as peppy on the gas as Harriet proved even harder.

We circumnavigated the estate, then veered back the way we'd come. Each time Harriet stopped at lights, I edged back behind buses or vans in the middle lanes, watching her between the traffic gaps and vehicle windscreens. Her right arm hung from the driver's window, a lit cigarette between two thin fingers.

From there, we headed towards central – Finsbury Park, Hornsey, Holloway Road – passing takeaways, vape shops and second-hand phone shops before I stopped noticing and had to focus to keep from losing the Skoda.

Near Camden, she gave way at a box junction when an oncoming white van cut through on red. I held back and changed to the far right-hand lane, curving behind a beat-up Vauxhall belching out hot grey smoke. This reprieve gave me a moment to think about my plan, and how I didn't have one, apart from follow Harriet and see where that led.

The lights changed, her car revved and I pedalled out the saddle to keep up. She took a sharp right, indicating late for the turn, and I nearly lost her in the melee of cars. I kept riding, cutting up a Lexus and catching a wanker sign aimed at me. Descending a sloping residential street, I let the bike freewheel and caught a welcome headwind that cooled my sweaty brow.

Another late right from the Skoda, and I held back, this time hovering behind a Land Rover loaded with kids. Over its bonnet, I could see Harriet was curving into a cul-de-sac with dead-end signs at the mouth. I kept my distance, and when I was close, dismounted and began walking.

We were somewhere in the poor end of Camden. Everywhere was cheap cladded housing, much of it boarded up or dilapidated; vehicles were abandoned, windscreens coated with dust and parking tickets.

Fifty yards ahead, Harriet was walking towards another cylindrical bin. I crouched behind an abandoned Datsun and watched. She looked around and removed another brown envelope, similar to the one Dominic had left. Again, without checking the contents, she deposited it in her boot, went back to the driver's side, manoeuvred a U-turn and drove back. I ducked down out of sight until she was gone, then mounted my bike. Off we went again.

Over the next hour, I witnessed two more collections, the exact same system for each – brown envelopes lifted from rubbish bins situated in dingy areas. By now, it had gone six, the sky was dusky blue and the air had developed a nip. I figured Harriet had thousands of pounds in the boot of her car, all blackmailed out of rich fools like Dominic Tyrell. The ink had barely dried on Tommy's death certificate, and she was still making a pretty decent whack from him.

We headed east again in the direction of Shoreditch, winding through more residential streets of terraced houses, maisonettes and social-housing blocks. I was getting sick of all this following malarkey, and my calves were starting to ache from the stop-start pedalling. But an instinct told me to ride this one out until the end. Sure enough, this proved the right move.

Near Old Street, we took a hard left on to another estate. Harriet inched the Skoda through a narrow archway. This time, I padlocked my bike to a rail and followed on foot.

It was a large estate, flat and sprawling, about as alluring as a cyanide factory. Square flats piled on top of more square flats, all bland and functional in design; greys and mustard-browns dominated the colour schemes; brick-dust cloyed the air.

Immediately to the left there was a skip overflowing with timber, gravel, a soiled mattress, chunks of polystyrene and broken glass, decaying fruit, an ironing board, a pair of slippers, a dishwasher loading tray and a bundle of soiled nappies. With no better hiding spot, I crouched behind it, covered my nose to mask the fetid smell, and watched.

Harriet parked in a bay to the far right, by a row of garages. I could hear the Skoda engine purring, and see her outline through the car window. She was smoking again. Only this time, there was no bin, no envelope, and she was staying decidedly put.

Just beyond the estate's northern exit, a figure was walking across the paving towards the Skoda. He was dressed entirely in black – black tracksuit bottoms and black boots, his top half swamped in a thick black puffer. As he drew close, I saw he had a Foot Locker plastic bag strung diagonally across his heavyset body. He stopped when he reached her car door, tapped on the glass and lowered his hood.

He had a square head, wide nose and piggish little eyes. His scalp was shaved, and he had the cauliflower ears of a brawler.

Harriet got out and looked up at him. He was dwarfing her, at least a foot taller and twice her weight. He said something, his neck swelling like an over-pumped inner tube. She walked to the car boot, opened it and began placing the brown envelopes into his bag, one by one. When she'd finished, he said something else and spat on the kerb before walking back the way he'd come. Thirty seconds later, he was gone.

I'd seen enough.

By the time Harriet was halfway into the car, I was behind her, just a few feet away.

She turned.

As I stepped closer, my eyes reflected in her aviators, wide and black.

'What the hell are—'

'No bullshit stories, Harriet,' I cut in. 'I want the truth.'

Her mouth started twitching like a plucked rubber band. 'Kasper, this is—'

'I watched you collect those envelopes for that lowlife,' I said. 'Now you're going to tell me why.'

'It has nothing to do with—'

'It *does* have something to do with me,' I butted in, pulling the sunglasses from her face. 'Now talk.'

Fear galvanised her eyes. 'I can't,' she said.

'Yeah, you can. If you don't, I'm dragging you straight to the cop shop. Let's see what they think about hidden camera pornos and defrauded bankers.'

Her face scrunched up. 'No,' she said. 'Oh God . . .' Tears ran from her eyes.

Suddenly I felt sick, like I'd drunk cheap wine on an empty stomach. She was scared. Shitting it, by the looks of things. Why?

'They'll hurt me if I talk. You don't understand these people.'

'Make me understand.'

'I can't!'

'Then you're going to prison, love, and Saul's going to hear about everything I saw today.' A voice in my head harped up, telling me this wasn't a hardened crook; this was someone who was afraid, just like her brother had been.

'I mean it, Harriet,' I said. 'I need the truth.'

She lowered her head. Wet mascara streaked from her eyes.

We stood there, neither of us speaking. An elderly man was walking a terrier maybe fifty yards from us. I waited until he was out of earshot.

'OK,' I said. 'You ready?'
She wiped her nose. Grimly, she nodded.
'Into your car then,' I said.
And in we got.

Chapter 12

I had Harriet drive us a few minutes from the estate, just in case the big bloke who'd collected the envelopes came back.

As soon as we were parked up on a dusty residential road, she lit a cigarette. Her citrus perfume failed to hide the smoke wafting up.

I opened the glove compartment.

'Hey!' she said. 'Stop that!'

I ignored her protest and had a rummage. Inside, I found a pair of nappa driving gloves, a road map, some biros, car sweets, a strip of Valium and several recent credit card bills. I picked out one of the larger bills, stating a debt in the region of twenty thousand quid in Harriet's name.

'You and Tommy racked up a lot of debt between you,' I said, holding it up. 'Shall we start here?'

She sucked the cigarette filter, lowered her window, flicked out ash and raised it again. Then she began.

'I've got financial problems. You figured that out already.'

'How much you owe?'

'Six hundred grand, give or take.'

'That's quite a bit. Who to?'

'Banks. Building societies. Creditors. But the biggest chunk is to a man I met who works off the books.'

'Who?'

'His name's Michael Napier. Sick Mick, as he's better known. He owns a gay bar.'

'Mick's Bar?' The name was becoming familiar.

She nodded. 'The place is a cesspit. Napier uses it for soliciting sex between his army of boys and rich customers, and for laundering money from his other interests.'

'Drugs, I assume?'

'Yes. He distributes in quantity. Wholesale.'

'How'd you hook up with him?'

'Through Tommy. He met Napier, found him glamorous, and started hanging around him. He didn't clock the man's into crime.' There was a pause as she inhaled smoke, held it, and let it seep out in a grey curl.

'What happened?'

'Last summer, Tommy took me along to the bar. "Harry, this is Mick, he owns the place . . ." Straight away, I saw through Napier's charm. But I also saw a way to make some money. So behind Tommy's back, I approached Napier. We struck a deal.'

'Let me guess. Napier subbed you drugs to sell?'

She nodded.

'Couldn't you pay off your debts some other way? Your dad said you've got some buff job in the City.'

She laughed humourlessly. 'I lost that job, Kasper.'

'Oh,' I said. 'Bad luck.'

She shot me a look.

'So you took up dealing as a new career path.' I shook my head. 'Not clever.'

She said nothing.

'Saul never twigged?'

'Dad's easy to deceive. He still thinks I go to work every day.' A fleck of ash fell from her cigarette, disintegrating on the gear stick. 'This car's on hire, paid with credit, like everything.'

'How'd you get into money problems in the first place?'

'Mum. Before she died, she racked up a heap of debt. I inherited it.'

'How'd she do that? Tommy made her out to be a saint.'

'Hardly. Mum went stark-raving mad.'

I waited while she smoked.

'It's a long story. In her final years, she splurged a heap of money. Her mind was warped from all the meds she was hooked on, and—'

'Hold up,' I said. 'Your mum was hooked on meds? Saul said she died from cancer.'

'That's just a cover story. Mum's addictions are what killed her. I was doing well with an investment bank at the time, working my way up the ladder. She confided in me, said she had some money problems. It was only after she died that I realised to what extent.'

'But you never told Saul?'

She shook her head. 'Dad's always been hopeless with money. After Mum died, he was bereft. I didn't want these debt problems coming out on top of everything else.'

'So you kept them from him?'

'Yes. I moved back home to save on rent and started paying the debts off, a little each month. It was going well. Another year or so, they would've been cleared.' She paused to light a fresh smoke.

'Then you lost your job?'

She nodded. 'Well, I got sacked. That's when I planned on telling Dad.'

'But you didn't. Why? Because of Tommy?'

She nodded. 'His problems were really flaring up by then. Dad started spending on psychiatrists and therapists from Harley Street, and when they couldn't help, he resorted to have-a-gos like you. He was spending money he didn't have. He even needed to borrow from *me*. The debts went up again, and I had no income. I needed a new way to make cash. Fast.'

Things were starting to make sense – Saul's dilapidated house, the financial difficulties he alluded to in his office, Tommy's bank card getting declined at that milkshake place – but there was a whole lot more I didn't know.

'So you and this Napier went into business?' I said. 'He gave you a few kilos to sell in the City, right?'

'Yes.' Another deep drag, and she said, 'I'd never done anything like that before, but I knew people who were into the whole party scene. They'd have paid top dollar for some decent gear. The plan should've worked. I'd have been able to pay Napier back *and* take a bite out of Mum's debts.'

I nodded – a perfect plan. It was like watching a car crash in slow motion. 'Things didn't go so well, though. Right, Harriet?'

'No.' She stared at the dash. 'The drugs got stolen, from the boot of this car.'

'How annoying.'

Another look came my way, her eyes like granite. 'This isn't funny.'

'And I'm not laughing.'

I took a deep breath and exhaled slowly. Times like this, I wished I still smoked.

'So, how did Napier take the good news his stash had been thieved?'

'How do you think? He went ballistic. He told me if I didn't pay him back, Tommy and I would suffer.'

'So Tommy stepped up to help?'

'Yes, yes he did.'

She lowered the window, tossed out her cigarette and lit up another. I wound down mine to let in some air and looked out at a bird-shit-spattered wall. At that moment, it was the less stomach-turning sight.

'First of all, Tommy maxed out all his credit cards and took out a high-interest loan. He wanted to help, and gave me all the cash he could get. But it wasn't enough. Napier demanded more. So then we tried to get the insurance money.'

I turned in my seat to face her. 'What's that?'

'Mum's life insurance. Tommy and I would both get ten grand on our twenty-first birthdays. I'm six years older, and mine was long gone. Tommy was due his in two years. But it's tied up in some stupid trust. He couldn't access it without the bank alerting Dad. So Napier suggested a different way to pay.'

She sucked on the cigarette stub.

'Keep talking,' I said.

'Tommy had a way with older men. They fall . . . I mean, fell for him. I knew it was wrong, but I swear, he offered to do it. I'd never have let him otherwise.'

'You were pimping him out?'

'It wasn't like that!' she snapped. 'I never asked him to do anything he wasn't OK with. I loved my brother.'

'Course,' I said. 'So how *did* it work, Harriet?'

She didn't answer.

'Let me hazard a guess. He began meeting men at bars and clubs, like Mick's. He'd spend the night at theirs and ask for a bit of money in the morning. Some company, followed by a bit of cash. It's the oldest trade in the book. Am I warm?'

She nodded grimly. 'The trouble was, Tommy wasn't very good at being on the game.'

'Go on?'

'You met him. He was cocky, but behind that front, he was a ball of nerves. Well, those nerves got the better of him. And when a few men refused to pay, he freaked. It just wasn't working.'

'What happened?'

'Napier came up with a better way of earning.'

Now we were getting to the meat of the story. 'The honeytrapping?'

'Yes. Napier owns these flats dotted around east London. The places have cameras hidden in the walls.'

'Why?'

'He's a voyeur, and likes filming people having sex without them knowing.'

'He sells the videos?'

She shook her head. 'They're for his amusement only.'

The sick taste in my stomach was returning. Ignoring it, I said, 'So he had Tommy flirt with a few wealthy men who had wives and kids, a lot to lose, get them alone in a flat, in front of the cameras, and make sure the footage was incriminating?'

Harriet didn't need to answer.

'Well,' I said, 'he did that bit pretty well.'

She looked over. 'Huh?'

'Dominic Tyrell showed me a sample of the video you sent him.'

Slowly, she nodded. 'Tyrell was one of the first. I didn't think it would work. But Tommy made the videos look good. So good, Tyrell and the rest of them had no choice but to cough up whatever I asked them for.'

'Tell me about this blackmailing system you set up.'

'That was Napier's idea too. He ordered me to send the videos out to the men Tommy went with. I sent a few anonymously and demanded money. If they didn't pay, I'd forward them to their wives. It worked. I made far more in one hit than Tommy usually did in two weeks. Napier was happy. He told us to find more men and carry on.'

'How many more?'

'What?'

'How many men have there been altogether?'

Harriet hesitated. 'Seventeen.'

'Christ,' I said, trying to stave off the image of Tommy with sixteen more Dominic Tyrells. I couldn't.

'Why cash?' I said, as calmly as I could. 'Why not bank transfers? Something safer?'

Harriet shrugged. 'Napier said it had to be cash so he could launder it. And he wanted *me* doing all the collections, driving around these grisly places, taking the risks.'

'Clever,' I said. 'That way, you're committing a crime and in his pocket. If he goes down, you're going with him. It's why you haven't gone to the police, isn't it?'

She nodded. 'I'd go to prison for extortion, intent to supply and God knows what else. Then they'd go after Dad. These people are serious, Kasper. That man you saw taking the money from me, he's one of Napier's thugs. You don't want to know what they do on his orders.'

A headache was beginning to suck the inside of my skull, making it hard to focus. Harriet's smoking wasn't helping either.

'I'll take your word for it,' I said. 'Back up to Tommy a minute. Why'd he kill himself, Harriet? This still doesn't make sense.'

It took a long time for her to reply. When she did, it wasn't much of an answer.

'Napier told us we needed more victims. He even gave Tommy a membership for that fancy gym where you two first met.'

'And he tried it on with me,' I said, 'till he realised I didn't fit the mould.'

'Of course. Napier said he was to go anywhere rich married men went, and hook them.'

'But it was only a matter of time before some of them tried getting revenge.'

'Yes. A couple of men I sent videos to turned violent. They assumed Tommy was doing the blackmailing and went for him.'

'Saul said he got attacked a few months back. That what he meant?'

She nodded. 'It was awful. Napier dealt with the men who did it. But it left Tommy traumatised. He wanted to stop. Napier said no. Told him he had to carry on.'

'Not long after came the first suicide attempt,' I said. 'Right?'

'Yes. He tried hanging himself over London Bridge. I hadn't realised how close he was to breaking down.'

'But you told him to keep going, knowing how vulnerable he was.' I couldn't mask the judgement in my voice.

'Just till Napier's debt was paid!' She grimaced. 'Then *you* appeared . . .'

'Me?'

'Yes. Putting ideas in Tommy's head. All of a sudden, he decided to quit. "Kasper will protect me," he kept saying. Napier flipped.'

Now, my headache was growing teeth and gorging to unearth an ugly truth – like it or not, *I* was involved in Tommy's death. Had it not been for *me* appearing, telling him about my daughter's death and offering him my help, he might still be alive.

'What about your father?' I said.

'What about him?'

'Saul must've guessed some of what you've told me, surely. He knew Tommy was being used. That's why he asked me to get involved, so I could find out who was responsible and put a stop to it. Don't tell me he's clueless in all this.'

She gave a limp smile, like I'd just made a bad joke. 'Come on, Kasper. You've met Dad. He's a kind man, but he's in cloud cuckoo land.'

'Then why not enlighten him?'

'I can't. If Dad found out the truth . . . on top of losing Mum, then Tommy . . . it'd finish him.'

'Well, that's very altruistic of you,' I said.

She looked at her knees.

I thought about Saul, the pacifist posters and paperweights in his office, his seemingly unflappable conviction on his radio programme; I thought of a man whose wife was dead, whose son was dead, whose family was close to bankruptcy, and who seemed unaware of a whole lot.

Now, all he had left was Harriet – the lying blackmailer sitting next to me who'd abused her dead brother's trust.

Could he really be that naive?

Harriet wiped her nose with her hand, the movement jolting me back.

'Napier wants his money,' she said. 'Tommy's dead, and he still wants it. I have to carry on collecting cash using the videos I have until I come up with a better way to earn.' She looked at her cigarette pack, running her thumb around the corners.

'No, Harriet,' I said. 'What you need to do is delete these videos and stop all this, right now. Understand?'

'I can't.'

'Why?'

'Napier will kill me.'

'I'll talk to him.'

'Talk? What will you say?'

'I'll tell him to back off. Trust me, I know how to speak these people's language.'

'No, you don't,' she said, and put her head in her hands. 'No one can help me.'

I lowered my window and looked up at the night. Dusk had started its descent, the sky a charcoal wash. Seeping into the car came a pervading darkness and chill. I shivered.

'Just go away,' Harriet said. 'Leave me alone.'

'Delete the videos,' I said again. 'Tell Napier I told you to do it. Understand?'

Shakily, she withdrew a fresh cigarette. The only sound was the spark of her lighter and the dry crackle of freshly burning tobacco.

'OK,' she said. 'OK, I will.'

Smoke danced towards the ceiling of the car. I watched it, thinking of how it broke into pieces, never to reclaim form.

Chapter 13

I probably should've stayed with Harriet a little longer and dug a little deeper, but in that moment I hadn't the strength to stay in that smoky Skoda a minute more. Something stank in there. It was more than her cigarettes.

I returned to fetch my bicycle and cycling away from her, I felt an emptiness expanding in my gut. As I joined the main hum of traffic, my hands began trembling on the handlebars of my bike, and I was struck by a sudden thirst.

I needed time out of my head. I needed a drink.

I ducked into the nearest pub I could find, one of those craft ale places loaded with beards, guitar music and plenty of tats. Six quid got me a pint of something cloudy. I drank that and moved on to the next place.

By pub number three, it dawned on me that a bar crawl wasn't doing the job. No amount of beer or whiskey could provide the anaesthetic I craved. A thought announced itself in my head, and there was only one way to answer it.

Twenty minutes later, I was in a side road of Shoreditch, half-cut, restless, and standing opposite a late-night drinking den. *Mick's Bar* shone in lurid red neon letters above its door.

It looked like most venues in this part of London – rammed with bodies, oozing heat and hormones, heavy bass music thudding against its walls as if a herd of animals was trying to escape.

A bouncer the width of a truck was standing beneath the bar's black awning. When he turned in profile, I recognised the face – he was the square-faced lump I'd seen a few hours earlier taking the blackmail cash from Harriet.

I began wandering over. A suited gent sidled ahead, palmed the bouncer a score and was let in. As he disappeared down into the bar, the blare of Euro-house stampeded out. Then the door closed, and the bouncer looked down.

Now, I'm six-one and bigger than most, but this bloke made me feel like I was a stick insect. I offered up my best attempt at a smile. It failed to stir him. He had the look of someone who flossed his teeth with a hacksaw.

'Help you, sir?' he said in a European accent I couldn't place.

'Here for a nightcap,' I replied, slurring slightly.

'Been here before?'

'Not for a while.'

'Got money?'

I handed over a crinkled twenty.

After pocketing the cash he said, 'Any dicking about, you're out. Understand?'

I gave a salute. He snarled, moved aside and allowed me down the steps and into Mick's Bar.

A puff of hot air hit me, followed by a blast of rapid-fire dance music pumping from mounted speakers. The place was packed, bodies everywhere: on the dance floor, propping up the horseshoe bar, filling out the low-ceilinged lounge and the booths. Some effort had gone into the decor – the floor was black laminate, the bar tops and tables marble – but none of the furnishings could mask the pervading seediness.

On the walls were lewd photos, Robert Mapplethorpe-style, showing pretty young men with little or nothing on and holding compromising poses, looking cheap and used in the process. One of the faces was unmistakable – a tall, fey boy with a floppy side parting, his bare back to the camera. He was peering over his shoulder, staring at the camera with a pair of puppyish brown eyes.

Tommy.

I felt a scrunching in my nape, as if I were wearing an undersized hat. I turned, and with my head down, I moved through the throng in the direction of the bar.

Posh, officious men seemed to make up half the clientele – financiers, advertising execs, senior civil servants, judging by the accents, mannerisms and wallet sizes. The rest were young lads, all around Tommy's age, clad in sportswear, vests, trainers and plenty of shiny stuff. Lights were dimmed, drinks over-priced, and discretion was a must.

The suit who'd entered before me had already found a blond boy to talk to on my left. In a different context, you'd assume he was his son. But dads don't generally caress their kids' knees like that. A tan-line showed where the man's wedding band should've been. The boy sipped a white wine and giggled enthusiastically.

The music sounded like Barbie yodelling over a power drill, a horrible racket, and it was already doing my head in. I looked around for the culprit DJ.

He was on a round podium situated in the centre of the dance floor, a short, squat man with almost-grey French-cropped hair, standing behind two elevated record decks. He was wearing baggy dungarees and a pink tee, a gold medallion and a sanctimonious smirk. Sweat glistened from his face, as if his skin was wrapped in cling film, and his mouth sparkled with gold-capped teeth.

A mecca of boys hovered around him, like he was a deity. Between spinning records, his hands were all over them. They seemed to love this, almost as much as he clearly loved himself.

I turned to the bar and held out a note to get served. Snippets of conversations caught me on both sides – lame jokes, bad chat-ups, sycophantic laughs. I tried not to listen.

A ripped barman wearing some kind of spandex vest served me. Over the din, I shouted for a beer. Nine quid got me a bottle of warm Heineken.

I started drinking and wondering what I was doing here. No two ways, it was stupid rocking up without some kind of plan.

But I guess something in me needed to see this place, to get a sense of the double life Tommy had led. My eyes kept flitting back to the photo of him on the wall, then to the dance floor.

It wasn't hard to picture him sauntering around, cruising unsuspecting men like Dominic Tyrell, luring them with those Bambi eyes. I necked my beer to mask the sour taste.

'You here alone?' came a voice to my side.

He was young, no more than twenty, but his eyes had the graveness of one much older; sandy brown hair cut in a Caesar crop, smooth skin, pouting lips drawn up into a seductive smile; but they parted to reveal bad teeth, tea-stained and misaligned, telling of a hard-worn life; a shiny black tee and leather pants clung to his thin lean body. I caught a whiff of the same strawberry perfume Tommy wore.

He held out a hand. I paused, unsure whether he wanted me to shake it or kiss it. I went for the former.

'I'm Chris,' he said, coming close to my ear. 'Buy me a drink?'

I smiled. Napier trained his boys well in their chat-up lines and toiletry tastes.

'OK, Chris,' I said, and put a hand in my pocket. 'I'll get you a drink, but only if you talk to me about one or two things.'

A wine spritzer for him and a second lager left me nineteen quid the poorer. After we clinked glasses, I said, 'So, are you friends with Mick?'

He tried masking his discomfort, taking a sip from his drink, brushing his hair, but once you know what fear looks like, there's no hiding it.

'Why don't we get to know each other?' he said. 'Maybe go somewhere private?' His hand glanced across my knee.

I leaned close so I could talk without shouting. 'Do me a favour, mate. Point Mick out. I'm dying to see who he is.'

'Mr Mick's busy,' he said. His eyes flitted to the DJ booth and came back.

I looked over, and took in the numpty at the decks more closely. '*That's* Mick Napier?'

Chris's hand went rigid and fell away. I turned back to see his expression. The smile was gone and he was making to stand.

Before he could go, I said, 'If you talk to Mick, tell him I popped by. Kasper's my name.' I spelled it. 'You can do that for me, can't you, Chris?'

His lips tightened. He nodded, took his drink and sashayed into the crowd.

I didn't stay much longer. The more I drank, the greater the chance I'd really put my foot in it, and I felt close to that edge already. After draining my lager, I went to use the gents and go.

At the urinal, while waiting for my natural flow of events to conclude, I heard laughter from the cubicle to my right. It sounded like a couple were having a good time in there.

Suddenly the main doors to the gents bashed open and in came the bouncer, presumably for me. Standing as I was, it dawned on me I was in quite a vulnerable spot, but I braced anyway, ready to redirect my pee on to him.

Instead of me, he kicked the door to the cubicle where the noises were coming from. It slammed open, revealing a rotund suited gent. His face was puffy red, and he was scrambling to pull his Y-fronts up. Behind him, sitting on the loo seat was a pale-looking boy, younger than Tommy, no more than sixteen, wearing a cowboy hat, leather waistcoat, blue jeans and desert boots. As the bouncer stepped towards them, a sheen of fear gripped the boy's eyes.

'No!' he said, holding up both hands. 'It's not what it looks like—'

'Out!' the bouncer said, pulling the boy's waistcoat, then grappling him into a mean deadlock.

Ignoring the suit's insistence that there was nothing awry, the bouncer heaved the boy out, eyeballing me along the way.

I zipped up and followed, jostling through the glut of bodies. Dancers dived aside like a parting sea around the bouncer, who manhandled the boy to the rear of the bar and through a back door. Briefly, I caught a glimpse of the DJ I now knew to be Napier, standing outside the club beside another thickset man. Then the door slammed shut. It was over in ten seconds.

'Why'd the kid get booted out?' I asked a different suit who was drinking something red with loads of straws and umbrellas in it. 'I thought this was a pick-up bar?'

'Bet he didn't get permission,' the guy said, eyeing me up and down.

'Permission?'

'Mick doesn't like his boys turning tricks here. And definitely not without him getting his slice of the pie.' He gave me a wink. 'You come here much?'

Blanking him, I thought about what he'd said. Napier wasn't as dumb as he looked. Assuming he was a money launderer, a wholesaler of Class As and a persistent voyeur and pervert, it made good sense for him to keep a tight ship.

I hung around a few minutes, wanting to see Napier again. No sign. He'd been replaced at the decks by a lithe fellow wearing loose denim and a floral shirt, who was blasting some speeded-up remix of a Scissor Sisters track I'd never liked. I took that as my cue to leave.

As I mounted the steps towards the entrance, I looked back a final time and froze. Through the rear doors, the bouncer was reappearing, followed by two others, Napier and the large man I'd seen. They stood at the furthest end of the bar, where Chris, the boy who'd hit on me, was leaning.

Napier was now wearing a cowboy hat. It looked distinctly like the one the boy who'd been booted from the gents had been wearing. The big man behind him was massaging his knuckles. I squinted so I could take him in more clearly.

The man had a poached, misaligned face, thick shoulders, and thick arms protruding from a tight polo. His eyes were black holes and his mouth was no more than a slash in a sheet of sandpaper.

The bouncer handed the big man a tumbler of spirit. A tattoo flashed around his neck as he took a drink. I remembered Dominic Tyrell talking about a thug with a tat.

But I didn't have time to ponder. Chris had spotted me. He said something to Napier and pointed my way. They all stared over.

Napier smirked. The bouncer frowned. The tattooed man simply lowered his drink. Our eyes met. Suddenly, the bar seemed to empty.

The bouncer headed across the dance floor. This time, he really was coming for me. Whatever Chris said had pushed his buttons. I could see this escalating, and turned to go.

Blocking my way was a portly man tapping into his phone. I shoved him hard to my right and he stumbled, yelled something, but I didn't hear it.

Outside, away from the noise and heat, the cool night was disorientating. I stomped ahead, putting distance between the bar and me, feeling a little dizzy and sick, just wanting to get my bike and be gone.

A few feet from where I'd chained it, something caught my eye. The cowboy who'd been chucked out was slumped in a doorway.

Blood pooled around both nostrils, as if he'd rammed berries up them, and there was a greying mouse of a bruise beneath his eye. He was clutching his right hand with the left, and when I looked closer, I saw the pinkie finger was sticking out at an odd angle.

This Napier wasn't just clever. He was cruel, too. The kid looked about ready to pass out.

'Want me to call you an ambulance, mate?' I said.

He glanced up, wide-eyed.

A flicker of recognition passed over him. 'You were in the bar?' he said, in the wavering voice of a child in the dark.

'Yeah. I saw you get dragged out.' I stepped closer. 'Why'd they beat you?'

'It's my fault,' he said. 'I need the money. But I shouldn't have broken Mick's rules. I'm stupid.'

'How about telling this to the police?'

'No, no,' he said, shaking his head. 'Please, no police.'

'Why?'

'He said he'd cut me if I did that.' He lifted his good hand to his nose, wincing. The fingers came back bloody.

I crouched down. 'You got money to get home?'

'Don't have a home,' he said.

'So where do you sleep?'

'Wherever.'

'You able to get back to wherever by yourself?'

He shook his head, slowly this time. 'Mick took all my money and my bus pass. As punishment.'

'Jeez,' I said, and reached for my wallet. 'Here.' I offered a twenty. 'Get yourself out of here and have that finger seen too.'

He looked at the money, at me, and took it.

I couldn't think of much else to say, so I stood and left him there, unchained my bike and pedalled away fast.

It'd been stupid, coming here tonight, and I might regret it in the morning; but right then I didn't care. The stuff I'd found out was cramming my head, all of it a jumble, none of it pretty.

Chapter 14

Thirst drew me from an unquiet sleep.

My tongue was furry, throat dry. I got up, had a wee, drank two pints of water, and before I could talk myself out of it, I jogged around Walthamstow Wetlands for half an hour, stopping midway to do a hundred push-ups on the reservoir banks.

By the time I got home, I was half-rejuvenated. My phone showed a missed call from a number I didn't know. I'd never been this popular.

I hit voicemail and listened to a softly spoken male. He said his name was Mani and he'd like a call back when I could. It took a few seconds to put a face to him.

Emmanuel. The train driver Diane mentioned.

He answered on the second ring. 'Thanks for getting back to me.'

'No problem,' I said, remembering his huge, bewildered eyes as we stood outside the train station the day Tommy died. 'So, how're things?'

He took a while to speak. 'Bad. It's hard to explain. I can't sleep. Can't be around my wife and kids. I keep seeing that boy. His face ...'

'Not so good, then. Why don't you stop by for a drink tonight? I work at a pub. We could grab a pint?' I gave him the address for McGovern's and said to come late.

'Appreciate it, man,' Emmanuel said.

I had eggs and mushrooms on the griddle by the time Dr Steiner emerged from her bedroom. She was wearing a pink fluffy dressing gown and banana slippers, and had a Dunhill already on the go.

'Good morning, Kasper,' she said, taking the glass of grapefruit juice I handed her.

Today's *Guardian* was on the counter – the latest Cabinet kerfuffle was the main story, but I couldn't tell you much more than that. Things need to get majorly bad in the news for me to sit up and notice.

She leafed through the first few pages, smoking methodically. Within a minute, she'd pushed the paper away.

'Abysmal,' she said. 'The world is doomed.'

To console her, I slid over a plate of eggs. 'Dig in.'

She lifted a fork with her left hand and held her cigarette with the right.

'May we eat while you smoke?' I said.

'Certainly,' came the reply, no hint of sarcasm. She impaled a small piece of mushroom and began nibbling miniscule bites between puffs. 'And what's been going on for you, Kasper?'

I sat at the breakfast bar, ate some eggs, drank some juice, and began telling Dr Steiner about yesterday's revelations. By the time I'd finished, she was on her third Dunhill, and my appetite had diminished.

'My God,' she said. 'This Harriet sounds quite the bitch. Pimping her brother and blackmailing wealthy men? It's pretty low down the scale.'

'Agreed,' I said.

Dr Steiner scrutinised me. 'How are you coping in all this?'

'I'm angry.'

'Of course you're angry. This has brought everything back. But anger can make you reckless. Take heed.'

She flicked ash into one of several ceramic receptacles dotted round the house for this very purpose. I could tell she was gearing up for something.

'I'll tell you a story,' she began. 'A few years before you came to live here, I caught wind that my girlfriend was cheating on me. For a few days, I was livid. I planned out ways to extract revenge that could have landed me in prison. And I came quite close to following through on them.'

I'd never heard Dr Steiner be this autobiographical and was intrigued. 'And?' I said. 'What did you do?'

'Oh, not a lot. I drank a bit too much wine, smoked a lot of cigarettes, and was able to vent to a few friends who calmed me down. Later, I found some solace by naming this contraption after *her*.' Almost with affection, Dr Steiner patted Mildred, her stoma bag, and smiled. 'But my point is, in some people, people like you in particular, I'm afraid anger can be dangerous, and not so easily tempered. I fear this bind you're in is taking you perilously close to the edge, because it's so close to your past. What do you think?'

I shrugged. Rationally, I knew what she said made sense: Tommy's death had exhumed Rosie, and I couldn't disentangle the two of them; but a part of me wasn't ready to turn my back on this thing, not yet.

'I still don't know what the hell happened to put Tommy under that train,' I said. 'On the phone message, he said he'd messed up. Before I quit, I want to know what he meant by that.'

'Perhaps he wasn't sure himself? Presumably he wouldn't have been in a coherent mental state in those final moments.'

'Maybe.' I thought back to last week, the day of his death, the sound of his voice on my answerphone. 'But I think something happened to push him over the edge. And Harriet's not told me the whole story. Their relationship was anything but normal. I've not got to the bottom of it.'

'Hm,' Dr Steiner said. She lifted her fork, ate perhaps a fifth of a hash brown, chewed slowly and attentively and swallowed. 'So, what do you plan to do?'

'I don't know,' I said. 'Saul deserves to hear the truth. You think I should tell him about Harriet's involvement?'

'You may not need to. A parent always knows when their child is lying.' She removed the filter from her cigarette holder and put the holder beside her Dunhills pack. 'But the real question is whether Saul can be honest about his own role in his children's problems. Doing so would mean acknowledging the mistakes he's made.'

'You think he's lying, too?'

She shrugged. 'How can I answer that? I've never met the man. Do *you* think he is?'

I lifted my empty juice glass and looked at the sediment in the bottom. 'I don't know yet,' I said. 'But something's wrong about him, too. All those right-on posters in his office, the radio programme, it doesn't wash that he could be such a do-gooder, yet have all this grime right under his nose.'

'So you think he's a charlatan?'

144

I shrugged.

'Hm,' Dr Steiner repeated.

She reached for her Dunhills and pulled out another, fitting the holder on the filter and lighting the end, drawing in smoke and letting it seep from her lips.

'I'll be frank,' she said. 'What I think you should do is to walk away. Pretend you never met this Tommy Berkowitz, and move on.' She paused a moment to smoke. 'Can you do this?'

I shook my head.

'I thought not.'

Marmite appeared and leaped on to the counter. He started purring as the doctor stroked his arched back. She pushed her plate aside and looked closely at me.

'So my advice is, tread carefully. There'll be risks in this. If the fight comes to you, be ready to fight back, or run.'

'All right.'

Now, Marmite had begun devouring the eggs, tearing them apart with paws and teeth. We both laughed.

'That wasn't meant for him,' I said.

'We'll share it,' Dr Steiner said, kneading the tom's rich velvet coat. 'Won't we, my second-favourite man.'

Chapter 15

How could I have recognised the foresight in Dr Steiner's words? As she predicted, the fight *was* about to come looking for me.

McGovern's was quiet that night, a scattering of old boys, oddballs, widows and widowers. Around six, I poured my first Stella and chatted with Hettie, an ancient Trinidadian I'd known since I was a teen. Every night since her old man's death, she came in for a double house brandy to help her sleep.

She started telling me about her eleven grandkids, all grown up now, doing apprenticeships and college courses, things like that. She asked if I was courting and I told her no way, I was holding out for her, and she lit up the pub with her laugh.

Not long after, I grabbed a break, took a stroll on the High Road and picked up a beef patty for my tea from a Jamaican place I liked. Walking back, chomping meat and pastry, I tried ringing Harriet. The call went straight to voicemail. Rather than leave a message, I sent her a text:

Call me.
K.

Turning the corner, I paused. A group of seven kids were camped outside McGovern's, trying their best to look mean. They hadn't been there when I'd left.

Now, I've seen enough mean-looking kids in my time to know which to take seriously – and these weren't serious. But in a pack, they could be intimidating, and chances were at least one had a weapon and was dumb enough to try using it.

They wore the usual street clobber – baseball caps, oversized hoodies worn up, concealing most of their faces, baggy track-suit bottoms, the latest sparkly trainers, hands plunged into crotches LA gang-banger-style – but they still looked scrawny, like schoolboys trying to act tough. Something was vaguely familiar about them; maybe they were boys from the flats or visitors at Savages, I couldn't tell. Whoever they were, they were in my way.

I caught a couple of screwball stares as I walked through them towards the pub. One kissed his teeth and said something I guessed wasn't a compliment. But they didn't try anything. Clever boys.

Inside, Paddy was by the window, staring at them balefully.

'Little gobshites,' he muttered, 'scaring off me customers.'

I looked around the pub. 'What customers?'

Ignoring me, he said, 'This area, Kas. It's worse than the Shankill Road during the Troubles. Rough as toast.'

'They're just kids, Pat. You were that age once.'

He tapped the window and made a shooing gesture with his hands. I heard laughter, a few expletives, and one hawked and spat on the pavement. Paddy cracked a knuckle and swore under his breath. For their sakes, I hoped they'd grow bored and leave.

They did. Ten minutes later, the pub entrance was deserted, and our meagre selection of customers could come and go with impunity.

McGovern's started filling around nine, mainly old folks in for a nightcap. I drank another lager or two.

Not long before ten, Paddy's sixteen-year-old daughter pushed through the doors. Suzanna was wearing a heap of make-up, tall platforms and some skimpy red thing that left much for the eye and little to the imagination. Heads turned as she sauntered towards me, plonked her phone on the bar and asked for a Smirnoff Ice. Before I could politely decline, Paddy appeared and pulled her brusquely towards his upstairs office.

A few minutes later, Suzanna came down, sullen-faced and without the make-up. Her heels were gone and the rest of her was covered beneath her dad's large Crombie. I poured her a consoling Coke from the gun. She drank it joylessly at the bar and began watching Netflix on her phone.

Not long after that, our customers began leaving, and I started scrubbing the tables, collecting glasses, loading up the glass washer. By half past, the pub was dead.

'You OK to close up, Kas?' Paddy said, totting up the till. 'I need to get Princess home for a serious chat.'

Suzanna pretended she hadn't heard.

'No sweat,' I said.

I shook Paddy's hand, gave Suzanna a fist bump and watched the pair head home, followed by the remaining drinkers sloping off. I topped up my pint, covered the draught barrels, and started collecting coasters and bringing in the signs.

It was still warm out, the sky an array of rich dappling blues. Steam from the glass washer was making the bar muggy, so I left the door ajar for a draught to ease in. After putting Dylan's *Blonde on Blonde* on the PA, I stuck a final half in my glass and ran hot water into the mop bucket. I left a couple of empty kegs by the door, gathered up the rest of the rubbish sacks and carried them out to the wheelie bins. I was back in the bar and crouching down to screw in a mop head when they came for me.

A high voice shouted, 'Hey, Kasper!' and a trainer crunched into my face.

I fell back hard, more shocked than hurt. Footsteps charged in beneath the shutters. Through a red cloud, I made out the boys from earlier, piling in.

They'd been waiting.

Fuck.

Fists and kicks started in and I was on my back, surrounded. These weren't hard blows, but they were coming from all directions, machine-gun fire, rat-a-tat-tatting. All I could do was roll to my front, cover my head and ride it out.

Now, I've been beaten many times and know the drill, but experience never prepares you for the rain of hurt and stripping of pride it always brings. When I covered my head, they kicked my stomach; as I reached for my stomach, they went for my head. Each time I tried to move, a new blow came from somewhere. Little bastards.

I managed to get on to all fours and tried to crawl away. A bit of distance and I could launch some kind of defence. No such luck. They were relentless, following me, kicking and stamping.

'Where you going?' one said, laughing shrilly.

More blows on my torso before a wild punch caught my temple and I cascaded into a fire extinguisher, pulling it and a chunk of plaster from the wall.

'Piss off!' I managed to say. 'There's no money here!'

I lifted my hand. A fuzzy beige thing was all I saw in front of me. Blood was pooling in my mouth now, warm and rusty. My body was trembling.

Hands came under my armpits, pulling me up.

A dry slap roused me.

Someone killed the music.

Silence.

I shook my head, forced myself to focus.

The tall, wide man I'd seen at Mick's Bar last night was in front of me. He was wearing a white Armani tracksuit, immaculately clean. The skin on his cheeks was peppered with scars and divots, as if he'd had smallpox as a boy, and the tattoo on his neck jutted out from under his collar. It was a Glasgow Rangers tat, dark blue and smudgy.

'Who're you?' I said, the enunciation sounding funny. My lips weren't behaving themselves.

'So you're Kasper,' he said, a gruff Scottish voice. 'How you doin'? What kinda name is that, anyway?'

'It's Polish,' I said.

'That so?' Casually, he pulled from his pocket a small triangular blade that slotted neatly over the knuckles of his right hand. He made a fist. The metal glimmered. 'You like my knife, Polish?'

I'd seen blades like this one – they were slick and cruel and meant for one thing.

'Who are you?' I repeated.

'My name's Vincent.' He was admiring his weapon. 'And I'm here to give you a warning. It's a one-off. You've been sticking your Polish trotters in other folks' business.' He raised the blade and pointed it at me. 'You need to stay away from the dead kid's sister. Get me?'

150

My shock was turning to anger. 'Says who? You? Or your little gimp of a boss, Napier?'

Vincent came closer. The blade seemed to double, then triple in size. It looked like it could cut gristle off meat like a spoon through jelly.

'I like the way it sparkles,' he whispered. 'Whadda you think?'

'I think if you tell your boys to let me go, you and me can sort this out the old-fashioned way.'

His black eyes fizzed. 'Reckon you're the hard man, aye?' He grinned. 'I've met men like you. They're all the same. Slice them a few times and they learn their manners. Hold him there, boys. Let's see how hard he really is.'

Everyone's focus was on Vincent and the blade.

He kept coming forward, and when he was close enough, I spat in his face.

He froze. Red foam webbed from his brow and cheek. He dabbed it with a finger, wiping it slowly across his cheeks like war paint.

'Not very nice,' he said.

Suddenly, the hands holding me clenched. I grit my teeth, bracing, looking into this maniac's eyes.

He wanted to cut me. I could see it.

Fear struck, for the deep, bottomless digging he was about to deliver. Death has never scared me that much. Torture does.

In spite of the fear, I forced myself to look. If he was going to slice me up, I wanted to stare the bastard out for as long as I could bear it.

'This is gonna hurt,' he said.

I knew it was.

But suddenly, my eyes were diverting away. Maybe it was a change in light or a movement in the periphery, but I found myself looking behind Vincent. There was a figure by the door, arms raised, holding one of the empty beer kegs I'd left outside the pub.

It took a second to recognise him – Emmanuel. The train driver.

I saw it before it happened.

The rest came fast.

Emmanuel lobbed the keg at Vincent, and I thrust my whole body forward and back, the surprise loosening my attackers' hands just enough to gain some leverage. I swept my head backwards and my skull crunched into someone's nose. A wet cry came from behind, but it was smothered by the thump of the keg hitting Vincent's side and thundering to the floor.

'What the—' someone yelled.

Quickly, I pulled away. Vincent was still standing, rubbing the shoulder that had taken the brunt of the blow, his face gripped with rage. I came up and swung a kick at his groin. He was fast, blocking it with an elbow, so I threw a clumsy jab to his face that split his lip. He hissed.

The keg was pounding along the pine flooring, the noise disorientating. I was about to hit Vincent again, but a pair of hands seized my neck, pulling back. I shoved an elbow into an attacker, once, twice, hearing grunts each time. The grip loosened. I reached back and grabbed an arm, lifted it up and careened backwards, crushing a body against a wall. I stepped forward; the attacker crumbled.

Two down.

I looked around at the others. They were just kids, not fighters. And I realised where I recognised them from – Mick's

Bar. They'd been working the floor, putting their stuff on display. Now they were here doing Napier's dirty work.

But I didn't have time for too much thinking. To my left came a Turkish-looking boy, charging in high and wide, making it easy to parry. I stepped back, feinted and hit him a hard cut above the eye, then hung low as another tried the same, jabbing this one in the balls. As they both staggered, I stretched out my arms and clothes-lined them into stacked tables and chairs, then pummelled them with a few roundhouse punches, back and forth, left and right, making sure they weren't getting up.

A fist to the back of my head caught me off-guard. For a second, my sight was darkness and stars. Shaking, I looked over and saw its owner – Chris, the boy who'd hit on me last night. I snarled and walked to him. He was bricking it. No doubt he was just another pawn in all this, but I had to put him down, and came in hard, reaching for his top and hurling him around before letting go. His side met the wall, taking another chunk of plaster with him.

A mist had fallen over my eyes. My perception was skewed, everything close up but far away.

I looked around. This Vincent was the one I wanted. He was out of sight.

By the dartboard stood the last two boys. There was nowhere for them to run.

'Let's get this over with,' I said.

They charged in unison, one managing to connect a poke above my left ear, but it wasn't enough. Not close.

I rammed them with my shoulders and pushed them back to the wall. The impact stunned them. A southpaw floored one, a right to the other's cheek sent him star-shaped and straight down. There they stayed.

I stepped back, panting. Emmanuel was standing rigid by the ladies' toilet.

'Where'd he go, Mani?' I said. 'The big one, Vincent?'

He pointed to the other side of the bar, where it curved around the room. I headed that way, leading with my shoulder. A moment later, I saw a figure in the shadows.

Vincent walked out. Both hands were in his tracksuit pockets.

I raised my fists. 'Come on,' I said.

He removed the right hand. Instead of his knuckle blade, it held a snub-nosed Smith & Wesson that looked real – and he looked like he could use it.

I stared at the barrel as he brought it up, and felt my hands flop to my sides. My heart fluttered, more exhilaration than fear. The round hole was infinite in its blackness. It was aimed at my face.

'Don't move,' he said.

'I called the police,' Emmanuel said, somewhere in the background. 'They'll be coming.'

Neither of us looked at him.

'I've had guns aimed at me before,' I said, my voice strangely calm.

Vincent flexed the weapon.

I stayed still, watching his finger caressing the trigger.

Whimpers started from behind us. To my right, I noticed the Turkish kid was pulling himself up using a stool, the legs scraping on the floor.

Vincent spat on the pine and walked further into the light. 'You've gone and fucked up tonight, pal,' he said. 'I came to give you a message. That's all. Now I may have to put you down for good.'

The barrel was a few feet away. From this range, it would blow a cavern in me.

Electricity crackled in his eyes.

Then came the sirens, distant but undeniable.

Vincent blinked. If he was going to shoot me, it needed to be now. We both knew it. For a split second, I thought that was it. Game over.

Then his crew began flocking to the door, scarpering. I'm sure their sudden movement saved me, for Vincent's attention darted to them, breaking the spell locking us.

'Come, Vinnie!' one said. 'Police!'

For a final time, he looked at me. 'You've had your warning,' he said.

'Get lost,' I said.

He kept the gun on me as he moved to the doors, only returning it to his pocket as he ducked under the shutters. Within seconds they'd all vanished into the night.

I stayed as I was.

After what seemed a long time, I called out, 'Mani? You OK?' No answer.

I turned and saw him, standing rigid by the bar. He looked petrified, but what normal bloke wouldn't after seeing seven kids beaten up and a gun get pulled?

'It's over,' I said. 'Relax.'

'You Tyson Fury in disguise?'

I couldn't help but laugh, even though it hurt like a bastard.

'Nope,' I said, inverting a fallen stool, picking a beer towel off the floor, rubbing my mouth with it and taking a seat. 'I'm just a barman. Now, let's get our stories straight before the police arrive.'

★

Two fresh-faced plods nosied in a minute later, responding to the 999 call Emmanuel had placed about a robbery. I told a female PC that my friend had mistaken an arm-wrestling competition for a break-in and acted with undue haste.

As I spoke, her partner wandered through the pub, looking at the dents in the wall, the beer keg Emmanuel had used as a weapon, which was now lying on its side by the bar, the spit and blood on the floor, and the fire extinguisher, which was hanging precariously.

'Looks like quite an arm wrestle, sir,' he said.

I gave a non-committal shrug and tried to smile, but my clotting lip was making it difficult.

They asked Emmanuel for corroboration. He nodded like a loyal dog. Then they looked at each other and shrugged.

Our story was rubbish. This pair knew it. But from my time as a uniform, I also knew how the opportunity to swerve writing up a meaningless pub brawl would be too much for them to resist.

Sure enough, after sharing a quiet word by the doors, they came back and told me the good news – I should keep out of trouble, and they planned to speak to the proprietor of the pub in the morning; but they wouldn't be pursuing the matter further. I wished them a pleasant evening as they stepped outside, then I pulled the shutters down fully and locked and bolted the doors.

'Why'd we have to lie to those police, Kasper?' Emmanuel said.

I looked at him, and shrugged. 'It's complicated. I'm investigating something. The law might mess it up.'

'But what if that guy comes back?'

'I don't think he will. Not tonight, anyway. He gave me his message.' I rubbed my jaw. It felt like I'd eaten a beehive.

'You hurt?' he said.

'I'll live. Thanks – for what you did. It took guts.'

I held out my hand. He shook it.

'So, Mani,' I said. 'How about that drink?'

Chapter 16

'**B**eer or whiskey?'

'What you having?'

I considered my answer. 'Both.'

I handed Emmanuel a couple of Becks and retrieved a bottle of Bushmills Paddy let me keep under the bar for emergencies. I'd say tonight qualified.

'Let's go outside,' I said, taking two glasses, the whiskey, and opening the back door.

Above us, the sky had turned navy black and cloudless, a bleached-bone moon its sole light. The pokey patio where we stood served as a makeshift smoking area, a square patch of mossy flagstones surrounded by slatted wood fencing on three sides and the rear of the pub on the fourth. A dozen or so empty kegs and crates were stacked in one corner, along with several Bass and Guinness ashtrays, all heaped with butts.

I took one keg, turned it on its side to act as a seat, and indicated for Emmanuel to do the same. Using a third as a table, I capped the whiskey, poured a couple of inches for both of us and drank mine in one. The booze fizzed in my war-torn mouth like chip fat doused in water. I sucked my teeth until the pain passed, then poured some more.

Emmanuel took a cautious sip from his and began sputtering.

'Drink, Mani,' I said. 'You'll get used to it.'

As he did, I considered him more closely. I put him about my age; a wedding band was on his finger, a crucifix round his neck. He was wearing suede Hush Puppies, baggy jeans and a faded beige jersey from Gap. Dad clothes. From his pocket, he withdrew a deck of Marlboro reds.

'You mind?'

I shook my head.

'Twenty-one years I'd been off the fags before all this. Now I'm getting through a pack a day.' He lit up. 'Why'd those thugs attack you, Kasper?'

'I told you – I'm investigating something. They'd prefer it if I didn't.'

'Investigating? You said you weren't police.'

'I'm not anymore. This is personal.'

'I don't get it.'

I shrugged.

The smoke rose around his face, but couldn't hide the uncertainty of his expression.

I poured and drank more whiskey. With each sip my mouth was growing accustomed to the sting. Pretty soon it'd like it; the rest of me already did.

'So, what're you investigating?'

'Why Tommy put himself in front of your train.'

'And them lot had something to do with it?'

'I'm guessing so.'

He nodded.

I gave a minute or so and said, 'So, Mani, what did you want to talk about?'

He cleared his throat and lifted his beer, held it to his lips but didn't drink any. Instead he put the bottle back down and stared ahead.

'Every night, it's the same thing. I keep seeing that boy, Tommy. There was nothing I could do. He was looking right at me. And then . . .'

His eyes glazed over, and I saw he was somewhere else, back in that tube tunnel, a moment that had changed his life irreversibly, and ended Tommy's permanently.

'I've been off work. Doctor's given me these pills for anxiety. Management says I need counselling. Everyone's telling me I need to talk to people, get this shit out my head. But I can't talk to nobody. My wife don't get it. My pastor says I need to talk to God. Well, God ain't listening. The only one who seemed to get me was you, a stranger, talking to me outside the train station. It don't make sense.'

It did to me. Sometimes there's an inherent understanding between those left behind after something like this.

He stubbed out his cigarette, put a hand over his mouth and closed his eyes. Breath shuddered through his fingers.

'I'm sorry,' I said.

He nodded. Tears were welling through his scrunched eyelids.

'How long you been a train driver?'

He waited a long time before answering, wiping his cheeks as he spoke. 'Eighteen years.'

'You like it?'

'Yeah, I do. Driving trains, you're with people, but you're with your own thoughts too. It suits a man like me.'

'This the first time something like this happened?'

'No. Six years ago, I had a similar thing. This young Asian boy took a jump just as I'm pulling into the platform. They said he had some mental problems, was off his meds, hearing stuff.'

'Did he die?'

'Uh-uh. Somehow he slipped under the tracks and they managed to fish him out alive. I said to myself, if this happens again, I'm walking. It took me three months to get my confidence back. And now this . . .'

'Yeah,' I said. '*This.*' I drank another finger of Bushmills. 'You know,' I said, 'when I was in the police, there were a few coppers who needed time away from the job. They'd done routine welfare checks and found people hanging or overdosed. It's the kind of stuff you're told about in training, but you never expect to see for real. My point is, there's no shame in getting help.'

He looked up. My last comment had interested him. 'That why you're not a policeman anymore? 'Cos of stuff you saw?'

'Something like that.'

A flurry of noises from behind the fence made him jump: sirens; a girl shouting in Arabic; the growl of a moped.

'Easy, Mani,' I said, pouring some more whiskey into both our cups.

He took his and returned to me. 'Mind if I ask you something?'

'OK.'

'Why do you think people do things like this?'

'Suicide, you mean?'

'Yeah.'

I took my time before answering. 'It's not always clear why. I know this kid Tommy was in a situation he couldn't get out of. And something happened to push him to breaking point that day.'

'What was it?'

'I don't know. But I plan to find out.'

'Case you hadn't noticed, Kasper, that fella had a gun. Why don't you just back off and let the police handle it?'

I shrugged. 'Tommy killed himself. A crime hasn't been committed. The police won't care.'

'Sounds like neither one of us can put him to rest.'

I let that one lie.

'You got kids of your own?' he said.

I saw where this was headed. I had no desire to talk about Rosie right now, but I couldn't see anywhere else to go either. Plus, this Emmanuel had just saved me from a slicing, and he seemed an honest bloke in a rut. Right then, he needed to hear something from a person who understood a little of what he was going through. That turned out to be me. So I took a breath and got it out.

'I had a daughter. Rosie. She died five years back, aged fourteen.' I lifted my beer bottle and began peeling the label from the glass.

'I'm so sorry, man. What happened?'

'She put herself in front of a train, Mani. Just like Tommy did.' I ripped the label away from the glass and scrunched it into my fist, then put the fist to my brow and closed my eyes. 'He copied her.'

'He copied her? You serious?'

I nodded. 'The day before it happened, I mentioned to him that my daughter had died. I didn't go into any details, and didn't think much of it at the time. The following night, the two of us were meant to meet up to talk about him. Instead, he left me some weird message, and jumped.

'After, I found out he'd done his research about how Rosie went. Getting details would've been easy. There're stories floating round the internet. He still had an article about her open on his iPhone. He went to the same station, the same spot where she did it.'

I paused to drink my whiskey, hoping the fiery water would quell the reality of what I'd just said.

No such luck. If I hadn't told Tommy about Rosie, Emmanuel and I wouldn't be sitting here. That was the cold hard truth.

'He knew what he was doing when he took himself to the train station last week.'

'I don't understand,' said Emmanuel.

'Tommy had no way out of the hole he'd dug, and if he told anyone about it, he'd put his family in danger. But by killing himself in this particular way, he could send me a message. He wanted me to start digging, to figure out what drove him to it. He knew I wouldn't be able to turn my back on a death just like my own kid's. And you know what? He was right.'

'Jesus,' Emmanuel said. 'Oh, Jesus.'

I kept my eyes closed. And in the darkness came the memories, emerging from the gloomy recesses of my mind.

Rosie leaving for school that morning, then stopping with the front door open, asking if she could stay back and talk to me about something. Me saying I was tired, had things I needed to do. I wasn't long home from a night shift, was in a funk after the latest knuckle-whacking I'd received from my sergeant, and still had to figure out with Carol when I'd be moving my stuff out. A serious talk with Rosie was the last thing on my mind. I told her to have a good day, keep warm, we'd chat at teatime. Half an hour later, she was standing on a platform, listening to music on her headphones. According to the witnesses, she waited, and as the train came, she just took a big step out.

Her tepid cheek a few hours later as she lay in the hospital ITU, tubes and pins and pipes poking in and out of her swollen body, machines breathing for her, keeping her alive; a squat doctor with a Russian accent telling Carol and me about some tests that showed little sign of brain activity. Little sign.

Her eyelids scrunched up, like she was a newborn; her forehead caved and purple, bandaged up where they'd had to burrow into the skull to release pressure; her lips a weird duck-egg blue, dry and cool when I leaned down and kissed them. She was cold, and smelled like disinfectant. Not my daughter anymore.

And after, when the life support had been turned off, there came the people, passing through our lives like clouds.

This psychologist woman who did her best to explain how the brain of a fourteen-year-old is governed by emotion, and in some teens it can be a driving force for these kinds of tragedies.

The neighbours and friends, colleagues and teachers, who left their flowers and cards, stews and casseroles, tiptoeing as if we carried some invisible disease. They assured us if we needed anything – *anything* – we should just ring. But they were all papier mâché faces, with vacant smiles and hollow stares.

Then the throaty coroner woman in her inquest summing-up, saying how suicide is a tragic problem facing our youngsters, and on this occasion, an impulsive act led to a girl's untimely death.

Words. Empty words.

I have no idea how long my eyes were closed. When I opened them, Emmanuel had a fresh smoke on the go.

'Hey, Kasper,' he said, 'if you don't want to talk about it, that's fine.'

'It's not that,' I said. 'It's just that I find it so hard to describe. Sometimes I remember everything, all the small, insignificant things. Other times, there's nothing. Just a gap. It's as if I never had a daughter and have always been like this. Ask about it. I'll do my best to talk, if that's what you want.'

'OK,' he said. 'Why'd your girl do that?'

'We don't know.'

'She left a note?'

'No.'

'She never done anything like that before?'

'No.'

'Was she sad about something?'

'Yeah. She asked to speak to me—' My voice broke, and I took a breath. 'I said I couldn't, we'd talk later. That was the last thing I said to her.'

'What do you think was getting her down?'

I shrugged. 'She'd been seeing a boy for a while, and it ended. She'd been upset about me breaking up with her mum and starting up with someone else. There'd been some bitchiness on social media about her putting on a bit of weight. But nothing major. It could've been any one of those things, or something else entirely.'

There came the sounds of the street and the crackle of Emmanuel's cigarette.

'This kid Tommy,' I went on, 'the last time I saw him, he told me how the world's a messed-up place and the people who *don't* have problems are the real nut-jobs.'

'You reckon that's true?'

I shrugged. 'I'm no psychiatrist, but my landlady used to be one, and she's helped me get a bit of perspective. Turns out there're plenty of people who do stuff like this. Leaping off buildings. Taking a load of pills. Tying nooses round their necks. Jumping in front of trains. Sometimes they die. Sometimes they don't. Sometimes they've got pretty obvious reasons to want to kill themselves. But other times, it's a mystery. But right then in that split second, whatever it is must be so real and painful they can't sit on it a moment longer. That's how it was with my daughter.'

Emmanuel nodded. 'But with this kid, Tommy, you're sure there was a reason he did what he did?'

'Yes,' I said. 'And I'm gonna find it.'

I topped up my whiskey. Emmanuel declined.

'What was she like?' he said.

'Rosie?'

'Yeah. Tell me about her.'

'Why?'

'I'd like to hear it.'

I smiled. 'She was like me. Tall and broad. Didn't say too much. She liked sixties music, the classics, none of this grimy crap kids listen to these days.' I paused to drink. 'She wrote poems and songs, stuff I didn't understand, but which sounded great when she read them. When she found out I was named Dylan after Bob Dylan she was made up. She hated aniseed and salt and vinegar crisps. She supported Spurs and played a mean Scrabble game. She could eat a raw onion without crying.' I laughed and shook my head. 'She was a normal kid. Nothing special.'

'Yeah.'

'But she was my baby, you know?'

I looked at my hands. The skin was frayed from the punches I'd thrown. Tomorrow I'd be in a valley of hurt, but right then I felt nothing.

'After the funeral, I set about finding answers. I thrashed it out with her mum, and we threw accusations at each other. Some of the stuff I said to that poor woman was unforgivable. But she was as clueless as me.

'Next, I tracked down her ex-boyfriend and roughed him up in front of his mates. The kid was so scared, he pissed his pants. But he didn't know anything.

'Then I went to her school. I told myself there must've been bullying or something going on. But after stomping about, kicking in doors, demanding to speak to the headmaster and nearly nutting the bloke, I left with nothing but a barring order.

'I thought I was going crazy. I was a policeman. I'd helped figure out lots of crimes. Why the hell couldn't I find out why Rosie did it? In the end, I had to accept what a part of me knew right from the start.'

'What was that?'

'That'd I'd let her down. She'd wanted to speak to me that morning, and I'd said no.'

'So what did you do? After something like that?'

'I did the only thing I could think of. I walked out on life. My job. A woman I cared for. My grieving ex-wife. I was useless to all of them, and they were better off without me. My plan was to get my affairs in order and check out of this sorry world.'

'But you're still here?'

I nodded.

'How come?'

'Guess I didn't have the balls to kill myself.'

'That bother you?'

I reached for the Bushmills and poured some more. Booze was in my blood now, rounding the edges. I drank and looked at him fondly.

'Yeah, it bothers me. It bothers me quite a bit, actually.' I heard myself chuckle.

'What's funny?'

'Oh, you've got to laugh at all this shit, Mani. Come on. Otherwise you'll end up topping yourself too.'

But he didn't laugh. He carried on staring and smoking his cigarette. 'You're a weird guy, Kasper.'

'Yeah, I've heard.' I reached down and picked up our empty Becks bottles. 'So, how about another beer?'

We carried on with the talking and drinking. Emmanuel told me about his wife, his church, his daughters, his love of fishing and oak carving and Alexander O'Neal records. I told him about Diane, my time with the Met, how I missed both but knew I couldn't go back to either.

By one in the morning, I was stiff, cold, bruised and pissed. Dark thoughts were circling my mind, but they'd lost their bite, and my drunkenness was giving way to a swathe of fatigue. I knew I needed to be unconscious soon, but I liked being here with this new unlikely acquaintance. In a strange way, I think it was helping both of us.

He gave me a hand clearing up the pub, piling stools back on to the tables and making the best of things, but the damage couldn't be hidden. There were two large gashes in the plaster-work and the fire extinguisher was done for. McGovern's was already a sullied pub, but even so, I'd have some explaining to do for Paddy tomorrow.

Unlocking the shutters and doors, I stuck my head out and gave a quick one-two to make sure no one was lurking around. Emmanuel exited, and I stood beside him outside the pub.

'Thanks,' he said. 'It's been good talking tonight.'

'No problem. It has.'

Again, we shook hands.

'I'd like to help the boy's family. It'd be good for me. If there's something I can do, will you tell me?'

I looked at his face, and saw he meant it. 'All right,' I said.

'And I'm telling management, I'll get back to driving trains in a couple of days. I'm ready for it.'

'Good for you, mate.'

He smiled a warm smile, then turned and started walking. After a few steps, he stopped and looked back. I hadn't moved.

'I'll see you, Kasper,' he said, and gave me a thumbs-up. 'Be lucky.'

I tapped my brow. 'Yeah,' I said. 'Lucky.'

Chapter 17

Not so lucky.

I came to the following morning feeling like a pile of nuts and bolts had been tipped down my insides. Pain reeled across my body, sharp and insistent, coming from all directions. I ran a hand across my face and wished I hadn't. It was puffy and raw, a blister ready to pop.

Staying in bed would've been the sensible thing, maybe emerging mid-afternoon to climb inside a bottle of Bushmills. Instead, I forced myself up.

Something grated at my side. I looked down and saw the source. The right side of my ribcage was a smear of dark grey, yellow and brown, like the countries on a map.

I hobbled downstairs to the bathroom, tiptoeing past Dr Steiner's room, from which her dulcet snores emanated. Blood had congealed in my mouth, the taste like lead filings. Crouching down to the sink, I drank water from the tap, spat into the basin and saw dark lumps of the stuff swirl down the plughole.

I kicked off my boxers and climbed under a steaming shower. I washed my hair, my face, and then my body, getting used to slow, cautious movements. Before long, the sound of my winces had grown familiar. The pain hadn't.

Back out, I drank more water, then wiped steam from the mirror and inspected my naked self with disdain. Day one after a beating is always the harshest, but it still came as a shock. There was a half-inch cut above my right eye the texture of grilled cheese. My upper lip was a swell of angry purple, and when I opened my mouth I heard a clicking that hadn't been there before.

I returned to my loft, gobbled some Nurofen, and dug out my Wayfarers. These, a pair of loose khaki cargo pants and a hoody would be today's uniform. Suitably attired, I went downstairs to percolate some battery-acid coffee and get my head into gear.

It was still early, not quite seven. A grey carpet of cloud hid the sun. A sparrow was rummaging on the lawn with a small twig in its beak, and trying, unsuccessfully, to become airborne. Eventually it gave up, left the twig and disappeared into the fog.

After three coffees, the pills started kicking in, the clouds began to shift, and I was able to think things through with a bit of clarity.

The kids who had jumped me all came from Mick's Bar. No question, they were there on Napier's orders and were led by the psycho calling himself Vincent, who I'd also seen in the bar. How did they know where to find me?

Elementary, dear Kasper – Harriet must've spoken to Napier about me, and he sent the heavy squad to scare me off. Only they weren't scary enough. Instead, I beat them up, and this Vincent character went and pulled a gun with enough horse-power to fell a bulldog on heat. Now I had them all pissed off.

This Napier was a dirty player. First, there was the beating of the boy at his bar, then last night's fight at McGovern's. People like him don't stick to a code; they just chisel and cheat to get what they want.

My gut told me he stole the coke from Harriet's car, or at least had a hand in it. This was a nasty trick that a particular breed of criminal goes for – sub some drugs to a green-skinned dupe, steal them back, then go bat-shit crazy when they break the news they've been robbed, and they're in your pocket for good.

Well, there was one way to find out. Ask him.

I left the house, jumped on my bike, and tried calling Harriet as I pedalled. It went straight to voicemail. No surprises there.

Next, I called Paddy and told him there'd been an attempted robbery at McGovern's yesterday not long after he'd left, but I'd managed to subdue them through sheer force of my character, and then hoodwinked two uniformed police with a made-up story. An inherent mistrust of authority meant Paddy was always keen to keep the law from snooping around his pub. He thanked me for dealing with 'those little wee bastards' and for fobbing off the cops.

Again I tried Harriet, and left a message this time, saying I was coming to find her. Last, I called Diane. 'I need another favour.'

'Go on?'

'Can you run a check on a Scottish bruiser calling himself Vincent? Big bloke. Face like a breezeblock. He's got a Glasgow Rangers tat on his neck.'

'Sounds like a guy I dated off Tinder. You OK? You sound wired.'

'I had a run-in last night. This Vincent's involved. It's all mixed up with the Tommy Berkowitz thing.'

'Maybe this is a good time to step back, Kas.'

'No can do.'

I heard her scribbling things down. 'OK, I'll call you on my lunch,' she said. 'Keep your phone on.'

'Thanks, Diane.'

Riding my bike against the headwind was energising. I was starting to feel half-human, even if I didn't look it, and I had a rough plan for what I'd do next.

Find Harriet.

Then the two of us would go talk to Napier.

But first things first, I needed a bit of protection. Last night had raised the stakes.

I unlocked the door of my dad's old allotment hut and switched on the gaslight kept on a hook. Sweeping shadows lassoed against the wood panels as the space became dully illuminated.

Kneeling down, I started rooting amongst the rusty tools, looking for a tatty Nike shoebox. It was easy enough to find, and when I lifted it out, it held a familiar weight.

Inside were photos, mainly of Rosie. I reached down through the snaps and felt the fabric of her old Spurs football sock. Carefully, I retrieved the sock and held it aloft.

It sagged heavily. With my left hand, I reached inside, touched cool metal. I gripped a butt, pulled the sock away and admired the black steel of a Beretta pistol.

I'd bought it from Neville, the father of my sparring partner, Ricky. He'd sold it to me a couple of months after Rosie's death – and a year or so before his incarceration for a hold-up. I'd known Neville since school, and he'd been surprised when

I asked if he could get me a gun – even more so when I told him I only wanted one bullet. One was all I needed for what I had in mind, I insisted.

At first he said no way, but Nev's substance and gambling addictions soon trumped any moral obligations, and after flashing a bunch of fifties, he'd sourced me the piece I now held.

And a handsome piece it was.

I'd told this Vincent character the truth last night as he'd held his Smith & Wesson level with my brow: his wasn't the first gun I'd had aimed at me.

During that first year after Rosie's death, I used to carry the Beretta with me day and night, concealed in a pocket, a thing of dark reassurance. I'd clutch the muzzle, touch the trigger and flick the safety on and off. Alone and out of sight, I'd hold it to my temple and sit with the knowledge that at any given moment, I could end things. It felt good.

I checked the chamber, the safety action and the solitary round. All in working order. Although one bullet wouldn't go far, if it came to it, anyone with a gun like this aimed at them would know I meant business.

I clicked the safety on, shoved it into the rear of my cargos and stood, adjusting my hoody to cover the bulge. Then I checked my watch. It'd just gone ten.

I locked the allotment hut, lowered my shades, retrieved my bike and cycled northeast in the direction of the Berkowitz house to fish out Harriet.

Chapter 18

Her Skoda was in the driveway, but no one was answering the Berkowitz front door. I pressed the bell. It ding-donged. I kept pressing and it kept ding-donging.

Thirty seconds later, I saw a flicker in the curtains.

'Open the door, Harriet!' I shouted through the letter box, my bruised torso berating me for leaning down.

'Go away, Kasper!' I heard. 'I'm sick!'

'Open the door!'

'No!'

Pretty fast, the flowery doorbell sound corroded into a meaningless blare. This was a childish torment that hadn't failed me yet; I once kept my finger on a bell for a whole hour at the home of a police informer who'd gone AWOL. He'd finally answered looking forlorn and slightly deranged. I reckoned Harriet couldn't last more than ten minutes.

'Leave me alone!' she yelled over the din. 'Please!'

'No!'

'I'll call the police!'

'No, you won't!'

Another minute and I heard the rattle of a chain, the turning of the key and then the door swung open.

'Well, hello,' I said, removing my finger from the doorbell and taking her in, 'and I thought *I* looked rough.'

Harriet was staring at me with a pair of puffy, bloodshot eyes. She was wearing a pink dressing gown that accentuated her hunched, twiggy frame. Her pallor was chalky white, and her mouth drooped forlornly; she looked steeped in insomnia and self-pity.

Without saying anything, she shuffled back into the hallway. Her movements had a peculiar stiffness, as if she had a trapped disc. As she locked and bolted the front door, I noticed the little finger on her left hand was bound with a bandage and splinted upright. The cowboy kid from Mick's Bar had had the same digit snapped as punishment.

'Looks like your friends did a number on you too,' I said.

She turned to me and leaned by the grandfather clock. 'I don't know what you mean.'

I removed my Wayfarers so she could see my bashed-up face in all its glory and pointed at her busted finger. 'What happened?'

She followed my eyes. 'I fell,' she said.

'Balls.'

'Kasper, I—'

'Harriet. Drop the act. I'm pissed off and you know why.'

Her lower lip started wobbling. She was scared. Bricking it, more like.

A deep, unsteady breath, and she said, 'They told me it was *you* they wanted, not me. But they hurt me anyway. Vincent broke my finger. He rammed it in a drawer.'

'Thought so. Where's Saul?'

'He's at the funeral parlour. For Tommy . . .'

'Good,' I said. 'It's best he doesn't hear this. How did you explain your finger to him?'

She wiped her nose with the dressing-gown cuff. 'I told him I had a fall at work.'

'And he believed you?'

'Dad believes everything I say.'

'Yeah,' I said, 'well I don't.' And I walked past her to the lounge at the rear of the house.

Any sense of organised clutter in the Berkowitz house had long since demised – the place looked like student digs. Used mugs, dirty plates and takeaway trays were scattered on the dining table and chairs; newspapers, opened and unopened letters and creased clothing lay strewn over the sofas and floor.

I went to the windows and stared at the eucalyptus in the garden. Foliage and dead leaves had clustered around its gummy roots, and a thin mist encircled its trunk.

'Have you got a cigarette?' Harriet said, behind me.

'No.'

'I need a cigarette.'

I turned. 'Start from the beginning. When did they grab you?'

'I . . .' she began, then faltered. I thought she was about to start crying.

She was.

I stood there and waited, resisting the urge to console her as she wept silently.

When she'd composed herself, she spoke with surprising bite. 'This is all *your* fault, you know.'

I felt a dint in my armour. Although I didn't want to admit it, the same thought had been churning round my head for days.

But I didn't want Harriet to see any weakness and clam up again.

'What do you mean?' I said.

'I did what you said. I messaged Napier and told him I was deleting the videos because *you* said I should.'

'And?'

'*And* his henchman Vincent hijacked me yesterday. He dragged me to the bar. Napier said someone called Kasper turned up there the previous night, asking questions. He remembered Tommy going on about you, and said I needed to be taught a lesson for opening my mouth. So Vincent assaulted me. They found it funny.'

'What time?' I said.

'Huh?'

'What time did Vincent jump you?'

'I don't know. Lunchtime, I think.'

'And what did Napier want to know about me?'

'He asked who you were, how to find you. I told him what I know. That you work at a pub in Tottenham. One of Napier's boys remembered you. Vincent took him and a load of others to find you. I went to A&E to get my finger seen to.'

Things were making sense. 'So they squeezed you for info, then Vincent and co. headed out, spotted me, and waited till I was alone before moving in.' I looked straight at Harriet and shook my head. 'Thanks for the warning.'

'I was afraid to let you know!'

'Yeah, right. What else did Napier say?'

'He said he'd break my neck if I step out of line again.'

'That'd make blackmailing cash from Dominic Tyrell a pretty tough gig. Wouldn't it, Harriet?'

To demonstrate exasperation, she flung her hands in the air, but the movement must've hurt something in her finger, and she let out a wince instead.

I returned to looking at the garden. An oblong of disparate light had cracked through the mist, illuminating a patch of yellowing grass. I tried focusing on that rather than the sound of Harriet behind me.

'There's more,' I said, 'isn't there? Tell me the rest.'

A long silence came, then she spoke. 'Napier phoned me again this morning,' she said.

'And?'

'He's added a ton of interest to my debt as a punishment for blabbing to you. He said I work for him exclusively. He'll take money off what I owe as long as I carry on collecting cash and running errands.'

'Poor you.'

'Kasper, this is serious!'

'No shit, Sherlock.'

'Can you help me?'

I shook my head. 'Harriet, why don't you bite the bullet and talk to the police? You're in way too deep.'

'Haven't you been paying attention? I can't go to the police!'

'Why can't you?'

'Because these people are maniacs! They'll kill me, and maybe you too.'

'Well, how very noble of you.'

'Piss off.'

I thought about what I'd just learned, and tried putting it together into a whole.

I couldn't. Bits were still missing.

'What aren't you telling me?'

'Look,' she said, calmer now, 'there's things to do with all this you don't know about. Horrible things. They come from the past. And they need to stay buried there.'

'Why?'

'It's none of your business. All that matters is, I need to start making money. Fast. Or else I'm done for.'

Too right. And whatever I thought of Harriet, her brother was dead, like my daughter. I wasn't prepared to let her – or anyone else – be the next to die.

'Tommy understood why I was doing this,' she added. 'That's why he helped me.'

I looked at a picture of Tommy on the mantle. He looked maybe nine. He was wearing a navy jumper over a collared shirt. It looked like a school portrait shot. His doleful eyes were gazing right into the camera lens, and his hair hung over his brow. It was hard matching that boy with the lascivious image of him hanging in Mick's Bar I'd seen two nights prior.

There were secrets in this family's past all right.

'OK,' I said, turning, looking hard at Harriet. 'We're sorting this.' I indicated towards the door. 'Get your coat.'

'Why?'

'We're going out.'

'Out? Where to?'

'Where do you think? To see Napier.'

'You're joking!' What colour remained in her cheeks seeped from them. 'He'll kill me.'

'Not if I stop him.'

She stared at me for several seconds, then her head collapsed into her hands and the tears began welling through her thin fingers, plopping on to the rug.

'Why's this happening to me?' she said. 'Why, why, why!'

*

Diane called ten minutes later. I was still at the Berkowitz's house, still looking at the garden, still listening to Harriet sniffling.

Diane had scored, digging up info about a repeat offender called Vincent Brown, aka Scottish Vinnie, aka Vinnie the Nut, who sounded like last night's visitor at McGovern's.

While she filled me in on his criminal CV, Harriet shuffled upstairs to tidy herself up. I probably should've kept a closer eye on her, but right then, I was glad of the reprieve.

'OK,' Diane said. 'This Vincent's a piece of work. Two stints in Brixton for aggravated robbery and intimidation, plus a spate of arrests for drugs and vice. Prior to that, I've got car theft, extortion, football violence, fraud. The list goes back to the eighties, lots of spells in YOIs. Before that, he was in foster care and a children's home, where he was suspected of a string of cat murders.'

'Cats?'

'Uh-huh. Animal torture. There's an adolescent forensic report from ninety-three when he was primary-school age describing him as an emerging asocial personality type. You know, a good old-fashioned psychopath. You've picked a beaut here.'

I rubbed my bruised chin, thinking. 'Vincent works for someone called Michael Napier. Napier runs the bar Tommy used to hook from. He's got flats set up with spy cameras. The name ring a bell?'

'Funny you should ask. I made a few calls, as there's no current address for Vincent. Seems his last probation worker lost contact and let things slide. I couldn't find much, so widened the search and got the last known whereabouts for a Vick Brown, who'd been living in a bedsit near Hackney.

Reason he's on file is he skipped three months' rent and chinned his landlord when the bailiffs came looking. Landlord gave a description to police of a big Scottish guy with a Rangers tat on his neck. I read the statement. On his tenancy, Vick put down a character reference – one Michael Napier.'

My grip tightened on the handset. 'That's him,' I said. 'That's our man. What've you got on Napier?'

'Not a lot. A few years back, there was an allegation of sexual harassment from a minor, but the victim withdrew his statement. There was suspected intimidation, but nothing concrete. Records show Napier used to have a fetish shop in Vauxhall, but the place got closed down by the council. Now he's got the bar in Shoreditch.'

'Anything to suggest he's serving drugs?'

'Nope. But maybe he's running a tight ship. His accounts and bar licence are all kosher. He's legit, Kas. On the surface at least.'

'Harriet assures me he's big time: wholesale Class As, the works. You believe it?'

'Who knows? Listen, you sure you want to be in the middle of this? It sounds as if these guys are proper undesirables. And *you* sound a bit off-key too, don't mind me saying.'

'Yeah,' I said. 'I think I am a bit.'

'Why don't we—' she said, but was cut short by the slam of the front door, the beep-beep of a car's central locking and the fire of its engine.

I ran out the house just in time to catch sight of Harriet's Skoda reversing over a potted plant and pulling away.

I didn't bother chasing. I'd done enough of that. Instead, I watched as she turned the corner and sped off, leaving a waft of dusty fumes in her wake.

'Damn,' I said.

'Kas!' I heard from the handset I was still gripping. 'Kas, you still there?'

I returned it to my ear and told Diane what had just happened.

She gave a dry laugh. 'Looks like your powers of persuasion are wearing off, big man.'

'She's scared,' I said, staring at the spot where the Skoda had been.

'So what's the plan now?'

I didn't reply.

'Kas? Don't do anything crazy, OK?'

I hung up before she could ask again, broiling with anger.
I knew Diane was right. That should've been that. I was more than a little off-key, and a bit of time to think would've helped.

But there'd been enough thinking.

On Napier's orders, this Vincent had come round to my place of work to send me a message. Had it not been for Emmanuel rocking up when he did, he'd have taken pleasure in filleting me with that blade of his. I was pissed off, and had good reason to be.

Dr Steiner's words came back, how anger could jeopardise my judgement and make me do something reckless. But I'd been acting reckless all my life. I was still here.

I checked my watch. Quarter past one.

A soft light had awoken, arcing through the clouds in ribbons of white. For reasons I cannot explain, my mind reeled back to the morning of Rosie's birth. I'd stared out the window of the maternity ward at an opulent blue sky much like this, holding the tiny kidney bean of a creature, my daughter, promising her I'd never let her down.

Yeah, right.

I lowered my shades, closed the Berkowitz front door and unchained my bike. The Beretta mashed my hip as I cycled away from the house and joined the throng of traffic heading east down City Road.

It was high time I made Mick Napier's acquaintance.

Chapter 19

Shoreditch again. In the seventies, my father was a labourer on sites round here, work that led him to the greasy spoons and boozers once synonymous with the East End. In one pub, now the site of a private dental practice, he'd lured my nineteen-year-old mother away from her nursing studies, before impregnating her with me a few weeks later.

When I was one, she passed from breast cancer, and Dad, bereft, relocated us north of the city to live near his brothers on the Paradise Towers Estate in Haringey. Here, I watched him decline into a black fug of depression and drinking, and when Rosie was just three, cancer had claimed him, too.

East London, like so much of the city, had changed staggeringly since his day, becoming a weird mishmash of the haves and have-nots, the scuffed-up and the sparkly new. Every week, a swishy new apartment building sprung up amidst the weather-beaten council flats, or some trendy pop-up wine bar encroached between the few remaining bookies, kebab shops and dead-end watering holes.

Today, you could buy crushed avocado wraps a few feet from scuzzy chicken takeaways, or get a turmeric latte opposite

185

the old pie 'n' mash shops that were still clinging on. One such place, Abe's, was open for lunch trade. Its owner and namesake was a liver-spotted old geezer who used to serve my dad. He clocked me from the window and gave a salute as I pedalled past. On a different day, I would've stopped to chat. Unfortunately, right then I had other business.

It was a little after two when I pulled up outside Mick's Bar. Without the filter of night and bustle of bodies, the place looked worn and tatty. Its garish neon lights were switched off, the awning drawn, windows blackened and the front door bolted.

I chained my bike to a lamp post and began walking over. A few feet away was a straggly male in brown corduroy trousers and a navy blazer. He was urinating against a closed-down pizza place, attending to business with one hand, eating a shawarma with the other. He glanced up at the sound of my boots.

'You know if this place is open?' I said, pointing at the bar.

He shrugged, zipped up and walked away, chewing.

Three hard knocks on the door and I got my answer.

A rustle of chains, the turning of a bolt and the door opened. A broad, square-headed man was standing before me. He was immediately recognisable – the friendly bouncer.

His eyes narrowed. He recognised me too. 'What *you* want?'

'I'm Dylan Kasper,' I said, raising my Wayfarers, smiling. 'I'm here to see Mick Napier, and I don't have an appointment.'

He looked me up and down and didn't say anything.

I gave him a moment, then said, 'Look, mate, there's two ways we'll sort this. Either you go back in there and tell your boss there's a bloke out here called Kasper wanting a quick word. Or else I come back here tonight, and every night, and start causing a real nuisance. What do you think?'

He pointed a finger down at me. 'Mr Mick don't want to see you.'

'I think he will,' I said.

He snarled. 'You don't want to do this.'

'Oh, but I do.'

He carried on staring, and closed the door abruptly. I stood for several long minutes, doing nothing, and was beginning to wonder if my charm had failed when the door unbolted a second time.

'In,' the bouncer said.

Without the clench of customers and that horrendous music, Mick's Bar seemed much bigger, but no less sleazy than it had two nights back. It was a gloomy place, with no natural illumination. The floor was sticky with last night's spilled booze, the air warm and fetid.

I followed the bouncer around the horseshoe bar, my eyes avoiding the image of naked Tommy mounted on the wall. A young male, Turkish-looking, was on a stool to my left. His lip was scabbing, and he was watching me furtively from beneath his hood, drinking lemonade through a straw. I recognised him. He was one of the kids I'd beaten up last night, and he didn't seem happy to see me.

Ahead to the right was the gents, and beside it, a bar table. Two men were sitting on either side.

Although both were steeped in shadow, I recognised the pair immediately. Today, Vincent was dressed down, black jeans, a Glasgow Rangers top and Timberland boots. His forearms were marred with faded tats, and thick hairs and veins corded the skin. The punch I'd chucked last night had left a slight swelling to his lip, but nothing more.

Beside him was Napier. He was older than Vincent, mid-fifties I'd say, with puffy lips, a beaked nose and rigid eyes, small and predatory. His peppery hair was styled in a George Clooney crop, and an inordinate amount of gold twinkled from his fingers, neck, ears and teeth. He wore a lilac crewneck and blue denim jeans ravaged with distress holes. On his feet were a pair of paint-splattered loafers that looked like someone had vomited on them.

I stopped ten or so feet away, sidestepped to the bar and leaned on it. The Beretta nudged against my hip. I'd half expected the bouncer to want to search me. But clearly this lot didn't think I posed a threat. More fool them.

Everyone was in sight, the bouncer a few feet right, the Turkish boy to my flank, and this pair in front.

Vincent was the first to move. Casually, he stood up and stepped forward. Napier followed.

'Afternoon,' I said, addressing Napier with a smile. 'I met Vincent last night. Your doorman and the lad at the bar I've encountered too. You must be Mr Napier. It's a pleasure to finally make your acquaintance.'

Begin polite. There'd be time for heavy hands.

'What the fuck do you want?' Napier said in a yappy, slightly effeminate Northern Irish voice. He stared at me as if I were an object.

So much for courtesy.

'I've heard about you, and thought we should meet in the flesh.'

'Shit,' the bouncer said.

The Turkish lad kissed his teeth.

Vincent kept staring.

Napier said, 'Vinnie gave you my warning to back off.'

I nodded.

'So there's nothin' more to talk about,' he said.

I shook my head, slowly. 'Not how I see it,' I said.

'Listen, boy. Remember where you are.' He pointed demonstrably around the bar with a stubby ringed finger, then back at me. 'This is a bar that caters for certain tastes. You've invited yourself in. I could have you beaten, drugged and humiliated by my boys. Vinnie would go to town. You'd be a changed man by the time we're through, an' the law wouldn't bat an eyelid.' He took a couple of steps closer. 'Or maybe it'd be simpler just to kill you.'

I stood my ground. I knew acting bolshie wasn't too clever – Napier was right, this was his turf, I had no real plan, and Vincent was probably armed and certainly dangerous. I didn't want this blowing up. Not yet, anyway.

'Maybe we've got off to a bad start, Mick,' I said. 'Mind if I call you Mick?' I didn't wait for an answer. 'See, I think we can come to an agreement.'

'What sort of agreement?'

'Harriet's told me about the system you came up with for repaying her drug debt. I'm sure it was just business for you. But now Tommy's dead. A line's been crossed. And I'm here to tell you, it's to stop.'

Vincent hissed, a sound I took for a laugh. He folded his wide arms over his chest.

Napier carried on staring. 'You're on thin ice here, Polski,' he said. 'Why should I give a shit what you have to say?'

I nodded, said, 'I'll make it simple. I'm not asking you to forget the debt. But I want you to back off for a bit, let

Harriet raise the money in her own way, and not hurt her again.'

'Anything else?' he asked, smiling.

'Yeah. I also need to be sure you're not going to send your boys to my place of work causing trouble again. Next time it'll get messy.'

'Shit,' the bouncer repeated. Clearly a man of brevity.

'Get a loada this fella, Vinnie,' Napier said. 'If I didn't know better, I'd say he's giving me orders.'

'He's got a death wish, I reckon,' Vincent said.

'That so?' Napier said. 'This how you get your kicks? A washed-up ex-plod persecutin' honest folk?'

'When those folk deal in vice and drugs and busting fingers,' I said, 'then yeah, it is.'

'Once a copper, always a copper, right?' Napier grinned. 'I heard about you. You had a bad rep. Couldn't obey no orders, an' liked to lose your rag when things didn't go your way.'

'You got friends in the Met?' I said with a sigh. Judging by Napier's arrogance and clean record, this was something I should've guessed.

'I know lots of folks in high places,' Napier said with a smirk. 'An' if I pulled a few strings, I could have you vanish. But I thought I'd do the right thing first, give you a warning. Looks like you're struggling to take it.' He pointed his finger at my chest. 'So what's stopping us putting you under the ground now?'

I shrugged. 'A couple of things. First, that would be stupid. Like you said, I'm ex-police. I've got friends on the Met too. Something happens, they'll be over you like a rash. A man in your line of work wouldn't want heat like that, would he?'

Napier's tongue darted from his mouth, left, right, then disappeared. 'You don't know anything about my work. I already told you, I'm a businessman. It's all above board.'

'Not what I heard.'

Ten seconds passed. Twenty.

'And what's the other reason?'

I slackened my shoulders and smiled. 'You're not good enough to put me under the ground.' I felt the kick of my heart, a tingling in my fingers.

Napier was the first to laugh. It was an unexpectedly low sound, wet and phlegmy, thoroughly unpleasant. His eyes stayed open, devoid of humour, just staring. Vincent was laughing next, then the bouncer.

I stayed as I was, waiting for the next bit.

'I'll hand it to you, Kasper,' Napier said, still chuckling. 'You got a pair. But this is getting boring. All's I care about is the money.' He wagged his finger. 'You come here, bringing your threats and attitude, dressed like a tramp.'

'Maybe you can give me some styling tips,' I said, 'once you've cleaned the puke off your shoes?'

His eyes widened. 'Piss off before you get hurt,' he said, his finger a few inches from me. 'I mean it.'

'Can't do that. Not until we sort this out.'

Vincent took a breath. My eyes flitted to him. His arms weren't folded now – they'd fallen to his sides without me noticing.

'What're you gonna do, Kasper?' Napier said, smirking again. 'Get rough? Put me over your knee for a spanking?'

'Maybe.'

'Sounds fun. But I got work to do.' He looked at Vincent, then the bouncer. 'Get this cunt out my bar, boys.'

Movement from behind me, the bouncer coming in. I stepped away, ready to sock him, then looked back in time to see Vincent's arms slip round his back, his shoulder flexing. He was reaching for something.

Instinct took over. I pulled the Beretta and aimed it at Napier.

Vincent was a split second slower, the Smith & Wesson in his right hand, held tense at his side.

'Careful,' I said to him. 'I'll pop your boss and you if you start getting trigger happy.'

Fire lit Vincent's eyes. But the gun stayed where it was.

'Whoa,' Napier said, his voice tight, shock widening his eyes. 'That's not very friendly, is it?'

'Put your hands where I can see them, Mick.' I looked squarely at him. 'Tell your boys to calm down.'

'Easy, boys,' Napier said, raising his hands slowly.

The bouncer appeared from my right. Then came the Turkish boy. Both had their hands up. Vincent was rock still, his body as taut as a crossbow, cocked and ready to fire.

'OK,' Napier said. 'So you got us. Now what?'

Good question.

'Now, I'm telling you how it is. Harriet's going to figure out a way to clear her debt. How she gets the money is her concern. But she'll pay you. Meantime, you're going to back off. Understand?'

The initial shock had washed from Napier. He began shaking his head.

'Fuck me,' he said. 'That little runt Tommy's dead and he's still causing me a headache.'

'I reckon he fancied the kid,' Vincent said.

Napier grinned. Gold twinkled from his capped teeth. 'He

was a pretty thing, wasn't he? Kinda fragile. That how you like them too?'

For a man with a gun pointing at him, Napier didn't seem all that perturbed. It bothered me. Vincent hissed another laugh. That bothered me too.

'But the reason you're doin' this isn't really about that boy,' Napier said. 'Is it?'

I flinched. The Beretta quivered from side to side.

Napier saw it. His eyes lit up.

'I heard about your daughter,' he said. 'Must've been hard, Tommy goin' the same way as her. What is all this? A way to say sorry to your girl for being a shitty dad?'

'You get one chance,' I said, my hand gripping the gun, palm slick with sweat. 'Next time you mention my daughter, you get a bullet in your skull. Now, have we got a deal?'

'No,' Napier said. 'No fucking deal.'

My arm was starting to ache. Through clenched teeth, I said, 'I'm doing my best to find a solution here. Another would be to shoot you.'

'That bitch owes me.'

'And I said you'll get your money.'

'Not good enough.'

'You know,' I said, scrambling for a counter attack, 'I'm wondering if *you* stole the coke from Harriet as a way to get her in your pocket.'

Napier's eyebrows hitched up. I had him intrigued. 'Reckon so, do you?'

'Yeah.'

He seemed to be considering something. 'Looks like Harriet and little Tommy didn't fill you in on everything, did they?'

'Meaning?'

'Meaning, you've not heard the full story, dickhead. If you had, you might not be charging in here like brave Sir fuckin' Galahad.'

Sweat trickled from my temple. Napier's comment about Rosie had thrown me, and something wasn't right in the way he was acting – it was too relaxed, like he was in on a private joke and was about to spill the punchline.

'All right,' he said. 'Now, don't kill me, but I'm reaching for my phone. You need to see what I'm about to show you.'

He went for his back pocket.

My finger drew tight on the trigger.

He came out with a Samsung smartphone.

After pressing a few buttons he said, 'Show time,' flipped the phone one-eighty and held it up a few feet from my face. 'Watch this, Kasper,' he said, and the video began.

The image was fuzzy at first – pale skin, the close-up of an acned chin, a thin wrist with a birthdate tattooed below the palm, a pair of brown eyes. Tommy's strawberry perfume hit me, even though I knew that was impossible. His face came into focus, eyes red and bleary.

The room behind him was recognisable. It was the one where the videos with Dominic Tyrell had been filmed.

Tommy was dressed in the same *Eat Me!* jersey and black skinny jeans he'd had on the afternoon we strolled by the canal.

'What is this?' I said, glancing up at Napier. 'Another sex tape?'

He shook his head. 'It was filmed that day, I was sure of it. A few hours later he was dead. Just watch.'

From the right of the camera came a slight woman with a jet-black bob. I recognised her clothes, too – the same dark blazer she'd had on outside the station when they pulled

Tommy out. Harriet. Her hands were knotted together, and she was shaking her head.

'Look,' she said, her voice tinny but clear enough to be heard. 'Napier's angry. Just keep going for a few more weeks. Please.'

'I won't,' Tommy said, turning to her. 'It's wrong, Harry, all of it. I'm stopping, from tonight.'

'Bloody hell, you're going to get us killed!'

'But I hate doing this. Going with strangers, blackmailing them. I want it to end.'

Harriet's hands broke apart. She came towards him, raised a finger and pointed it at his face. 'You're so fucking selfish. Everything I did for you when we were kids, and this is how you repay me.'

He took a step back, clearly burned by this. 'That's not fair—'

'Oh, grow up, Tommy. Life isn't fair.'

He shook his head. 'Mum wouldn't have wanted this. She'd be ashamed of you.'

'You always bring Mum into this, like she's some saint. She's the reason we're in this mess.'

'Don't say that! Mum loved you! She loved all of us!'

'Love? She loved us so much she brought that man into our house. She loved us so much she got hooked on drugs, racked up a heap of debt and left me to sort it out. Is that what you're saying, little brother?'

'She couldn't help it! After everything that happened—'

He didn't get to finish. Harriet slapped him. Although shorter and slighter, her blow made him wither back and almost topple.

'It's always been the same with you,' she said, turning her

back. 'Poor Tommy, such a delicate thing. You're weak.'

'I'm not!'

'Yes, you are! Face facts. Mum died because she couldn't live with the guilt. She was a bitch!'

His long arms hugged his frame, as if a sudden draught had blown into the room. He started crying, rocking back and forth, a young, bewildered child. Although I was watching a video on a small handset, the tension was palpable.

'No,' Tommy said, his voice wobbling. 'This is wrong . . . Kasper's going to help me. We talked today, and I'm meeting him tomorrow. You could come, Harry; he can help both of us!'

I felt a jolt up my spine at my name being said. Napier giggled.

'*Kasper?*' Harriet spat. 'That oaf from the gym you've been going on about?' She pointed accusingly. Tommy clambered back from her finger as if it were a knife. 'What the hell have you told him?'

'Nothing. But I will. I'm going to tell him everything. About Mum and Dad and what happened to us, and how it was me who stole your drugs!'

I thought the video had paused. They were both frozen.

Then Harriet spoke. 'What did you just say?'

'You heard.' Tommy wiped his eyes. '*I* took the drugs from your car, Harry, and *I* flushed them down the toilet. It wasn't some random thief. It was me.'

She covered her mouth. 'Why?' she said. 'Why, why?'

'Because I was scared!'

'Scared?'

'I knew you'd lost your job. I knew you were stressed about something. I just wanted to know what it was, to see if I could help. So I took your keys and searched your car.

But all I found were these packs of white powder in the boot. I freaked. I thought you were a drug addict, going the same way Mum did. What was I supposed to do?'

'So you destroyed them?'

Tommy nodded. 'Then when you told me they were Napier's drugs, I realised I'd made a mistake. But you must believe me, I did it because I love you, Harry. I owe you my life. But don't you see? All this, it's wrong. It needs to stop!'

Harriet was visibly trembling. She took her hands away from her mouth. 'You idiot,' she said, still quiet, but with bite. 'This is your fault.'

'We'll talk to Kasper,' Tommy said. 'He can help us—'

Something must have snapped in Harriet, for she pounced, slapping him with both hands again and again. It was hard to watch. She hit his face and head. When he lifted his hands and crouched to protect himself, she went for his neck and back instead. The sound was awful, like raw meat on a slab, interspersed with Tommy's whines and pleas.

'You're so selfish,' she said, anger braying her voice. 'So. Bloody. Selfish.'

'No!' Tommy said. 'Please, Harry, no—'

A cruel dash across his scalp sent him to his knees and he fell out of view. But I could still hear his whimpers.

Harriet was pacing in a circle, her hands fists. 'I need to think,' she said. 'I need to think this through. In the meantime, I want you to stay calm and do exactly what I say until I've worked things out.'

A moment later, Tommy got back up. He was rubbing his red, tear-streaked cheeks.

'You're right,' he said quietly. 'This *is* my fault. And I know what I need to do to fix it.' He sounded calm; the same calmness I'd heard on the voicemail he left the day he died.

Harriet must've heard it too. 'What's that supposed to mean?' she said. 'What do you *need* to do?' She had the finger back in his face. Only this time, he didn't recoil from it.

'You'll see,' he said.

'Tommy?'

He didn't reply. Instead, he turned and walked.

'Tommy! Come back!'

Off camera, I heard a door opening and closing. He was gone.

Harriet didn't pursue. She didn't run to the door or screech his name. She just stayed where she was, and after a pause, she put her head into her hands and wept.

The film stopped abruptly. Napier lowered the phone.

A light, airy feeling was draughting through me. I took a step back to balance, but my vision kept swaying.

How'd I been so blind? Tommy's aversion to alcohol, his refusal to take medication – he'd taken the coke from Harriet's car. He'd been mortified at the harm addiction had done to his mother, and thought his sister was going the same way.

'That was an interesting night, all right,' Napier said. 'Tommy came to the bar, but he was acting funny from the off. I told him to go with a bloke who had an eye on him. He refused. Instead, he kept talking about some big fella who was going to help him out. I'm guessing he meant you.' He pointed the phone at me.

'Yes,' I said, my voice hoarse. 'Then what?'

'I called Harriet and told her to get over and sort her wee

brother's head out. She came sharpish and they went to talk in one of the flats. They didn't know I was filming. But my cameras are always on. You never know what you're gonna see.' He returned the phone to his pocket. 'But this video, it *was* a bit of a surprise.'

'What happened,' I managed, 'after that video ended? To Tommy?'

Napier shrugged. 'What do you think? He bolted.'

'And then?'

'Then, I sent Vinnie to bring him back. But he'd vanished. Next thing I hear, he's jumped under that train.'

If I'd wanted to ask anything else, I don't think I could've, so constricted was my throat. It didn't matter, though – I was too numbed to speak.

Napier was grinning, his mouth a mix of puffy lips and gold teeth.

'So now you know,' he said defiantly. 'It was Tommy nicked my coke from Harriet's car. He pinched it and flushed it down the loo, all because of some mummy issues. That's one messed-up family, what's left of them, anyway. And if I don't get what I'm owed, I'll come after that bitch, and send this video straight to her professor dad to see.'

Vincent cackled. The sound clawed something in me. I'd almost forgotten his Smith & Wesson.

'So tell me,' Napier went on, 'why get involved? Snooping around won't bring Tommy back, or your daughter. It'll just get you and the people you care about hurt.'

I stared. A part of me knew he was right. This had nothing to do with me.

But it did, and confirmed everything I knew.

I'd failed Tommy.

Like I'd failed Rosie.

Who was next?

For a moment, the desire to murder Napier was consuming. I'd pop my single bullet between his eyes and watch the back of his head blow out like a pink sponge.

Then what?

Vincent would kill me.

Tommy would still be dead. Rosie too.

And Saul and Harriet would be screwed.

No. Napier had the upper hand, and knew it. The Beretta dropped to my side.

'You look a bit queasy, boy,' he said. 'Hassan, get the man a drink.'

The Turkish lad started towards the bar. His movement made me spin round, and I flashed him a look.

'Stay where you are,' I said.

He stopped dead.

Napier snorted. I turned back. He was looking at his watch.

'OK, Kasper,' he said. 'You told me your offer. Here's mine.' His stumpy finger pointed at me again. 'I want you to crawl back to whatever shithole you came from and never come back. Forget everything. It's none of your concern. Harriet works for me. Try anything, I'll bury the pair of you.' The finger went to my face. 'Understand?'

Blood was pounding in my ears. It was hard to think.

I managed a nod.

'Good,' he said. 'Now fuck off.'

The silence beat out.

I turned and was walking hard and fast around the bar,

passing the bouncer, hearing Vincent and Napier laughing again, everything quaking in front of me.

I reached the door, pulled the handle, and dived into the harsh sunlight, then ran from the bar and didn't look back.

Chapter 20

'Harriet!' I yelled into my phone after enduring her voicemail for the third time. 'Call me, now!'

From Mick's Bar, I'd cycled north along the canal towards the Berkowitz house, stopping every few minutes to try her mobile as I was doing now.

I removed the handset from my ear and looked at it dismally. Anger swirled through me, aimed at her, Napier, Vincent.

But mostly it was aimed at myself. I'd messed up today. Big time. Chucking my weight around like Billy Big-bollocks at Napier's bar was a dumb move. I'd underestimated him, and had come out with my tail between my legs.

There'd been too many revelations today, and none of them made sense. I needed to root out Harriet for the answers. Off I pedalled.

Fifteen minutes later, and for the second time that day, I was at the Berkowitz house. Her tatty Skoda wasn't in the drive now, but that didn't mean anything. I did the doorbell-holding trick, assuming she'd be cowering behind the curtains like before.

When I heard the rattle of the door chain, I braced myself, ready to wade in.

This time, Saul answered.

'What on earth's going on?' he said.

It'd been a week since I'd seen him, but the man had aged a decade. His skin was creased and colourless, hanging from his face like tissue paper, accentuating lines and deepening the shadows.

'Kasper,' he said. 'What's the matter?'

'I didn't know you were in, Saul,' I said, and felt a sudden self-consciousness as he eyed me with his own concern.

'What happened to you?' he said. 'Have you been fighting?'

I'd forgotten my pulped appearance, and was too riled to make something up. 'Yeah,' I said, 'I have.'

He looked aghast.

'Saul, listen, I need to speak to Harriet. Do you know where she is?'

'Work, I suspect. It was her first day back at the office today, after Tommy. Why?'

In that moment, the temptation to tell him everything pulled at me: how Harriet wasn't at work; that she'd racked up a whopping drug debt and had a hand in Tommy's death. It would've taken a couple of minutes, tops.

But I held back, like I'd held back at the mortuary. I don't quite know why this was – maybe it had to do with the brittle state Saul was clearly in, and the knowledge that this, on top of Tommy's death, could break him. Or maybe it was old-fashioned guilt: by telling him, I'd be revealing my own part in Tommy's death.

'If you speak to her,' I said, 'can you tell her to ring me?'

Saul tilted his head. 'Yes. But I'd like to know why.'

'There's something I want to ask her. It's nothing to worry about. Take care.'

I didn't wait for a response, just turned and headed quickly away from the house, sensing his eyes on me until I fell out of sight.

I kept trying to reach Harriet, but by teatime had to face facts – she'd vanished, and I was out of ideas. With a swollen face and a loaded Beretta still in my pants, hanging around residential streets probably wasn't the best idea.

So, desolately, I headed home, thinking the day couldn't get much meaner.

Wrong again.

Sometime around eleven, my phone vibrated.

I was stretched on my mattress with my hands behind my head, looking at the ceiling. I lifted the handset. Number withheld.

Harriet, no doubt.

'Nice of you to finally ring,' I said. 'So you got my message?'

At first, I heard breathing. Then came the voice of Vincent.

'A'right, Kasper,' he said. 'What message you talking about?'

I gripped the handset and sat up. 'What do you want?'

'Jesus, you've got it in for me. We should be pals. We're not so different.'

'I'm nothing like you.'

'That so?'

My temperature spiked. I had to restrain the urge to chuck the phone against the wall. 'Say what you've got to say, Vincent.'

'You shoulda backed off.'

'Well, I have now.'

'Not good enough, pig-fucker. See, me an' Mick been talking. We know how men like you think. You need to be sent a proper message, shown who's in charge.'

'What are you getting at?'

He chuckled. 'I've sent you a message.'

'What message?'

'That pub of yours.'

'What about it?'

'It might look a bit toasty tomorrow morning. Catch my drift?'

He hung up before I had time to reply.

Adrenalin pumped through me. I grabbed my keys, my coat and the Beretta, jostled down the stairs and thundered to the door.

The roaring was audible before I made out the faint amber glow in the distance, and then I caught the unmistakable reek of fresh smoke. I swerved on to the High Road, pedalling hard, almost toppling over the handlebars when I saw McGovern's pub in flames.

Up close, the smell was pungent: melting plastic, burning wood and belching black plumes, all of it attacking the night.

Paramedics, police, firefighters were everywhere, spraying water, cordoning, doing what they could. I chucked my bike and came towards a policeman who pushed me back.

'No!' I said, pathetically. 'Christ, no!'

Crowds had gathered, some in dressing gowns and pyjamas, others the night-dwellers, drinkers, street kids, all bearing witness to this atrocity.

A few of the pub's locals were outside too. Their usually ruddy faces were starch white.

I moved backwards, circling round to the right so I could get closer. No good. Another policeman planted a hand on my chest.

'Let me through!' I shouted. 'I work here!'

'Step back, mate,' he said into my ear.

I looked at him, and saw it was useless. 'What can I do?' I said. 'I need to do something!'

He shook his head. 'Nothing, mate. Just let emergency services handle it.'

But they weren't handling it. There were at least a dozen firefighters, blasting high-pressure sprays, doing what they could, but it wasn't enough – whatever fuelled this blaze was unrelenting, and for an old pub like McGovern's, filled with aged oak bar tops and pine floors, and stocked up with liquor and flammable cleaning products and God knows what else, there was no hope.

Windows started shattering, followed by an outraged crack as the roof began to keel. People gasped and retreated. McGovern's was being pulverised from the inside.

I looked at the faces, maybe sixty people now. One of them I recognised: a slight, elven teenager dressed in pink pyjamas and a blue dressing gown. Her wet eyes were transfixed on the carnage.

I pushed towards her, crouched down and touched her shoulder. She jumped, as if woken from a fugue.

'Suzanna!' I shouted at Paddy's daughter. 'Suzanna, you OK, sweetheart?'

She nodded. 'I was in bed, at the flat. Then someone phoned, said Dad's pub's on fire.'

'Where's Paddy now?'

Her expression said it all.

'Suzanna, where is he?'

She stared at McGovern's before shouting the news I'd been dreading. 'In there.'

I had to look. And when I did, I pictured Paddy somewhere amidst all that, and knew there'd be no way he was coming out alive.

'You're sure?'

She nodded. 'He was in the cellar, doing a stocktake.'

I stood and watched and didn't say anything else.

Time passed agonisingly until the fire was finally subdued; the flames cowered, the crackle receded. A black, mangled mess was left where a pub should've been. Steam and smoke wafted from its charred body.

'Jeez,' someone said to my left. 'Fuckin' state of the place.'

They were right. All the windows were blown, with glass dangling like broken teeth from the frames and sills. Inside, chairs and tables poked up from the floor, forming warped and tortuous shapes, like alien furniture. The rendering and balustrades were a mush, and even Paddy's licence certificate above the door was indecipherable.

There was an unnatural silence around us, as if there'd been a power cut. Every tiny sound resonated – the dripping water from the hoses; the crackle of police and ambulance radios; firefighters' boots as they ventured into the ruins; and then the howls from Suzanna as Paddy's bloated body got pulled from McGovern's and laid out to smoulder.

Chapter 21

Back in my father's allotment, a rank taste was swirling in my mouth, and my hands wouldn't stop shaking, no matter how much Bushmills I drank.

And I'd drunk some. After leaving the devastation of McGovern's, I stopped at the offy and bought a large bottle. The whiskey attacked my throat and I coughed and drank more, pacing around the small plot like a caged animal, trying to stave off the image of Paddy getting zipped into a body bag and the police and paramedics trying to console his daughter.

I couldn't.

Paddy was dead. Little Suzanna, two years older than my Rosie, had just witnessed her dad's corpse getting dragged from the wreckage of his beloved boozer. I knew what this would do to her, how time would never heal the scalding effect a death like this has.

It was my fault, all of it, and I had no idea what to do.

Go round to Mick's Bar and chuck a petrol bomb through the window?

Hunt down Vincent and Napier and kick seven shades out of them both?

Or maybe I should just stay here and drink myself into a stupor?

Yeah, that sounded about right. And that's what I did.

Sometime later, a vibrating in my pocket caught my attention. I think it'd been going for a little while before I finally noticed it. I lowered the whiskey bottle and looked at the handset, squinting to make out the caller.

Harriet's number flashed on the screen. 'Kasper?' she said.

'Well, at least Vincent didn't incinerate you too,' I slurred.

'Are you drunk?'

'I am. Where are you, Harriet?'

'A service station, near Watford Junction. I've been driving around for hours. I shouldn't have run away like that. I panicked when you said we were going to talk to Napier. I didn't know what to do.'

'A lot's happened since then.'

'What?'

'I went to see Napier alone.'

She gasped. 'What . . . what happened?'

In as few words as possible, I described the afternoon's events. When I got to the fire and Paddy's death, her breathing became harsher, as if she were hyperventilating.

'Your friend is . . . dead?' she said.

'Yeah. Dead.'

'That's not my fault! You can't blame me!'

'I don't. I blame Vincent. He set the fire. And I blame Napier for ordering it.' I paused to drink. 'But this is on me. I got involved with your brother. And I underestimated those two bastards.'

Silence followed.

'Napier showed me the video,' I said, 'the one of you and Tommy the night before he died.'

'Oh God,' she said. 'He swore he'd delete it if I did what he said.'

'Guess he lied,' I said dully. 'I reckon we're both going to have trouble sleeping with all this on our consciences. Aren't we?'

'Yes,' she whispered.

I gazed upward. Paradise Towers Estate shuddered, the ziggurats black against the moonlit sky.

I could hear the click of a lighter as Harriet lit a smoke. She started saying something else, but I'd stopped listening. My head was full.

She was mid-sentence when I said, 'Good luck, Harriet,' and dropped the phone in the soil.

But her voice kept whining from the earpiece. 'No! Kasper! What about me?' I think she was crying. 'You can't just abandon me! Please, Kasper, please . . .'

I reached down, found the phone and hung up.

When she tried calling back, I hung up again, and when she tried a third time, I turned the damned thing off. I rested my elbows on the roof of the hut and put my head in my palms.

Time passed.

The Beretta was still in the waistband of my cargo pants. I'd almost forgotten about it. Clumsily, I retrieved the gun, swivelled the barrel towards my face and clicked the safety off. The black circle stared up at me longingly.

How easy it would be.

Put it to my temple.

Squeeze.

Done.

Was this how they both felt? Standing on that platform, waiting for the sparkling eyes of a train to light the tunnel?

'Idiot,' I said, and thudded the butt of the gun against my brow, two, three, four times.

Pain speared out, a momentary distraction. I chucked the gun into the hut and out of sight so I couldn't do anything worse.

But I wasn't getting off that easy. No way.

I crouched down and retrieved my father's old garden shears from a toolbox. Kneeling, I spread the blades out to full reach and brought one on to my left forearm. Then, adding force, I began dragging it over the skin, very hard.

Slow. Steady. Pressure.

Ah . . .

My teeth ground and I pushed harder. A scream came from beneath the surface, a hundred firecrackers exploding at once. Then came the first warm trickle.

I held my arm aloft, examining the wound. An inch of skin was parted, gaping in a black grin, the blood quickly turning cool in the night. It began to run and split near my elbow like the branches of a tree.

It should've hurt. The pain was supposed to give some reprieve.

But there was nothing. All I felt was the kick of my heart, a reminder I was still alive and Rosie, Tommy and Paddy were not.

'Kasper,' a familiar voice said.

It was a little while later, and I hadn't moved.

Turning, I made out the blurry figure of Dr Steiner. She was at the gate of the allotment, cocooned in a green parka with the hood up, a lit cigarette in her hand. So rarely had I seen her out of the house, and never in the middle of the night like this, that the sight drew me away from my slumber, and into the now.

'What're you doing here?' I said.

'Looking for you,' she said. 'You rushed off earlier and weren't answering your phone.'

'Is something wrong?'

'You tell me,' she said. 'I found this tacked at the end of my porch.'

With the cigarette balanced in her mouth, she withdrew from her pocket an A4 sheet. My heart clenched as she unravelled it and held it up.

It was a grainy photo of Dr Steiner. She was tending to her plants, smoking, clearly unaware that she was being scoped. Above the image were the words:

NEXT TIME IT'S HER

'Fuck,' I said.

'Indeed,' Dr Steiner said, returning the sheet to her pocket. 'For the last hour, I've been scouring the streets looking for you, hoping you might shed some light on this. I went past your place of work and saw the wreckage there. The hospitals confirmed you hadn't been brought in. Then it dawned on me that you'd be here. Which you are.'

She opened the gate and walked in, stopping about halfway along the dirt path. Even in the darkness, her eyes were clear and precise from behind her glasses. I could feel them taking in my swollen face, my wounded forearm and my wretched expression.

'So,' she said, first inhaling, then blowing out smoke, 'where shall we begin?'

I hadn't anticipated this. Now, I realised how much I needed to speak.

I drank a finger of Bushmills from the bottle and told her everything that had happened – the fight at McGovern's, going to Napier's, the video of Tommy and Harriet, Vincent blazing McGovern's, and Paddy's death. I told her how I'd been stupid and cocky, blindsided by anger and my own messy past, and that tonight's misery was all my fault for going in guns blazing.

Dr Steiner kept silent, her focus steady on my face, her only movement the lifting of her cigarette to her mouth.

'I'm sorry for your loss,' she said when I finished. 'I know you thought highly of Paddy.'

'Yes,' I said.

'And what will happen now?'

'The police will investigate the fire. But I doubt they'll find anything suspicious. Meanwhile, Harriet will carry on running errands for Napier until she cracks up, gets arrested or jumps in front of a train like her brother.'

'I mean with *you*. What will happen with *you*?'

I looked at her. Although I was drunk, I realised that before me was a sight I'd never seen before – Dr Steiner was on edge.

'I thought I could handle this,' I said. 'But I've been careless. People have died. Now they're threatening you.'

'Yes,' she said, 'but I'm more concerned at what this is doing to *you*. I've never seen you like this.'

I looked at my hands, mired in blood and soil, shaking.

'Call the police,' she said. 'Even if there's no evidence, it's the right thing to do, surely?'

I thought about it, and shook my head. 'This crew Harriet's mixed up with are predators. They'll come after her and Saul, and you too.'

'Saul must have his suspicions about her, surely?'

'A parent always knows when their kid's lying, right?' I said, quoting her remark from a few days back.

'There you go.'

I looked up at the night.

'Answer me something, Dr Steiner,' I said. 'How's it possible for a couple of kids to get as messed up as these two?'

She took a long drag and breathed out a stream of smoke before answering. 'Self-destructive traits can grow from any number of places. But from what you've told me, I suspect somewhere in the Berkowitz family history, there's been a significant trauma.'

'Yeah,' I said. 'And now little Suzanna's got her own dose of trauma to keep her awake.'

'You *must* walk away from this ghastly mess,' Dr Steiner said. 'For your protection. And now for mine. I'm not going to let these people scare me. But at the same time, I won't be threatened.'

She stepped closer and I looked down at her small, slight frame. Her eyes were arrow-tips.

'You've done all you can.'

I didn't answer.

In front of me now, she placed a hand across my forearm, covering the syrupy cut.

'Look what this is doing to you, my dear.'

The touch of her brittle fingers softened something. I stared down at the hand.

'Please. Walk away.'

'I don't know . . .' I said, but didn't finish the sentence. My head was a wreck. I was so bloody tired.

She removed the hand, took a final pull on her cigarette,

stubbed it out on the fencing mast, removed the filter from the holder and returned the holder to her pocket.

When she spoke again her voice was stiffer. 'I was a psychiatrist for thirty-one years. In that time, I saw many patients destroy themselves. It was hard enough in clinic. I can't bear it in my own home. If this carries on, I'm afraid you'll have to find dwellings elsewhere.'

I took this in. What she was saying made sense, and was fair enough.

'OK,' I said, and looked at her. 'OK, I'll stop.'

'Good,' she said, and linked her arm into mine. 'Then let's go home.'

Chapter 22

Dr Steiner was right. Finding out why Tommy put himself under that train had been my reason for getting involved in all this. Well, I'd done that, and survived. Now it was time to step back.

The following morning, still knackered, and with a bastard hangover to boot, I thought about calling the police and telling them everything I knew. With the fire at McGovern's, Paddy's death, and the threat tacked to Dr Steiner's porch, there should be enough to nab Napier and his crew.

But I refrained. If Napier caught wind, he'd blow his lid, come after Harriet, and send Vincent for Dr Steiner and me. Tommy would still be dead, Paddy too, and Saul would lose everything. For what?

I also suspected that a sociopath like Vincent would've covered his tracks, and sure enough, when Diane called a little later, she told me that an electrical fault was the probable cause of the blaze.

'But I'm not ruling out arson,' she said curtly, and paused. 'The whole thing looks wrong to me, Kas. Like a murder. If you know anything and you don't—'

'I don't have a clue, Diane,' I broke in.

'Kas, seriously, if this is to do with that Berkowitz kid, you could be in danger.'

'I'm tired,' I said. 'And I'm not doing anything about Tommy anymore. Drop it.'

'OK,' she said. I could hear the hurt in her voice. 'Sorry about your friend.'

'Yeah,' I said, 'cheers for that.' I hung up.

Weighing heavy on my conscience was Suzanna, Paddy's daughter. What torment would the poor girl be waking to this morning? No matter how painful it would be to hear, she deserved to know that her father's death was no accident, and that I was involved in it.

But now wasn't the time to let any of this stuff out the cage. She'd be grieving. And I was missing my friend.

For the second time in as many weeks, I plucked a bunch of lilies from Dr Steiner's garden, bound them with tape and cycled to McGovern's, or what was left of it. I placed the flowers on the doorstep beside a sizable collection of bouquets and cards, spirit bottles and beer cans other well-wishers had left.

In daylight, the demolition left by the fire was even harsher. Head to toe, the place was gutted: a black skeleton, obscene and garish beside the bookies and takeaways. Boarded steel covered the shattered windows, the doors were sealed with chipboard, and yellow police tape circled the entire site, there to keep the squatters, looters and prying eyes at bay.

A dozen or so of the pub's regulars were standing around the site, staring mutely, their heads bowed, flat caps removed, like mourners at a funeral. I gave some nods, shook some hands, but didn't want to hang around. I guess I was scared someone might start with the questions.

Then I noticed Suzanna. She was standing in front of the deformed entrance of the pub, wearing Paddy's old Crombie. It dwarfed her, and made her look like the child she was. Behind her was one of Paddy's many sisters from Donegal, a rotund, stern-faced woman I'd once met, Sharon I think her name was.

My heart was in my throat as I wandered over. Suzanna's eyes found mine.

Up close, I realised she wasn't crying. She'd gone beyond tears, passing through the shock and into the frozen stage of grief that, for some, never thaws.

'Kasper,' she said, and held out a small hand. Her fingers were cold as I cupped them.

'Hello, sweetheart,' I said.

We stayed there a long time.

I went back to my loft, kept the lights off, the door closed, cracked my first lager and sat on my mattress, looking out the window at the sky. Two pigeons had settled on the ledge. Before long, they were watching me watching them.

It was coming up to lunchtime. I had nothing going on, no job, no family, just a heap of death weighing me down. Outside, kids were learning stuff at school, parents were out doing jobs, old people were doing whatever old people like to do. I was drinking warm beer, looking at a pair of pigeons, and feeling more alone than I'd done in a long, long time.

By one, I was wondering when it would be a reasonable time to have my first taste of Bushmills. By half past, the thought had turned to action.

But I didn't have long to wallow.

My phone was vibrating.

'Kasper?' The voice on the other end of the line was raspy. Still, no mistaking that familiar patter, just as terse as when we'd first met at the Equilibrium.

'What is it, Jazz?' I said.

A few seconds later, I was out the door.

I try to avoid hospitals. The last time I'd been in one was five years ago, the day Rosie did what she did.

But psychiatric hospitals are a different beast. I'll be honest – the places freak me out. These places always seem to carry the same malaise: it's ingrained in the walls, the sparse furnishings, the flat expressions worn by staff, but most of all, in the lingering boredom, sadness and anger etched into the patients' faces.

My time as a policeman had led me to mental institutions on many occasions, usually to deposit voice-hearing criminals who'd been bashing their heads on cell doors, or the waifs and strays we scooped up off the street who were convinced the government had planted microchips under their skin.

There's nothing subtle in psych wards. It's a grim business, and the ailments they contain – bouts of melancholia, extreme disorders of thinking, the peaks and troughs of mania – seem to strike all kinds of people in all walks of life. And on this occasion, the recipient was Jazz.

They'd taken him to a hospital in south Westminster; a tall, imposing building plotted halfway along the Vauxhall Bridge Road, and ten minutes by foot from Pimlico tube. Whoever designed this place must've had a predilection for the macabre, for there were black iron railings circumnavigating the entrance and windows, and red terracotta brickwork leading to its peak. The only things missing were a couple of gargoyles and a Christopher Lee look-alike outside.

After signing in at reception and being issued a panic alarm to wear round my neck, I was told to head to the fifth floor. A cramped lift took me up. I passed Saturn Ward on the first floor, Mercury on the second, then Neptune, Pluto, and a moment later, I was pressing the buzzer of a heavy-duty, magnetically locked door to be let into Jupiter Ward.

A male nurse with a Nigerian accent answered. He wore an NHS lanyard around his neck that told me his name was Rupert. A wave of school-dinner smells wafted from behind him.

'I'm visiting Jazz,' I said.

Rupert frowned.

'Jasper,' I corrected, realising I didn't even know the kid's full name.

'Follow me,' he said, and led me into a low-ceilinged hall. As soon as I was inside, he closed the door, and it clicked locked.

Jupiter Ward didn't look much like the wards on *Holby City*. It was more like a care home, and not a classy BUPA place, either. All the walls and surfaces were an off-grey colour; the ceilings grubby white, the floors grey lino, and there were no windows anywhere, making the air warm and close and meaty.

Four hallways splayed from the nursing office: one led to a lounge and dining room, one to an activity space and medication room, the other two towards patient rooms. Along each, the lighting was dim, the colours drab and listless. It all helped reinforce a peculiar kind of dreariness.

A few patients were dotted around these halls, men and women, shuffling aimlessly. They either wore loose, casual clothes – tracksuits, jumpers and jeans – or green hospital gowns that hung like kaftans. Superficially, they looked like a diverse bunch – colours, ages, levels of self-care or neglect – yet they seemed to share something: a displaced look. Strangely, most were shoeless, either barefoot or in socks. None seemed interested in me.

Rupert showed me along one of the two hallways of private rooms. Halfway up, we passed a female patient of indeterminate age, shuffling. She was obese, had a wispy beard and small marble eyes, and wore a vast hospital gown and apparently nothing else.

'Fuck, fuck, fuck,' she began muttering, her enunciation clipped, almost RP.

I gave her a wide berth, and we moved further along.

Near the end of the hall, I asked about the circumstances of Jazz's admission.

'Boy took an overdose,' Rupert said. 'He was found by his dad. Close call, by all accounts. Got taken to A&E for stomach-pumping, then sectioned here under the Mental Health Act for his own safety.'

The way he spoke was weirdly impersonal, like he was reading the instructions for a food processor.

We stopped outside a room. 'This is him,' Rupert said. 'He know you're coming?'

'Yeah.'

'OK. You got your alarm. Call if there's problems.'

I told Rupert I would, and thanked him for taking care of Jazz. He shrugged and smiled, like I'd said something amusing, and left me there.

I peered through the round plastic window in the door. It was a plain room, square and spartan. There was something unusual about it, but it took a moment to realise what.

Then I saw it – no sharp edges or hooks, and nothing to tie a ligature to. The door handles sloped, as did the bedposts, the table edges, the chair legs; even the coat hangers on the wall appeared to be made out of rubber.

I pushed the door open, walked in and closed it behind me. Suddenly, all was quiet.

Jazz was lying in the bed with his eyes shut. His tanned skin looked sallow, and his buzz cut was flecked with dry skin. Blankets covered his body, outlining his muscular frame, yet he seemed to have shrunk.

The sound of my footsteps made his eyes open. He looked up through half-mast lids.

'Thanks for coming,' he croaked.

I nodded.

He blinked, and I saw his eyes focus. 'What happened to your face?'

'Had a run-in with a few undesirables,' I said. 'They look worse.'

There was a chair beside the bed. I sat in it, interlocked my fingers, and looked at Jazz. Now I was here, I had no idea what to say. *How are you?* It sounded ridiculous.

So we shared a silence. But right then, silence seemed enough.

'You're the only person I wanted to visit me,' he eventually said.

'What about your family?'

He shook his head. 'I told them to keep away.'

'How about mates? People from the gym? Want me to contact someone?'

Another shake. 'It's a madhouse here. The fuck-fuck woman might try and eat them. I couldn't think of anyone to call but you.'

'All right,' I said, not sure what this said about me. 'Want to tell me what happened?'

He breathed in and out, slowly. 'I'd just had enough.'

'Enough of what?'

'Everything. You understand. I know you do.'

I guessed I did.

'After we talked, it hit me. I realised I loved Tommy, and he was gone. I was too late. I suppose I should've reached out and spoken to someone about how I was feeling. But I didn't want to. When you look the way I do, big and tough, it's not easy to say this stuff aloud. So I kept it to myself.'

I waited, knowing there was more.

'Then yesterday, my dad started giving me a hard time, telling me to cheer up, go and take a girl out, stop being such a misery guts. I just got sick of it all. I realised I could never be who I really was. So I drank half a bottle of vodka, got all my steroid pills and ate the lot.' He sighed. 'It was dumb. Dad found me, called 999. I woke up in hospital.'

I nodded.

After a moment, Jazz's eyes flitted down to my forearm. I'd stuck a plaster over last night's cut, but there was no hiding it, or the expression tarnishing my face.

'What's wrong with you?' he said. 'I'm the one who took an overdose, but you look worse than me.'

'It's nothing.'

'Don't lie. You're sad too.'

Sad? I suppose I was. It was that simple.

'Tell me,' he said. 'Please. I like hearing you talk.'

So I did. I told Jazz everything, right from the start. I told him what I'd learned about Tommy and Harriet yesterday at

Napier's, and about Paddy's needless death; I told him how I'd contemplated blowing my head off last night, but sliced my arm with a rusty garden shear instead; how I was a jobless, despondent, pissed-off semi-alcoholic man, and hadn't a clue what I was doing with my life.

I'm sure there are many who'd condemn me for burdening someone in his fragile condition with stuff like this. All I can say is, in that moment, I sensed he wanted to hear it.

The only thing I held back on was Rosie. Tommy had found out about the circumstances of her death, and look what happened there. I wasn't about to repeat the mistake twice.

I could see a change in Jazz, an alertness in his eyes.

'Help me sit up,' he said when I'd finished.

I stood, lifted him under the armpits. He wheezed. Although his deltoids and trapezius were rock hard, the muscles felt like a suit of armour, encasing a soft, vulnerable body.

'Thanks,' he said, and I returned to the seat. 'So what are you going to do now?'

'Nothing,' I said.

'Aren't you going to get those bastards back and help Tommy's sister?'

I shook my head.

'Why not?'

'Isn't it obvious?'

'No.'

'This thing's got way out of control. Every time I get involved, people seem to die.' I paused. 'I need to step back. It's dangerous.'

Jazz looked away. His silence seemed to be asking a question.

'This stops now,' I said, answering it. My voice had risen in volume.

'No,' Jazz said. 'That's a cop-out. I don't think it's your involvement that's to blame. It's the stuff you haven't done that is.'

'What? You don't know anything about me.' I was getting angry now.

Jazz didn't seem to notice, or care. 'I know what I can see. Tommy saw it too. That's why he picked you. And that's why you should deal with this mess. It's the only way you'll clear your conscience and move on from whatever's holding you back.'

Maybe the pills they had him on were screwing with his head, or maybe he'd blown a gasket or two when they revived him. Either way, what he was saying was crazy.

I tried coming up with a gentle rebuke of some sort, but I had nothing.

Jazz turned to the bedside table, where a plastic jug of water rested, and filled a beaker. He sipped through its straw, returned the beaker and placed his head back on the pillow. Then he looked directly at me.

'There are more boys from Mick's Bar working at the gym,' he said. 'I've seen them cruising, trying it on with some older johns. They're all pretty and bolshie and full of front. But beneath it all, they're scared. Like Tommy.'

'Stop,' I said, my voice shaky. I tried to block it all out. 'Those boys aren't my problem. None of this is.'

'You're right,' Jazz said, and paused. 'But think about what Tommy said. There's only one way to fix this. You'll know what to do. Those were his words, weren't they?'

I nodded.

'Tommy knew what he was doing. By then, he'd decided to die. But he was talking about you, too. And what you needed.'

I was starting to get worked up, and had to fight the urge to bolt.

'Weren't you listening?' I said. 'Harriet used Tommy, her little brother. You said you loved him. Now he's dead. And you want me to *help* her?'

'I know what you're saying,' Jazz said calmly. 'There's no excusing what she did. But that doesn't matter anymore. This isn't really about her, or her dad, or even Tommy. It's about you putting something right. Because who else is going to?'

I flung up my hands, tried to shake off the truth in what he was saying. I'd come here hoping to be a bit of support to this suicidal steroid-munching meathead, nothing more. Instead, he'd turned into some kind of oracle.

The swaying sensation from Mick's Bar was back with full force, as if I were in a dinghy caught on choppy waves. I reached for the arm of the chair, gripped it and clenched.

What I was hearing made no sense at all.

But Jazz was right. Bloody hell, he was right.

'Sod it,' I said, pushing myself up to standing. 'I'll do it.'

'Good,' Jazz said, looking up, smiling.

I held up a finger. 'On one condition.'

'What's that?'

I pointed at him, said, 'No more of this feeling sorry for yourself and overdosing bollocks,' and wagged the finger like a headmaster. 'It's not a good look for us hard-nuts. OK, young man?'

'OK,' he said, and laughed.

Chapter 23

Right then, if I were to help Harriet get out of her mess, ensure no one else got killed, and not get evicted by Dr Steiner in the process, I needed a pretty robust plan that involved brains as well as brawn. And the following day, standing by the rain-streaked conservatory window and watching the morose grey sky stretch into morning, it dawned on me that I had the bones of one.

Or two, to be precise.

Harriet arrived at Sally-Anne's Milkshake Shack late, pushing through the doors and retracting her umbrella. An ankle-length mac and aviators couldn't mask her haggard look.

I was at the bar, finishing a chocolate malt. 'You've got to try one of these shakes,' I said, as she took the stool to my right. 'They're yum-tastic.'

The rain hadn't kept people away from Sally-Anne's Milkshake Shack that morning. Most were young professionals and kids with parents. Bacon smells wafted from the open-plan kitchen to the rear of the bar, and Jerry Lee Lewis jived from a retro jukebox.

A bouncy waitress came over. I ordered two of Sally's Special Breakfasts. She brought us a jug of coffee and said our food would be with us in a jiffy. I poured coffee into two cups, drank some and looked at Harriet.

'So, how've you been?'

She shook her head, staring at the bar. 'What did you want to talk about, Kasper?'

'You.'

'Me?'

'In case you haven't noticed, you're in a mess. And without help, you're screwed.'

'Why do you care all of a sudden?'

'Because all this has bled into my life, and for some stupid reason, I've decided to help you.'

I drank some coffee.

'OK,' I said. 'Here's how it is. You did a shitty thing, using Tommy, and you're going to have to figure out a way to live with yourself for that.'

She said nothing.

'But let's face facts. Napier will chew you up and spit out the bones when he's done with you. We both know what kind of man he is.'

Again, nothing.

'I'm not happy with that outcome. So I'm going to sort something out. But afterwards, you're on your own.' I drank some more coffee.

'What are you going to do?' she said.

'I've come up with two possibilities. The first: you come clean with Saul. Tell him everything. If he forgives you, maybe he can get some cash selling his house or something. Who knows? Once you've got some money for Napier,

I'll make sure he doesn't rip you off when you pay him back.'

Our breakfasts came, two loaded servings of fried stuff. Harriet removed her aviators. Her eyes were pinched red. She looked at her food like it was a plate of manure.

I smiled at the waitress, added a dollop of HP and waded in.

'Eat, Harriet,' I said, cutting toast, loading up bacon and mushrooms. 'You'll need the energy.'

She just shook her head. 'You said there was another possibility?'

I wiped my mouth. 'Have you ever worn a wire?'

Her expression dropped. She was pale as a sheet.

'Look,' I continued, 'I know it sounds risky, turning police informant, but if we get Napier to confess to supplying drugs on tape, he's done. Give him a dose of his own medicine. Except we don't want his money. We want him sent down, and then you can walk away.'

That was the final straw. She covered her face with both hands and started crying.

'You liked that idea better, didn't you?'

By now, a few customer heads had turned, adults and kids looking warily at us. I stared at them until they turned away, and then got back to my breakfast.

Harriet pulled an inhaler from her coat pocket and took a few hits.

'I didn't think . . .' she said, 'I didn't think police . . . did stuff like that . . . in real life.'

'They do. And of the two, I think it's the better option.'

'Napier's not . . . stupid, Kasper. He's got police in his pocket.'

'I know. We'll need to be careful.'

'He'll know.'

'Not if we do this right.'

Her breathing tempered. 'I don't understand.'

I pushed my plate aside. 'If I tried to sting Napier alone, he'd smell a rat. I've got plenty of reasons to want revenge. But with you, I think we can trip him. See, he knows you're scared, and he reckons he's holding all the cards. You wouldn't have the balls to double-cross him because of the evidence he's got on you. Well, we can use that confidence to hood-wink him.'

'We?'

I nodded. 'Like I said, I'll help you.'

She lifted her coffee, tried a small sip, pulled a face and put it down, sloshing half into the saucer.

'No,' she said. 'I can't go through with it. I appreciate your efforts, but there must be another way.'

I shrugged. 'None that I can think of. You're in a tight spot here.'

'I can't do it!'

More heads turned.

'Stop shouting,' I said, 'and eat some eggs.'

'I feel sick.'

'I'm not surprised.'

She scowled and placed her elbows on the counter and her chin in her palms. I drank the rest of my coffee.

Finally, she said, 'OK.'

'OK, what?'

'OK, I'll do it. I'll talk to the police, and go through with this entrapment plan, as long as you're there with me. I mean, what choice have I got? But it's insanity, Kasper. And if it goes wrong, it's on *your* head.' She pointed her index finger, using the same hand where her busted pinkie stood rigid in its splint.

On a different day, this would've dampened the effect she was going for, but in the pit of my gut, I knew what she said was true. If something went wrong – and someone else got hurt – it *was* on my head.

Even so, I was sure this could work. And with Napier and co. locked up and Harriet off the hook, somehow everything that had happened might count.

'Fine,' I said. 'I'll make a few calls and get the ball rolling. Leave your phone on, Harriet. Don't do anything stupid.'

Stiffly and without a word, she lowered her aviators over her eyes, stepped off the stool, headed for the doors and walked back out into the steady drum of rain.

Through the window, I watched her stop by the bus depot opposite, where she raised her umbrella and sparked a cigarette. Sam Cooke's 'A Change is Gonna Come' came on the jukebox. I reached for my phone, dialled a number, and waited for a familiar voice to answer.

'Kas?'

'We're on, Diane,' I said. 'Set up the meeting.'

Chapter 24

It didn't take Diane long to arrange a meeting with the National Crime Agency. When I was an officer, organised crime was combated by SOCA, the Serious Organised Crime Agency, but since my time they'd been absorbed by the NCA, a national gang of policing bigwigs whose remit was to disrupt serious villainy and invariably piss off local plods in the process.

On Saturday, the night before the meeting, I texted her and confirmed I'd be outside Holborn police station bright and early. Then I lay back in bed with the lights off and tried to rest.

I couldn't. Something was bugging me.

I discovered it wasn't the usual baggage of my past, or Tommy and Paddy being dead; it wasn't nerves, or the pelt of rain on the ceiling and windows.

There'd been a niggle for the past few days, but I'd never given it my full attention until now.

It was to do with Saul, his late wife Judith, Harriet and Tommy, and their weird messed-up relationship. The whole Berkowitz clan smelled decidedly off, and I still hadn't a clue why.

Harriet said there were things from the past that needed to stay buried. And the night before he jumped, Tommy said something too – about all the things that happened to them.

What things?

Dr Steiner had been pretty clear: trauma was the probable root of the Berkowitz kids' destructive behaviours.

But what had happened that was so traumatic? What had led them to this?

I closed my eyes and tried to quieten my thoughts. Maybe the truth would come out if I prodded this cage enough; or maybe it wouldn't, and I'd have to settle for not knowing.

Whatever happened, we still had Napier to deal with. His next cash instalment was due in seven days, and according to Harriet, he wasn't giving any leeway.

If my plan worked, he and his crew could be in custody before the weekend, leaving her debt-free.

If it worked.

My last visit to Holborn police station had been a decade ago, back when I was still an officer, but from the outside, the place was pretty much as I remembered – big, brown and ugly.

Harriet was hiding from the steady rain beneath a concrete overhang. She was wearing her black mac, the collar popped up, and had sharp heels on her feet. Aviators concealed her eyes. She was pulling on a wet cigarette.

As soon as I was in earshot, she said, 'I can't go through with this, Kasper. You'll have to think of something else.'

I lowered my hood and shook rain from my brow. 'It's all there is, Harriet,' I said, coming under the shelter, stopping beside her. 'Just breathe.'

'Oh God,' she said.

I waited for her to finish the cigarette and power-smoke through another. The rain kept on, a steady drone that filled the silence.

Through the glass of the station window, I could see Diane at the main desk. She looked good. Tight figure, tight suit. Our eyes met.

'Let's go in,' I said, and walked past Harriet, pushing through the double doors.

London police stations are much the same, and this place followed suit – grey walls matching grey steel benches, the tables bolted to the floor. Everything was washed out, old, grubby-looking, the kind of grubbiness no amount of scrubbing can clean.

I gave Diane a nod, reciprocated with a cautious smile as she took in the bruises still marring my face. At the desk, she slid over a form and biro. Harriet, beside me now, raised her sunglasses, looked at the form, then at me.

'Fill it out,' I said. 'Your details.'

She took the pen and began scribbling. A drop of rain trickled off her nose, smudging the ink.

'Thank you for offering your help, Ms Berkowitz,' Diane said, her voice fair but with a don't-piss-on-my-chips edge.

'I hardly *offered to help*,' Harriet said, tossing the form back at her. 'I haven't got a choice. *He's* made that abundantly clear.' She gestured at me with a head flick.

I shrugged.

Diane stayed poker-faced. 'We'll do our best to make the process as painless as possible,' she said, not attempting to sound convincing. 'Come this way.'

We went past the desk and through a set of security doors. A uniformed copper with a thick ginger beard guided us into a poky lift, and we began the descent into the bowels of the building.

A thin passage met us, made up of white walls, brown carpets and amber fluorescent lighting. Diane led, Harriet and I were in the middle, the officer to our rear.

We stopped at a tight, square room. Inside, it was hot and smelled stale, like boiled cabbage. A table and four metal chairs were the only furniture. Mounted on the table was a digital recording machine that looked like an industrial-sized microwave.

I took one of the seats.

Harriet leaned against the wall. 'Can I smoke?' she said.

'No,' Diane said.

Harriet reached into her bag, pulled out a strip of nicotine gum and began chewing. Neither of us said anything more until the door opened abruptly.

Two suited men entered the room. They wore big plastic badges on their lapels informing us they were from the NCA. Neither exuded the confidence these regalia implied.

The first was a bald, heavyset man about my age. He had blotchy cheeks, rubbery lips and a walrus chin; he carried his pear-shaped frame in a grey suit that pinched around his middle and did little for him, but to be fair to the suit, he did little in return. He took a seat, and his whole body seemed to groan.

The other one was younger, thinner and beadier. He looked like Harry Potter.

Diane rested against the wall to our left. I looked at her, smiled, then back at the two detectives and smiled some more.

'Hi,' I said.

Ignoring me, the big one pressed buttons on the recorder and it whirred to life. He pressed something else that gave a buzz and a light on the machine turned green.

Harry Potter took the seat next to his colleague and cleared his throat. To Harriet, he said in a crisp Estuary voice, 'Ms

Berkowitz, my name's Detective Sergeant Hargreaves. This is Detective Sergeant Wilson. We're with the NCA's Organised Crime Division. Please sit.' He gave a theatrical pause while she positioned herself beside me. 'I've had a chance to liaise with Detective Sergeant McAteer about your offer. We'd like to discuss the finer details.'

DS Hargreaves had nice white teeth and cool minty breath, a puffy red tie and some stubble he was working a bit too hard on. His hair was slicked back in a precise side parting, and his round-framed Tom Ford glasses looked more expensive than everything I had on put together.

'As I'm sure you're aware,' he went on, 'we can't guarantee immunity or safety—'

'Why not?' Harriet said, affront in her voice. 'I'm the one taking the risk. What about witness protection?'

'This case doesn't warrant anything like that. However, *were* your actions to secure a significant arrest, we *might* be able to disregard law-breaking on your part.'

Her chewing rose in speed. 'My part?'

'Correct. You've admitted intent to supply drugs and involvement in an organised blackmail ring. All serious offences.'

'That does it,' Harriet said, standing. 'I'm not going to stay here and listen to—'

'Chill, Harriet,' I said. 'It's OK. He's just showing off.'

She looked at me, her chewing now fever pitch. Then she returned to her seat and popped in another piece of gum – petulantly, I thought.

'You're not under arrest or caution,' Hargreaves said. 'You're here to offer information. How we act on that information remains to be seen.'

'When you say significant arrest, what's that mean?' I said.

Hargreaves turned to Wilson, who gave a nod. 'What I'm about to tell you is strictly confidential. Michael Napier has been on our radar for some time, but has persistently evaded arrest.'

'How?'

'Tipped off by senior officers on the Met. Our sources tell us that these men have been compromised by Napier with the same extortion tactics described by Ms Berkowitz.'

'Jesus,' I said. Videos of senior police paying for sex would bring a whole heap of shit down on the Met. Public trust in the force was already hanging by a thread.

'We've been waiting for an opportunity to arrest him, but until now, he's always been one step ahead of us.' Hargreaves paused. 'Perhaps you can tell me a little bit more about how you came to know Napier, Ms Berkowitz? We're familiar with the outline, but further details would help.'

Harriet stayed mute.

I nudged her under the table.

She looked over.

I nodded, and she began.

It took her twenty minutes to describe the mess. To be fair, once she started, she did a pretty good job. Her focus remained on the table the entire time, and she paused only for breath or to replace her gum. Wilson remained straight-faced, while Hargreaves listened with reptilian interest, his eyes blinking mechanically behind his glasses.

'Napier and his crew are bastards,' Harriet said as she drew to an end. 'Insane, criminal bastards. All this drove my brother to suicide. You have to stop them.'

Hargreaves nodded and tapped a biro between his teeth. I couldn't tell if he was thinking or showing off his nice dental work.

'It's not enough,' he said. 'We need some assurance that Napier will implicate himself on tape in serious criminality, not just the smutty stuff.'

'There are no assurances,' I said.

Ignoring me, he went on: 'Ms Berkowitz, do you have any information about where he keeps his supply? Distribution routes, tactics? Anything that would strengthen our chances of a conviction?'

'Look, Hargreaves,' I said, 'this is the best you're going to get. Do you want it or not? Because we can take care of this ourselves if you aren't willing to get your hands dirty.'

For the first time, he looked at me dead on. His eyes narrowed behind his lenses. 'It's *Mr* Kasperick, isn't it?'

I tapped my brow deferentially. 'Kasper to my friends.'

He gave a plastic smile. 'It seems you're quite a recalcitrant.' He produced a manila folder from his bag, licked his index finger, withdrew a sheet and started reading aloud. '"A committed but volatile and insubordinate officer" was how one psychologist described you when you were serving with the Met.' He leafed to another sheet. 'And here, I have transcripts from a disciplinary investigation. It cites "undue heavy-handedness with suspects of serious crime, and a tendency to deal out his own version of the law".' He looked up. 'Hardly a glowing CV, is it?'

I cracked a knuckle under the table and began counting to ten.

He snapped the folder shut. 'You're here as an advocate for Ms Berkowitz, that's all. This is police business. I'll have you removed if you don't remember your role.'

'Whoa,' I said. 'Seems I touched a nerve.'

Diane sniffed.

Hargreaves looked at Wilson again, and Wilson looked at me. Neither said anything.

I figured this was as good a time as any to say my bit, so jumped in. 'Listen, in my role as Harriet's advocate, as you put it, there's some things you need to know about this guy.'

'Such as?' Hargreaves said through a smirk.

'Napier may look like a joke, but he isn't to be underestimated. He's got some undesirables working for him, including an enforcer called Vincent Brown. Look him up. He carries a Smith & Wesson and a knuckle blade and likes setting fires. He makes this thing serious. Understand?'

'We're aware of Brown, and—'

'See my face, Hargreaves? This was just a taster, as was Harriet's bust finger. Brown's a killer. He burned down my mate's pub, with him in it. You'll need to go into this with more than biros and posh specs to pull it off.'

I was getting rattled, and Hargreaves' expression wasn't helping. What we were proposing came with a hefty dollop of risk, both to Harriet and me. I'd already underestimated Napier once, and look where that got me. I needed to be sure the police were taking this seriously.

'Leave the manpower to us,' Hargreaves said. '*If* this goes ahead, you just focus on getting *your* bit right.'

'Don't worry about us,' I said.

He gave an even longer pause, then said to Harriet, 'I'll need to speak with my seniors. But in principle, we can make this work.' He smiled. 'Ms Berkowitz, what do you think? Assuming I get the green light, are you happy to proceed as discussed?'

I looked at Harriet. Her face was empty.

'Harriet?' I said.

She nodded.

'For the record,' Hargreaves said at the recorder, 'Ms Berkowitz is nodding to indicate consent.' He looked at us both. 'This seems a good place to end.'

Wilson hit a button and the recorder gave a beep. We stood.

Hargreaves shook hands with Harriet, hesitated, and offered the hand to me. As grips go, his was a firm one. I held his palm a little longer than needed and squeezed it quite a bit harder too. Childish, I know.

The two detectives left, and by the time we were exiting, they'd all but vaporised.

'I need the toilet,' Harriet said, rushing up the hallway towards the sign for the loo.

'John, can you go with her?' Diane said to the uniform, who cantered to keep up.

There was a water dispenser outside one of the rooms. I leaned down and filled a paper cup.

'That could've been handled with a bit more diplomacy,' Diane said, 'but I think you got your point across. What do you think of Hargreaves?'

'He's barely out of Pampers. And if he keeps tapping his teeth with his pen, I may need to snap his glasses. Apart from that, he's grand.'

Diane's laugh echoed up the windowless hall. Her eyes looked big enough to fall into, and for the briefest moment it was just the two of us and none of this stuff mattered.

'Want to meet tonight?' she said.

No hesitation. 'All right.'

She slid a finger against mine, then away.

'Listen,' I said, 'I know I'm out of favours. But can I have one more?'

'Depends. Let's hear it.'

'It's a long shot, just something that's been bothering me about the Berkowitz's past.'

'What is it?'

'That's just it. I don't know. But I think something may've happened to Harriet and Tommy when they were kids.'

'You're not giving me much here, big man.'

'Yeah, I know. So I was hoping you'd have a bit of time to do some digging. Plug their names into the PNC database from ten to fifteen years back, see if something comes up. Berkowitz isn't a common name. There can't be many.'

'But what am I looking for?'

'Haven't a clue.'

'You realise that's a needle in a haystack?'

'Yup. But I also know you're the finest detective I ever met.'

'Sweet talk will get you nowhere,' she said. 'All right, I'll have a go. Don't hold your breath, though.'

'Thanks, Diane.'

We started walking up the hall, and a moment later turned a corner. Officer John was outside the ladies toilet, standing like a sentry. The sound of running taps came from inside, along with groans and sloshes and spits.

'I think she's vomiting,' he said helpfully.

'Should I go in to see if she's OK?' Diane said.

I shrugged. 'If I was her, I'd be puking too.'

Suddenly, the door flung open and there was Harriet. Her face was like melted wax, and her breath smelled of baby sick.

'I need a cigarette,' she said.

'Drink this first,' I said, and offered the cup of water.

She swigged it down, much of it spilling around her collar.

'Come on,' I said.

241

Shuffling, dragging her feet, she followed us to the lift. No one spoke as we ascended to ground level, but the silence had the density of clay.

From the lift, we were ushered by Diane back the way we'd come, through security doors, past the main desk and into the waiting room, to return to the mid-morning gloom outside.

Chapter 25

A few hours later, Diane and I were sitting at a small round table in a swanky wine bar called The Salisbury, a short walk from her flat. She had a Chardonnay. They didn't do beers on draught, so I settled for a bottle of Magners served in a tall glass loaded with ice.

We clinked glasses. 'Cheers,' she said, and took a sip, watching me over the rim.

Diane still had piercing eyes. They bore a faint smattering of lines around the edges, adding depth and meaning to her face. Tonight she was wearing a neat black dress that hugged her frame like a surgeon's glove. Heads had turned when we walked into the pub, and I was aware of more eyes following her when she bought the first round. Her frizzy hair was pulled back again, and she wore small silver earrings that sparkled each time she laughed, which she liked to do, and which seemed to illuminate something inside her.

I was wearing a black shirt and black jeans, had argan oil in my hair and Cool Water on my wet-shaved cheeks. The cuts and swelling around my face were calming, and from a distance I could've passed for a Colin Farrell lookalike. Maybe.

'You think Harriet can hold it together for a sting?' she said. 'The woman seems pretty unstable to me.'

'She'll probably crumble or try to leg it again,' I said. 'That's why I'm going in with her.'

'This can't be easy for you, Kas. I still don't get why you're helping her like this?'

'It's hard to explain.'

'Want to try?'

I drank a couple of inches, swirling the ice and thinking about the answer I wanted to give. Recounting my conversation with Jazz and the realisation that I was on a quest for redemption over Rosie sounded pretty hokey, and I doubted Diane would understand my logic. To be honest, I wasn't entirely sure I understood it, either.

'I know what it's like to lose a kid,' I eventually said, 'and I don't want Saul Berkowitz having to arrange the funeral for a second one. Will that do?'

'The pacifist professor's not entirely clueless in all this, you know.'

I looked up. 'Meaning?'

She hesitated.

'What, Diane?'

'I did some digging into the Berkowitz family like you asked.'

I put down my drink. 'And?'

'And, turns out you're right. A decade and a half back, the family got mixed up with a Professor Robert John Riding. Heard of him?'

I shook my head.

'Riding was an American academic originally from California. Records show he was in Saul Berkowitz's social sciences circle, until his arrest.'

My stomach was already constricting. 'Arrest for what?'

'Two counts of child abuse, plus a load more for downloading and distribution of underage porn. The guy was wanted in Thailand and the States for similar offences, but managed to hide under the dark web and a bunch of pseudonyms. He liked to travel, securing posts at universities all over. His specialist area was child exploitation, of course. Riding was prolific, Kas, one of those career paedophiles you read about. Whenever the heat came down, he did a geographical somewhere else and carried on.'

She reached into her bag, pulled out a slim A4 folder, slipped out a sheet. 'Here he is,' she said, and handed it to me.

I stared at the police mugshot of Professor Riding. It was black and white, blurry and heavily pixelated, but still recognisable. The pale skin, deep stare, Burt Reynolds moustache – it was the same man I'd seen in the photo under Tommy's bed.

'Jesus,' I said. I gave Diane the sheet and drank heavily, but the cider couldn't quell the sour taste in my throat.

'There's more,' Diane said, putting it away. 'Apparently, Riding used to threaten the kids he abused to keep them tight-lipped. He said he'd have them shipped to other countries and sold into the slave trade if they squealed. It worked. He was able to carry on for years until one of his victims blew the whistle. I looked up the report to see who it was.'

My heart kicked. 'Tommy?'

'Nope.'

I waited.

'It was Harriet. Aged twelve. I read the transcripts. She did a brave thing, telling the police how that bastard abused

Tommy and her. Probably saved a lot of other kids in the process.'

I shook my head. 'So that's what Tommy meant when he said he owed her.'

'Saul never mentioned any of this, I'm guessing?'

'No, he didn't.' It was still sinking in. 'Where's this Riding now?'

'Dead.'

'How?'

'Some dopey judge granted him bail. He went on the run. Year before last, they found a body in north California at the foot of a rock face. He was in pretty bad shape from the drop, but dental records proved it was him.'

'He jumped?'

'Who knows? However he went, we know he's brown bread.'

I kept shaking my head. Childhood abuse. An apparent suicide. Why had Saul never mentioned any of this? When I showed him the photo under Tommy's bed, he'd lied about not recognising the man. Everything was a muddle.

'So now you know,' Diane said. 'Does it change anything?'

I looked at her, and away. 'Not really. But it helps me understand a bit more about these two kids. Why they turned out the way they did. Their lives had been torn apart long before I rocked up.'

'That's right. Maybe you can let yourself off the hook a little.'

Diane's fingers were under the table, touching my trembling hand. 'You OK?' she said.

I didn't want all this pulling me away from her, so looked for a distraction. 'I'll get the drinks in,' I said, even though Diane's wine was hardly touched.

Returning with a fresh round, I tried changing the subject. 'So, how're your sisters?' It was the first thing to pop into my head.

Diane smiled. 'Poppy's still at John Lewis. Tomika's finishing up her social work degree. And Francesca's expecting her first in August.'

'Auntie Diane?'

'I know. Mum's made up.'

'Tell your mum I said hi. And tell Fran she'll make a great mum.'

'I will. She likes you, Kas. All my family do.'

'What's she having?'

'A boy. She plans on calling him Ezra.'

'Cool name.'

'It's biblical. The father's a minister. It's either that or Ezekiel.'

'Fair enough,' I said. 'Ezra's better.'

'You ever hear from Carol?'

I shook my head. 'She's moved up north somewhere. We send each other a text on Rosie's birthday. I heard she's been working part-time in a GP practice, answering phones, booking appointments, stuff like that.'

'Good for her.'

'Yeah. After what happened . . . well, I'm glad she's getting her life back on track. It flattened her.'

'It knocked the stuffing out of you too, Kas.'

I looked at my drink.

'Do you ever think about us?' she said.

'All the time.'

'We had something. Didn't we?'

'Yeah.'

'You know, when you dropped me like you did and walked out on life, I was so angry. Course I was hurt for you, but more than anything, I was pissed off you'd just disappear out of my life. I wanted to help you so much, but you were unreachable. Don't you think I had a right to feel that way?'

'I can't give you a better answer than the one I gave five years back, Diane.'

'What? That you couldn't be with anyone? That after what happened to Rosie, you needed to be alone?'

I nodded.

'So why're you seeing me now? What's changed?'

I drank more cider and waited until it'd gone down. 'Maybe I should go,' I said.

'No,' she said, her voice sharp. 'Don't you run off again.'

I looked at her. 'I don't think I'll ever be that man you knew.'

'Meaning?'

'Meaning, a part of me died with Rosie.'

'Ah, give me a break. Any second now, the violins are going to kick in.'

A couple of heads had turned. Diane didn't notice or care. Leaning in, she said, 'Listen, what happened to your girl was a tragedy. But it *wasn't* your fault.'

I drained my glass and looked at the sloshing ice. 'I need another drink,' I said.

I returned from the bar with a third cider, and my loping thigh hit the table, spilling some of Diane's wine.

'Sorry,' I said.

She mopped it up with a napkin. 'Slow down, big man.' Her voice had softened. She smiled.

'Christ, it's good seeing you,' I said, sitting back down, my words a little slurry. 'I've missed this.'

'Me too.'

I saw the gap between her top two teeth, the freckles around her cheeks, and remembered nights like this, the two of us talking and drinking and laughing together. Good times. Not perfect, but always *good* . . .

But those times were in the past, and the past belonged to Rosie. To go back there now felt like betraying her somehow.

I should've finished my drink and called it a night then, but beneath the table, Diane's hand found mine again, and drew me back.

'It's OK. I'm here,' she said.

I nodded.

'Come home with me. Just for tonight.'

'All right,' I said.

She put Nina Simone on the stereo and her arms around my neck. I let my hands slide down the curve of her frame, and we began undressing each other.

I carried her to the bedroom and looked at every bit of her. Her palms ran across my shoulders, my scarred arms, the yellowing bruises around my side. She moved like a dancer, slick and elegant, not a wasted move, and I wanted her so much right then.

But I couldn't. Something was in the way.

After a while, we gave up trying and stepped on to the balcony. Murphy the dog stirred from her cushion by the sliding doors, watching us, her pregnant tummy now the size of a watermelon. I stood behind Diane. Her fingers reached back, found mine. We looked at the clouds as they changed shape, joining together, moving apart.

'Sorry,' I said.

'Don't be.'

'It's not that I don't want to—'

'I know, Kas. Maybe you had a bit too much to drink.'

I breathed in the familiar coconut scent of her hair.

'Looks like more rain,' she said.

We listened to the first patter on the balcony ledge. When her skin began to pimple and I felt her shiver, we went back inside to her bedroom. No more words.

I lay there in the darkness of her bedroom, thinking about what had just happened, and waiting until the cadence of her breathing changed and I knew she was asleep. Then I opened my eyes and sat up.

My watch said quarter to one. If I went home now, I'd be lying awake, alone and in bad company. I wasn't up for that.

Truth was, I felt lonely. Here I was, next to a woman I still loved, and even though I craved her intimacy more than anything, I was a million miles from her. What the hell was wrong with me?

I dressed in the dark. As I was putting my socks on, I heard Diane stirring.

'You OK?'

'Sorry,' I said. 'Didn't mean to wake you.'

'That's all right. Can't sleep?'

'No.'

'Why don't you read a book or watch TV next door? It won't bother me.'

'I fancy a walk,' I said. 'I've had a great night, Diane.'

She sighed. 'I'll see you, then.'

I zipped my jeans, laced up my boots and left quickly. As I was exiting the lift and stepping through the foyer, I had my phone out and was calling a number I hadn't rung for some time.

A European voice answered. I told her what I wanted, she told me a price and gave me an address in Dalston where someone called Rosette would see me.

Thirty minutes later, a peroxide blonde answered a chipped red door and took me up a flight of narrow stairs. She smelled of hairspray and cigarettes; her teal eyes were strained with fatigue. Six months back, I'd been with her. Her name had been Danielle then.

She asked what I was called and I shook my head.

'No name,' I said.

She understood.

Her workspace was a prefab studio. A bathroom partitioned off by a dented stud wall was to the left; to the right, there was a kitchenette, separated by a row of hanging beads. Centre stage stood a low-slung king-size bed. On a bedside table there was an ashtray and a lump of hashish resin. The sweet smell of cannabis cloyed the air.

I took out my wallet and paid her cash. She counted the notes and took them to the bathroom. I sat on the bed.

A moment later, she came back, stood in front of me and began undressing before my eyes. She smiled, revealing the dry gums and greying teeth of a smoker. Her eyes stayed flat.

With nothing on but her bra and knickers, she lifted my hands and invited me to touch her. I felt the fleshy bits, the stretch marks, the silky white scar around her navel where she'd had a C-section, all signs of a life I didn't want to know about.

'How you want me, baby?' she said.

It took a while to speak. 'Can I just hold you for a while?'

Something seemed to soften in her. She came around to my left and sat beside me on the mattress. Gently, she cupped my head and lowered it to her breast.

'It's OK,' she said, stroking my hair.

I could hear her heartbeat.

Chapter 26

A little after nine that morning, I took a call from Detective Hargreaves.

'I've had a chance to discuss your proposal with my seniors. They've decided to authorise a covert entrapment. Security will be tight in order to avoid any leaks, and I will personally vet every officer involved. Napier won't find out.'

'Good,' I said.

His voice sharpened. 'For this to work, Kasper, we'll need a confession from Napier on tape. He must clearly implicate his involvement in drugs and vice. Only then can he be taken into custody and a warrant issued to search his premises.'

'What prep have you made for Vincent Brown?' I said.

'Our tactical division will provide armed backup during the op,' he said, then added, 'all under my direct supervision, of course.'

'I feel safer already,' I said.

'Rather than concerning yourself with *us*, how about you worry about getting Napier to spill. All right?'

'Sir, yes, sir.'

*

An hour later, I was helping Harriet write a text message to Napier.

We were back in Holborn nick, now in a room they called 'the snug'. There wasn't much that was snuggly here – the only difference from the interview rooms was the addition of the bobbly brown sofa we were presently sitting on.

Three plastic chairs stood opposite us. Hargreaves sat on the one furthest away. He was wearing an earpiece that was digitally connected to Harriet's phone, allowing him to listen remotely when a call came in. His green eyes were fixed on us, blinking behind his glasses like the shutters on a camera.

Harriet's message read:

I don't have your money. I can't do this. Find someone else.

'Send it,' I said.

She hit the button and gave a whine.

'Shouldn't take long.'

Two minutes, in fact.

Hargreaves went rigid as her phone started ringing. He put a finger to the earpiece, looked over, and nodded at us to answer. With shaking hands, Harriet took the call.

Immediately, I could hear Napier's yappy voice through the handset. Although I couldn't make out what he was saying, I caught enough to know it wasn't complimentary. Harriet's knees began trembling.

'Mr Napier,' she said, 'Mr Napier, if you just—' but she couldn't get a word in.

I gave it a moment, but saw it wasn't working, so reached over and slid the phone from her hand. When I put it to my ear, Napier was mid-sentence, saying something about 'burying your bony arse in the ground—'

'Mick,' I cut in. 'It's Dylan Kasperick. Top o' the morning.'

A pause. 'The interfering pig-fucker. I shoulda guessed.'

'Listen, Mick, Harriet's having problems. Big problems. But we've put our heads together. There's a new offer on the table. You'll love it.'

'You remember my warning, fella?'

'I remember.'

'Sounds like you think you're running this gig.'

'It's not like that, Mick. I know the score. But since my place of work burned down, I've been out of pocket. And Harriet still owes you. So I've been thinking of an opportunity. Something that'll pay off nicely for all of us if we stop messing around and work together.'

I heard Napier's breaths, a click of a lighter, the heavy flow of smoke.

'Go on,' he said.

'Not over the phone. Let's meet to discuss it. All of us. Face to face.'

'All right. Get yourself over to the bar. We'll talk here.'

'No, thanks. You might recall last time I was there, our conversation got a little heated. I'd prefer to speak somewhere neutral.'

'Where?'

I waited, pretending to think. 'There's a big supermarket round the corner from your bar.'

'I know the place. So?'

'They've got an underground car park with four levels. Let's talk in the bottom one. Tomorrow morning. Seven.'

'Make it six.'

'Fine.'

He paused. 'You fucking with me, Kasper?'

'No.'

'If you are, I'll bury you – and that dotty old shrink you live with. You know that, right?'

'I know, Mick.'

He hung up.

I gave the phone back to Harriet and looked at Hargreaves. He gave the thumbs-up.

Twenty minutes later, we were at the car park to prepare for tomorrow's sting.

It looked like any supermarket car park – concrete walls, concrete ceilings, the whole enclosure colourless and utilitarian. Thuds echoed above our heads, along with crashing trolleys, car horns, a few muffled voices.

'You're not serious?' Harriet said.

Hargreaves and I looked at her.

'You want to meet Napier in this . . . this *dungeon*?'

'Yes,' I said.

'I don't like it. It's not safe.'

'No, it's good,' Hargreaves said, scanning around. 'Everything's open-plan. It's easy to block off exit routes, and there's sustained radio contact. Well done, Kasper.'

'Aw, thanks,' I said. 'Do I tape the wire to my chest or something?'

'*You* won't, Kasper,' he said. 'After your last run-in with Napier, he's likely to search you.' He turned to Harriet. 'Therefore, *you* should wear the recording device, Ms Berkowitz.'

'You can't be serious!' Harriet squealed again.

I sighed. As much as I didn't like the idea, Hargreaves was right.

'It'll be OK, Harriet,' I said. 'Just stay close to me.'

'I don't like it,' she said. 'Where will the backup be hiding? In case something goes wrong?'

'This isn't Hollywood, Ms Berkowitz,' Hargreaves said.

'She's got a point, though,' I said. 'There should be a signal. A nod for you to send in the cavalry.'

'A code word, you mean?' Harriet said.

'I think we'll know, Kasper,' Hargreaves said, folding his arms.

'Sorry, mate. I want to be sure you've got my back when I say you do, not when you decide. No offence.'

He smiled stiffly. 'What would you suggest?'

I thought. 'When I start whistling, that's your cue.'

He lolled his head, expecting more. When I didn't give anything, he shrugged.

'Fine,' he said.

We shuffled round for a few more minutes, but there wasn't much else to see. Hargreaves took some photos, checked the radio signal again from different spots. Everything worked.

Not long after, an elderly parking attendant appeared and came to inspect the Fiesta Hargreaves had left in a disabled bay, looking for the car's non-existent blue badge. The young detective strolled over and flashed his police ID as if he were the town sheriff.

'Don't care if you're the Pope, son,' the attendant said, looking at it blankly. 'Still can't park there.'

In spite of the gloom, I saw Hargreaves' face darken to an unmistakable red.

'Let's go,' he said brusquely. 'There's nothing else to see here. Six tomorrow morning, Kasper. Try to be punctual.'

Chapter 27

I told Hargreaves it'd be in everyone's interest for me and Harriet to stay in a hotel, ideally within walking distance of the car park where tomorrow's sting was to happen. She was looking decidedly off-key, and I knew that if I left her unsupervised, she'd scarper again.

To my surprise, Hargreaves agreed. He made a few calls, and with a smirk scribbled down the address of a bed and breakfast nearby called the Luxury Inn that he said would meet our needs.

Luxury Inn proved to be a misnomer. It was a rickety old dosshouse, gnarled and peeling. A thin, jaundiced man, barefoot and wearing a decrepit brown blazer, was sitting outside on the steps beneath the awning, clutching a Diamond White, staring at the can affectionately.

'Here?' Harriet said as we passed him. 'You want us to stay *here* tonight?'

'Relax,' I said. 'I bet it's fine inside.'

It wasn't. The interior was steeped with grime. A smell like wet dishcloths hit me as I pushed through one creaky plastic door, then another, and led us into a narrow hallway that ended at a reception desk. To its left was a payphone. An obese white male wearing flip-flops, tracksuit bottoms and a string vest was making a call from it, shouting into the receiver something about '. . . gettin' my money back off that bitch . . .'

Sitting behind the desk and watching the man on the phone with malign interest, there was an old, pucker-faced geezer with cataract eyes and cheeks sponged with burst capillaries. He was chewing Bombay mix from a paper bowl, his fingers twisted with arthritis, the tips tobacco yellow.

I gave our details. He checked the booking in a diary, reached below the desk and produced a rusty key for a top-floor room.

'We're sharing a room?' Harriet said behind me, not hiding her disgust.

'Looks that way,' I said. 'Hope you don't snore.'

The lift was broken, so we took the narrow staircase up three flights. Twice, Harriet needed to stop to catch her breath and take a few slugs on an inhaler.

My guess, our room hadn't been redecorated since the eighties. It had cork flooring and some kind of radioactive-green floral wallpaper, ripped and scuffed and daubed with stains. Two single saggy beds stood by the wall, separated by a cabinet peppered with cigarette burns.

Aside from some turned milk and instant coffee sachets on top of the fridge, the only other complimentary item was a Gideon Bible I found in the cabinet. Flicking it open, I saw a previous guest had defaced it with images of male and female sex parts. The artist clearly had some talent.

Harriet sat on the bed nearest the window, still puffed from the stairs. She pulled off her sunglasses and looked around, then at me, then at the floor.

No two ways, this place was a shit-heap, and neither one of us was thrilled to be here.

'Kasper?' Harriet said. 'What do we do now?'

Opening my backpack, I pulled out a bottle of Bushmills and a six-pack of Export. 'I don't know about you,' I said, cracking a lager, 'but I'm having a drink.'

It kept raining as the evening ground on. We spent a bit of time going through who'd say what to Napier tomorrow, but that didn't take long. After that, there wasn't much to talk about.

Around seven, I ordered up some Chinese takeaway. I wasn't hungry, but figured we should eat and it would pass a bit of time. I'd had a couple of the beers and a finger of the whiskey, as had Harriet, who drank cautiously from one of the teacups.

I sat on the bed and ate rice, vegetables and some kind of meat from a tin tray. Harriet picked at her fried noodles and looked at a prawn cracker as if it were a deep-fried beetle before tossing it. She cranked open the window, sat on the ledge and lit a cigarette.

'Try to eat,' I said.

'No, thank you,' she said.

Instead, she burned through two smokes and then switched on the TV. Sipping her drink, she perched on the edge of her bed, staring at the screen like a toddler watching cartoons. We both fell quiet.

After maybe an hour, she broke the silence. 'I'm scared, Kasper.'

I looked up. She had her back to me, so all I could see was her jet-black bob. She was very still.

'I know,' I said. 'It's normal to be scared.'

'You don't understand. I'm scared about tomorrow, but I'm more scared of what'll happen after, if this plan of yours actually works. What do I do with myself then?'

'You could tell your dad the truth. He might surprise you.'

'The *truth*? And have an *honest* father–daughter relationship with him?' I heard the incredulity in her voice. 'I've not had an honest relationship in years. I've never opened up or let anyone get close. I'm not a real daughter. I'm not a real person. I'm just a shell.'

I think the whiskey had gone to her head a little.

'When this is over,' I said, 'maybe you two could get some counselling together, help you communicate.' It sounded limp, even to me.

'Come on. It's too late for all that. I pimped out Tommy, my little brother. I forced him to keep going, and it drove him to suicide. I despise myself. If Dad finds out, he'll despise me too. You know what? I wish *I* was dead.'

She was crying. A childish mew, battling with the sound of the rain on the window and the drone of the TV. It was stifling. For a second, my mind flitted back to the previous night, lying with the prostitute, and the comfort that came with that anonymity. I knew where I'd rather be.

I stood, walked around the bed, turned off the TV set and stood a few feet from Harriet. She looked up, breathing slowly through her mouth. Her eyes were glassy with tears.

'I know about Robert Riding,' I said, handing her a tissue from my pocket. 'What he did to you both when you were kids.'

She inhaled sharply. Her pupils dilated, two inky saucers filling the irises. Bones seemed to protrude through her skin, small jagged shapes, like machine parts.

Then she exhaled. Her body grew slack and she looked down.

'How . . .' she said, and stopped to wipe her nose. 'How did you find out?'

'Does it matter?'

She shook her head. 'I suppose not.'

'It's not an excuse for what you did. But it explains a lot.'

I felt cumbersome there, a burly man standing above a crying woman nearly two decades my junior, so I took a step back and leaned against the wall, sliding till I was on the floor.

'Dad's never talked about the abuse,' she said. 'He and Bob were friends, you see. The whole time I was giving evidence, he was either mute or flew into a wild rage when Bob's name got mentioned.'

Again, I thought back to Saul's reaction to the photo of Riding, insisting he didn't recognise him.

'What about your mother?' I said. 'How did she handle what happened to you and Tommy?'

'Mum was devastated. She blamed herself, thought it was neglect.'

There was a word I knew. Although Judith Berkowitz was dead, a part of me identified with her. There's no pain quite like seeing your child suffer, even more when they can't understand the hurt themselves.

'And when Bob went on the run,' I said, 'how did your mum react then?'

'How do you think?' Harriet said. 'She became furious.'

'Furious?'

She nodded. 'At Bob for hurting us, and at Dad for being so blind. Most of all, she was furious with herself. That's when she began to self-destruct.'

'What was your family connection with Bob?' I said. 'How did he weasel his way in?'

Harriet gave a thin smile. 'Mum knew him from Berkeley campus, in California. They were undergrads, both from pretty freethinking, hippy-ish families. They bonded over gender politics, queer theory, anti-fascism, free love and all that social science-y stuff. There was a lot of drug-taking and bed-swapping going on. At one point, I think Mum was in love with Bob. Or certainly in lust.'

'Yet she ended up with Saul. Why?'

'Dad was the opposite of Bob. He was straight-laced, a junior researcher visiting from London, and a few years older. He fell for Mum, and she knew he'd be good for her, a solid, reliable man.

'After Tommy and I were born, we all moved to England to settle in Dad's old family house. But we'd always go over to the States and see Bob. Mum insisted on it. I think she still cared about him.

'Then, as we grew up, he started to visit us. He'd stay at the house sometimes. Eventually, Mum suggested Dad should find him a job at the university as a lecturer. He came to live in London, a few roads from us. We were a happy little unit.'

'You sound like you loved him too?'

'Bob? He was this funny, clever American with a big bushy moustache and an amazing laugh. Course Tommy and I loved him. He was so much cooler than stuffy old Dad in his tank tops and sandals. We called him Uncle, and he gave us nick-names. I was Matilda, like the Roald Dahl character, because I was clever.'

'And Tommy?'

'Cupcakes. Bob said his plump cheeks were good enough to eat.'

I nodded, remembering this as the nickname Dominic Tyrell said Tommy had asked to be known by. Some memories die hard.

'How did the abuse start?' I said.

'It's hard to remember exactly. I know I've stored it all up here' – she pointed at her head – 'but there are huge bits missing. Mostly it comes back to me in nightmares.

'Mum was spending more and more time in America, caring for her sick father. Dad had just taken a professorship at the university and was immersed in that. So they asked Bob if he'd look after us now and then. Of course, he said yes.'

A long minute passed.

'First, he'd come over to the house in the mornings or afternoons, when it was just Tommy and me there. Then he'd stay over the whole night. He'd do bath time. Pyjama time. And cuddle time. That's what he called it. He started coming into our rooms, saying he was checking up on us. Tucking us in. I never knew it was abuse. I didn't know what it was, and still can't find the words to describe it. I just knew it hurt each time he touched me. It made me feel sick. I'd hear Tommy crying in the other room and knew he was doing the same to him. I just lay in bed, too scared to move. After, Bob said it was his way of showing how much he loved us.'

'Christ,' I said. 'How long did it go on?'

'One year, three months and eight days,' she said, as if the numbers were ingrained in her. 'And I remember every second.'

'I'll bet. Why didn't you tell anyone sooner?'

'Bob said he'd punish us. He'd tell stories of child slaves, and said that's what would happen to us if we told anyone.'

'So what changed?'

'It got to the point where I didn't care about the consequences. I just needed it all to stop. I was twelve. Tommy was six. We were trapped. It was killing us. So I told Mum. Everything. And she took me to the police.'

I rubbed my brow, taking this all in. There were more questions I wanted to ask – about how two bright parents could be so deceived by a prolific sex offender, and why Saul never mentioned any of this when he hired me – but right then, there was a bigger elephant that needed pointing out.

'Harriet,' I said, 'Bob was found dead in California.'

'I know.'

'It could've been a suicide.'

'Yes.'

'Or perhaps someone killed him.'

'So?'

'So, I'm wondering if your mum had a hand in what happened to him. You said she was furious. Maybe it drove her to act out her revenge.'

I watched for a reaction. Nothing.

'You must've considered it?'

There was a faint yet undeniable nod. Then she turned her face away.

In a sense, I knew this didn't matter. Bob was dead. Judith was dead. Tommy too.

But at the same time, it did matter. This was the real reason we were here. Saul and Judith Berkowitz had let a monster into their home. Had he not interfered with their two innocent kids, Harriet and I wouldn't be sharing a dingy hotel room and her brother would still be alive. I was sure of it.

'Tell me about your mum,' I said. 'How she got into debt and died.'

'I've told you, she was an addict. The pills killed her.'

'Tell me again. In detail.'

'It was gradual. After Bob vanished, she started taking painkillers.'

'To numb herself over what had happened,' I said, glancing at the Bushmills bottle and the scarring on my forearm. Who was I to judge?

'Yes,' Harriet said. 'By then, Mum's dad had died, and she had a stockpile of his cancer meds. Pretty soon, they got a grip on her. When they ran out, she started ordering more online, paying exorbitant fees on the black market for Oxycodone and Valium. The tablets made her crazy, paranoid, and she was spending more and more time by herself, in the attic. We used to hear her, pacing around, shouting and swearing at all hours of the night. She became thin and haggard, like a witch. It used to mortify Tommy to see her like that.'

I leaned in, my intrigue getting the better of me. 'What was she doing in that attic, apart from smashing herself on drugs?'

'She was plotting how she was going to catch Bob. It became an obsession. That's how the debts really built up.'

'Explain that bit.'

'She employed these bogus investigators all across the world. She blew thousands, splurging money on any possible sightings. Sometimes she didn't come down for days. It got out of control fast. Dad, Tommy and I didn't know what to do, and all reacted differently. I ran off to university. Dad buried himself in his work. And Tommy . . . well, you know what he started doing.'

'Yeah,' I said.

'Every few months, Mum would travel somewhere. Dad told us she'd gone to visit her mother in California. But I knew she was out there, looking for Bob, following up on her leads. Even though her health was failing, it was her mission to punish that man.'

I thought about this, putting the pieces in order. 'It was two years back when they discovered Bob's body,' I said. 'Your mother died that same year. Right?'

'Correct,' Harriet said. 'She passed a few months after they found him.'

'What were those months like?'

She bowed her head and seemed to stare at a grubby spot on the cork floor. 'Strange. Artificial. The house was suddenly quiet. It was like she'd already died.'

'Did you ever speak to your mother about how Bob got found? The details of his death?'

She shook her head. 'We never mentioned his name.'

'What do you think happened to him?'

'The same as you,' Harriet said matter-of-factly. 'Mum finally did it, she found him and killed him. She never took credit, but I'm sure it's true. It was like she was finally at peace, just before she died. Tommy and I talked about it a few times. And we were happy. She didn't have to fight anymore.'

'What did you do? After she passed?'

'I tried to bury myself in work. I saw how much financial trouble she'd left us in. I was twenty-four, working for a good firm in the City. I told myself if I could address that problem, then I'd have done some good for the family.'

'But you got sacked?'

She nodded. 'It was a few months after the funeral.'

'What happened?'

She looked at her splayed hands, pale and bony. 'There was a man at work, a colleague. It's embarrassing . . .' She pursed her lips and suddenly flinched, as if singed by a memory.

I waited while she found her words.

'I can't *do* physical relationships, Kasper. Not after what Bob did to me. It was stupid of me to try getting involved.'

'Did this man hurt you?'

'No, no. It was the other way round. I just wanted to feel normal. He was a nice guy, but wanted more than I could give. When he tried progressing things, I reacted appallingly . . .' She put a hand over her mouth, stifling something. A moment later, she removed it and said quietly, 'He invited me over for dinner. After the meal, he asked if he could kiss me. I said OK. Then he asked for a cuddle. And suddenly, he became Bob.'

She put her palm to her brow and pushed, as if she were kneading a scar.

'He told the police I threw a glass in his face. The injuries were awful. He'll be scarred for life. I was charged with assault. I never knew . . . sometimes, people don't realise what they're capable of, do they?'

'No,' I said, remembering some of my own shameful behaviour in the wake of Rosie's death: roughing up schoolboys, kicking down doors, shutting out all the people who cared for me. 'They don't.'

'Anyway, I got hauled in front of management and was sacked. I tried to apologise to my ex, but he wasn't having it. Instead, he ran my reputation into the ground, telling people I was nuts, deranged. No one would employ me after that.'

'But you still couldn't tell Saul? Why?'

'It would've meant dredging up everything again. By then, Dad had erased Bob from memory, and created the cover story about Mum dying from cancer. He was using that to explain why Tommy was acting out. I suppose denying everything was his attempt to make us feel safe. But he couldn't.'

Safe. The word had off-sided me.

Harriet must have noticed a change in my expression, for she gave a peculiar half-smile. 'It sounds ridiculous, doesn't it? Even though Bob was dead, he still had this power over Tommy and me. I became shut down and frigid, unable to get close to anyone. And he went the other way, turning into a needy man-child, always wanting strong people around him, like Napier. And you.'

'Me?'

Harriet looked at me incredulously. 'Come, now, that's why he took to you, Kasper. He told me he manipulated someone to pick a fight with you, right?'

'Yeah.'

She nodded. 'That's Tommy all over. I loved him and I miss him, but I'm not going to sugar-coat my little brother. He could be a sneaky git to get what he was after.' She took a breath, and exhaled slowly. 'But it wasn't his fault. He was a product of his experience. His nightmares were far worse than mine, you know.'

'That's why he kept his bedroom door locked?'

'Yes. He was afraid someone would sneak in and hurt him. He preferred to wake up next to a random man rather than by himself in the dark. Poor boy. He really was more damaged than me.'

'I don't think Tommy was any more damaged than you, Harriet,' I said. 'You were both royally fucked up by that man. It just came out in different ways.'

She looked at me and smiled again, more fully. It was one of the saddest smiles I'd seen in a long time. In her eyes, I recognised the same wounded child I'd seen in her brother.

'What are you thinking?' she said.

'I'm thinking the same thing that's been going round my head since all this started. Why the hell didn't Saul step up and help you two kids? He's absent in all of this. When I showed him a photo of Bob I found under Tommy's bed, he pretended he didn't know who he was. It makes no sense. Surely he could've done more before your lives blew up.'

Wearily, she shook her head. 'Dad's more deluded than anyone. The lecturing, banging on about love and forgiveness on the radio, that's become his focus.' She rubbed her eyes. 'I think he's convinced himself none of what I've told you ever took place. Bob never existed. Mum died from cancer. I go to work every day. And Tommy's problems were down to grief.'

'Don't you think a small part of him wants to hear all this, even though its ugly?'

'The truth would kill him.'

'Doesn't that make you angry?'

'Angry?' She laughed. 'Yes, it does. The whole thing makes me so angry I could scream.'

'Perhaps you should.'

But she didn't, and neither of us said anything for a long time.

In the silence, I weighed things up. Something still didn't fit.

Saul was an intelligent man. He couldn't have been so blind. In the same way that a part of me must've known my daughter was suffering, something deep inside him knew all this. It was why he'd asked me to look out for Tommy, why he'd let me dig around his bedroom – and it was why he'd asked me to tell him whatever I found out.

I thought about putting this to Harriet, but her eyes were brimming again.

'How do I put this right?' she said. 'Tell me. Please. What do I need to do?'

I didn't want to lie or fob her off with some useless platitude. Not after the things she'd just told me.

I wanted to tell her I was the last man she should be asking, that my own child had chucked herself under a train, Tommy had copied her, and I regularly thought about joining them.

But I held back, and for the next minute or so, there was just the drum of rain and the rhythm of our breathing.

'Try not to think about this stuff anymore,' I said, and returned to my bed, avoiding her eyes. 'Let's just get through tomorrow. OK?'

Not a lot more was said after that. I chucked out the Chinese food and lay down on my bed. A little while later, Harriet did the same. Somewhere around midnight, I turned off the lights.

Chapter 28

My eyes pinged open at the sound of my phone vibrating. I reached for it in the dark.

'Kasper?' Hargreaves said.

'Yeah.'

'Are you up?'

'Almost.'

I checked my watch. 4.30 a.m.

Harriet was standing, silhouetted against the window. She was very still.

'I've got a tactical team poised,' Hargreaves said. 'We're ready. Don't be late.'

'We won't.' I hung up.

'Morning,' Harriet said. 'I didn't want to wake you.' She wedged the window up a few inches and lit a cigarette.

Outside, the pre-dawn sky was a morass of grey-blue, the colour of a bruise. A few birds were chirping somewhere, but that was all. The rain had stopped, but the air that whispered in was damp and peaky, and I felt the hairs on my neck begin to bristle. Harriet seemed impervious to it.

I rolled out of bed, switched on the bedside light and stood.

I was wearing tracksuit bottoms and a T-shirt, and felt a little exposed opposite Harriet, who was dressed – black heels, black trousers, white shirt. She looked like she'd been awake for a long time.

'Couldn't sleep?' I said.

'No.' She finished her cigarette, turned and headed to the bathroom.

While she was there, I made us two cups of strong instant coffee. When she emerged, I went to hand her one, but faltered when I saw she'd unbuttoned her shirt, exposing her bra, along with the small microphone Hargreaves had given us, taped discreetly around her sternum.

'Have I done this right?' she said.

I put down my coffee. 'Let's see,' I said, and came to her.

Up close, she was even thinner and paler than I imagined, like a child, her ribs protruding like xylophone keys. She'd added some eye make-up and was wearing citrus perfume.

I did my best to put aside any awkwardness, along with the knowledge that the last man who'd viewed her in an intimate way had ended up scarred for life.

The fastening was secure. I pressed a small green light on the mic, like Hargreaves had shown me and it came on, telling me it was charged and ready.

'Looks fine,' I said, stepping back. 'Just keep it covered. OK?'

She nodded, and began buttoning up her shirt.

In the bathroom, I had a pee and splashed water on my face. Then I put on a clean white vest and a black flannel shirt, and tucked both into black jeans.

Back in the room, I finished my coffee. Harriet's lay untouched. She was wearing her mac, aviators covered her eyes, and she had a fresh Marlboro on the go.

'All right?' I said.

'Yes.'

'Then let's go catch a crook.'

Vast puddles of rain had formed outside the Luxury Inn, pooling between the cracks, creating a glassy sheen on the uneven paving. In the quiet damp air, we began walking east in the direction of the Aldi car park. With each passing moment, the sky was changing colour and shape, moving from grey into mauve, and from mauve towards a strange lilac stippled with slowly moving cirrus clouds.

Already, there were people dotting the street, stragglers from the night or early risers for the day to come. We passed a trio of hipsters clad in spray-on jeans, jumble-sale jumpers and moccasins; we passed a svelte woman wearing skyscraper heels, sashaying to the train station while immersed in her smartphone; we passed a pair of homeless men curled in a Cash Converters doorway, gazing aimlessly at us.

The nearer we got to the car park, the more Harriet seemed to wither. She kept stopping to light cigarettes, adjust her sunglasses or simply freeze, as if struck by a thought.

'Harriet,' I said, starting to worry these interludes would make us late. 'I need you to keep your shit in one piece. OK?'

Her mandible clenched and her lips spread around her teeth. She swallowed audibly, and nodded, but it was clear the woman was white-knuckling it.

'It'll be fine,' I said, doing all I could to keep my voice measured. 'Just stick to the plan and say what I told you to say.'

She kept nodding, lifted her smoke and pulled hard on it.

A few minutes later, we came to a Ladbrokes. A red Fiesta was parked outside. I saw Hargreaves' reflection in its wing mirror. He was wearing a red and black checked lumberjack shirt, the sleeves rolled up. His right elbow hung from the car's open window. Like Harriet, he was hidden behind sunglasses. I wished I'd brought mine.

A few feet ahead of the Fiesta there was a tatty white removals van. I guessed this contained Hargreaves' backup.

As we passed, I asked Harriet to give the microphone a tap, just to double-check it was working.

Instantly, Hargreaves reached for his ear and grimaced at the harsh noise coming through.

It worked.

At ten to six, Harriet and I were standing inside the lower level of the car park. The supermarket didn't open until six, so we'd had to climb under the gate to get in.

It was cool and dark; our footsteps and breathing echoed off the low ceilings.

The only vehicle was a white Astra. Parking tickets were splayed over its window. Crushed lager tins, fag butts, a used nappy and other unidentifiable crap lay scattered around, remnants from the night-dwellers who used the space to shelter from the rain.

'What if Napier doesn't come?' Harriet whispered.

'He'll come.'

'His contacts in the police could've tipped him off.'

'That case, I'll think of something else. Just chill.'

At six, the supermarket opened.

At five past, Napier came.

A plain white tradesman's van descended the slope. Harriet inhaled and took several steps back.

Driving the van was the square-faced bouncer from Mick's Bar. He swung the van round and parked in a bay seventy or so feet in front of us. As soon as the engine died, both side doors opened. Out came Vincent, the bouncer and finally Napier.

Napier was wearing a Burberry sweatshirt, tight jeans and white Reebok Classics. A gold medallion hung around his neck. In his right hand was a Samsung, the same mobile he'd shown me the video on. He hooked his nose in our direction, as if caught by a scent.

'Over here,' he said. 'Both of you.'

I walked, not hurrying. Harriet's footsteps scuttled behind me.

The bouncer was leaning against the van. He wore bovver boots, scuffed combats and a loose white polo. His arms were folded over his wide chest. He was big, knew he was big, but his was a mix of brawn and fat: he wasn't the threat.

Vincent was another story. His knees were soft, a shoulder-width apart, hands sunk loosely in the pockets of an Everlast tracksuit; but there was nothing relaxed about him. With each breath, the tendons in his neck strained like lift cables, as if the skin wasn't strong enough to contain them. As I drew close, the intensity from his eyes seemed to harden the air between us.

Next to his two companions, Napier looked positively infantile in stature, but the man was no kid, and definitely wouldn't be a pushover. Last time we were face to face, I'd had a gun aiming at his temple. Even if he hadn't had a tip-off about today's sting, he'd be frosty around me, and quick to smell a rat.

When I was ten or so feet away, he said, 'That's close enough.'

I stopped. Harriet shuffled beside me to the right.

'Raise your shirt. Let me see if you're packing.'

I lifted the hem of my shirt and vest to show I had nothing to hide and swivelled around three-sixty. 'I'm clean, Mick,' I said. 'I come in peace. Nice medallion, by the way.'

Napier pointed the phone at me. 'Stop being a dick, and say what you got to say.' Even at this range, I could smell his breath, a mix of minty gum and stale smoke.

'I like it,' I said. 'Skip the niceties. You're a straight-talker.'

'One chance,' he said. 'Talk. Or we're gone.'

'All right.' I opened my palms, a sign of kinship. 'Here's how it is. From today, Harriet's out. She's cracking up, and can't get you any more money. Right, Harriet?'

She nodded, her hands wrung together. 'I'm sorry, Mr Napier,' she said. 'He's right. I can't keep doing this. If you make me carry on, I'll hurt myself like Tommy did.'

'Shit,' the bouncer said.

Vincent and Napier stared.

'There you go,' I said. 'To be frank, since Tommy died, I've been spending a bit of time with Harriet. Trust me, she's falling to pieces. I don't want you hurting her, and I don't want her hurting herself, either. So I've been thinking of another way to get what you're owed.'

'What's that?' Napier said. 'You gonna start working tricks like her brother?'

'Actually,' I said, 'you're not far off. Let *me* get you the rest of the money.'

'How you plannin' to do that?'

'Simple. I'll join your firm.'

'Shit,' the bouncer repeated. If a line works for you, why not milk it?

Napier's lips drew apart into a toothy, gold-capped grin. 'You're crazy, man,' he said. 'Have you on my payroll? Why'd I agree to something like that?'

'Think. I know the police. I could find out what they've got on you. Don't forget, I was a copper for years. Still got friends there. I could make sure you're one step ahead of the game.'

'I got my own police contacts. They done me OK so far.'

'True. But they're in your pocket because you've got sleaze on them, right? Trust me, no one likes to be blackmailed forever. Eventually, they'll figure out a way to bite back. Even Escobar got his comeuppance.'

Napier's mouth screwed up and he scratched his chin.

'Mr Napier,' Harriet said, 'just listen to what Kasper has to say. Please.'

Don't push too hard, Harriet, I thought. A sniff of desperation, and Napier would know something was off-key – then the plan gets blown apart, and quite possibly, so would we.

'That it?' Napier said, aiming the words at Harriet. 'You wanna swap your skinny self for this man and let him do your dirty work?'

'There's more,' I said.

Napier swung me a raking glare. 'What else you got?'

'I'm offering you protection.'

'Protection from what?'

'I'll scare off anyone who gets in your way.'

'I got Vinnie for that.'

'I know.' I looked at Vincent and back to Napier. 'But I'm scarier than him.'

I sensed Harriet shrinking back a step. *Good*, I thought. She'd said what she was meant to say, and kept herself together. *Leave the rest to me.*

'Hear that, Vinnie?' Napier said. 'This man reckons he's got the edge on you.'

Vincent smirked. 'Wanna test me out, do you, pal?' he said.

'Yeah,' I said. 'I do.'

'OK, OK,' Napier said, 'enough of this macho crap. I know why that daft bint wants out. But what the fuck's in this for you, Kasper?'

I shrugged. 'As you know, I've not had the best few years. To be frank, I've been in a bit of a slump. Well, I'm ready for some excitement. And I want to make some money. Real money. You could pay me whatever you're giving Vincent. Trust me, I'm worth it.'

'You got a lot of confidence.'

'I guess I do.'

I could almost hear the cogs turning in Napier's head. So far, I was pretty sure, he hadn't clocked us – but I didn't like the way Vincent's hands stayed in his pockets.

'Harriet?' Napier said, directing the words at her again. 'You happy for this man to take your debt?'

This time she gave less of an answer, more a whimper.

It fed into Napier's cockiness; he grinned, and I saw he was coming round.

'All right,' he said, back at me. 'You got me intrigued, I'll give you that. And you're right about one thing. That woman behind you, she's lost the plot. But she's a big girl and got herself into this mess. I gave her drugs to sell in good faith. Instead, she leaves them in her car and her fuckwit brother flushes the lot, then kills himself.'

'Harriet's unreliable, Mick,' I said. 'I'm not.'

'That so?'

'It is. You heard how I beat up your little gang. And you

279

saw me at your bar. Outnumbered. Outgunned. I don't scare easily. Take me on and you won't regret it.'

Napier wet his lips, breathed in, held air, and blew it out. He was interested. I could feel a tingle in my belly.

'Let's just say I was able to find you a bit of work,' he said. 'You could begin paying back what's owed straight away?'

I smiled. 'Tell me more.'

Napier lolled his head from side to side, weighing things up. 'I've had a run-in with the Turks from Blackhorse Road. They say I'm encroaching on their patch. What the fuck's encroaching? This is a free country, last I heard.'

'What're we talking about here, Mick?'

A mist of greed spilled over his eyes. 'What you think I'm talking about? Distribution. Coffee and sugar. Brown and white.'

I nodded slowly, attentively. Now, I had him. Just stay calm, don't give anything away.

'I got four big shipments arriving each year. The last one nearly ended in a fuckin' blowout when the Turks caught wind of the delivery date. My boys on the Met reckon they have their own police contacts. They thought I'd start stealing their business, so they tipped off the drug squad. Before I knew it, a load of my product got seized. One hundred large, that cost me. I can't have that happen again, Kasper. I'm a businessman, understand? Can't have it.'

'Course you can't.'

He rubbed his chin again, flashed me another golden grin. Clearly, he was beginning to enjoy himself.

'See,' he said, 'with an operation like mine, organisation's key. That's why I've never got caught. Cos I'm organised.'

'Uh-huh.'

'I like to know everything that's going on, in public, an' behind closed doors.'

'Indeed you do,' I said, 'hence the hidden cameras.'

He nodded, and held up a stumpy gold-ringed finger like he'd done in his bar. 'But you're right. Eventually, someone's gonna stab me in the back. An' I don't got eyes in the back of my head.' The finger pointed at me. 'So I could use an extra pair, from someone who knows what's fishy. You think that someone could be you?'

'Yeah,' I said. 'Sounds right up my street.'

'Mick . . .' Vincent said, leaning down to Napier, a crease lining his brow.

'It's OK, Vinnie,' Napier said, and I saw I had him. 'We're just talking. Right, Kasper?'

I nodded.

Yeah, Mick, like a couple of old mates.

He'd already implicated himself on tape. But I wanted more, to seal the deal.

'When's your next shipment?' I said.

With another sparkly smile, he proudly said, 'June fifth, I got two lots due from Holland. Vinnie's to sort out the pick-up and my boys will do the distribution and use the bar to wash the cash.' He paused, looked up and pointed his phone at me again. 'You could be the tactical branch? Making sure nothing smells wrong along the way?'

'Sounds good,' I said. 'Really good.'

Napier beamed magnanimously.

I took a step back. Then I circled my lips and began whistling the first tune I could think of. It was a Dylan song, 'Idiot Wind', one of Rosie's favourites. I guess it must've been rattling around my head somewhere.

By the time I got to the chorus, Napier's smile had begun to fade. He could sense something.

Behind me, Harriet made a gargling sound. I looked at Vincent – a vein in his brow pulsated. At the first squeal of tyres, his eyes sparked red.

'Mick!' he yelled. 'It's a trap!'

Napier looked round, registered Vincent's panic, and spun back in time for me to say 'Surprise!' and lunge forward, slamming my fist into his nose, busting it. It was a great punch, full of shoulder, connecting just right. He caved like he'd been hit with a cannonball and went straight down, his arms splayed out, legs in a V-shape, his Samsung springing from his hand and clattering to the ground.

The unmarked police van careened downwards and Harriet ran past me towards Napier.

'Bastard!' she screamed, and before I could do anything, she stamped hard on his balls, once, twice, grinding down with the heel of her shoe like the dot of an exclamation mark.

Napier howled.

When I saw she was about to move to his face, I grabbed her shoulder and pulled her back. She kicked and writhed, possessed with an incredible strength, her aviators toppling off.

'Easy!' I said, holding her, while scanning for the bouncer and Vincent, who'd both fled. 'Cool it, Harriet!'

She breathed hard and fast, but began to calm. After a moment, I let her go.

She looked up. Her face was stark, eyes open wide, like someone had flashed a strobe at her.

'Stay with the police,' I said, and she sped away. Officers spilled from the van. She stayed with them. When I saw she was safe, I ducked down, and started looking for Vincent.

His flashy tracksuit gave him away. He was making for Napier's van, planning on zooming off before the police had the area secure.

Staying low, I went to its front. As he appeared, I punched him with a sharp uppercut to the face: another cracker that would've put most men down, but it felt like all I'd hit was a slab of pebble-dash.

He took a step back. Blood darkened his lips. He pulled the Smith & Wesson from his pocket. With no time to retreat, I stepped in and booted the gun. A loud shot went wide, the sound ricocheting off concrete. He hissed, went to aim again. Before he could, I kicked his shin and he fell to one knee, exposed.

Seeing an opening, I moved in.

Suddenly, a thick forearm was around my neck, squeezing. Vincent grinned as the air left me and I was pulled back. Next thing, my feet parted from the ground. Bells started ringing.

'Vinnie!' I heard the bouncer yell, right next to my ear.

Vincent stood back up. The gun glinted at his side.

'Shoot him!'

'Police!' someone shouted. 'Drop it!'

Vincent didn't drop the gun or shoot me. Instead, he turned, and he bolted.

The bouncer hesitated, and it bought me a second. I elbowed him twice in the gut, the blows loosening his grip enough for me to drive my heel on to his toes and mash down. He screamed. A third elbow and he slackened. I threw him off for the police to deal with.

Stars floated in my vision, and my ears still pinged from the gunshot. I looked around, disorientated.

By now, Hargreaves and other uniformed police had cordoned the area. Two had guns out, and were in combat positions. Harriet was watching from the van, her face a tangle of fear.

Napier was on his feet, staggering like a drunkard towards his van, clutching his balls and bloody nose. I was about to move in on him until something else caught my eye. In the far-left corner of the car park, the flash of a track-top, moving low, heading for the fire exit this time.

'Vincent!' I yelled.

He turned.

Our eyes locked. Something primal passed between us.

'Armed police!' someone yelled.

I sensed the officers take aim. I didn't want them blowing Vincent away, not until I'd had my own go at him for Paddy. I charged forward, not checking blind spots.

Big mistake.

An arcing fist from my right blasted my temple. I hit the ground, tasted dirt and concrete.

Spinning over, there was the bouncer again, looming above, his eyes ablaze. Two uniformed officers lay floored behind him, rubbing their bloody faces.

My ears pounded. I flipped on to my belly to escape his feet, then mounted to a knee. Ignoring the pain and shakiness flooding me after the blow, I feigned right as he dived in with a lumbering stamp. It gave me space to spin round and slam him full on the chin. It felt like punching a garden spade, but something cracked and I knew I had him hurt. He staggered back and I came in hard, two jabs to the kidney and a sweep to the knee. Another kick to the gut and he rolled down. Two more uniforms moved in, this time disabling him with a taser shot to the spine, sending him into a paroxysm of pain.

I could taste blood now, hot and rusty. The energy beneath my skin was caustic, sending my senses into flux.

I looked left, right.

The police were spreading out, taking control of the area. Vincent was gone. Dammit.

But Napier wasn't. He'd do.

I went to him, grabbed his collar and heaved him around to face me. Bloody snot drooled from his nostrils.

'Kasper!' someone shouted. 'Kasper, don't hurt him!'

Napier whimpered. I slammed him into the rear of his van. He grunted.

I let him collapse, lifted him back up, repeated the movement.

'How's it feel, Mick?' I said. 'You afraid yet?'

'Kasper!'

Another slam. He lay in a foetal position, covering his face. Crying.

I stepped back. Immediately, armed officers took my place, grabbing Napier, scooping him up and cuffing him. There was a dent in the bodywork of his van.

I looked around. The bouncer was cuffed and was being frogmarched away by police. One of their cars contained Harriet, cowering down in the backseat. The rest of the team were talking into radios, sticking evidence tape on Napier's van, or massaging bloody lips and cheeks.

Hargreaves strolled past me and came face to face with Napier.

'Ged me my lawyer,' Napier said, his broken nose streaming blood.

'Michael Napier,' Hargreaves said, 'you're under arrest.'

Napier gestured my way. 'Me? Arresd him! He adacked me!'

Ignoring his objections, Hargreaves read him his rights.

Bloody foam appeared between Napier's gold teeth.

'You're dead, Kasper,' he hissed.

'Bye, Mick,' I said, turning my back on him. 'Wear something respectable in court.'

A moment later, Hargreaves was seeing Napier into the police van sweatbox, where he sat alongside the bouncer. The door slammed, the ignition fired, and the van headed off.

Wiping his hand on a tissue, Hargreaves came to me. 'Job well done,' he said.

'Not quite. Where's Vincent Brown?'

'He assaulted an arresting officer.' Hargreaves gestured towards a burly uniform nursing a nasty gash above his eye. 'We'll find him. Don't worry.'

'I told you, the man's dangerous. He's armed.'

'And I'm telling you he's got half the Met after him. He'll be in custody by the end of the day. Trust me.'

'Let me know.'

We watched the van ascend from the car park, followed by the car containing Harriet. Within a minute, they were gone, leaving only me, Hargreaves and two other uniforms. The place seemed unusually quiet.

'Make this stick,' I said. 'If Napier gets out, he'll be gunning for revenge.'

'Don't worry,' Hargreaves said. 'There's enough on tape for warrants to enter his premises. The CPS can't say no, even with the best lawyers and friends in high places. We'll have him charged by tonight.'

I nodded. 'Will his broken nose and swollen balls cause problems?'

Hargreaves gave a dismissive hand sweep. 'Those injuries were sustained resisting arrest.'

I nodded. 'Thanks. What about Harriet?'

'She won't need to testify. And there'll be plain-clothes officers guarding her house until Brown is arrested. I give you my word.'

'Good,' I said. 'She's been through the wringer. Go easy on her, OK?'

Hargreaves said he would, and paused. 'Can I give you a lift somewhere, Kasper?'

I shook my head. 'I fancy being alone.'

He hesitated, and nodded. 'Right then.'

We shook hands. He got into the remaining Fiesta, fired the ignition and drove off to street level.

The car park was quiet. I checked my watch. Six-forty.

All the adrenalin in my system was starting to flush, my heartbeat to temper. I felt strangely subdued.

The plan had worked. Napier had incriminated himself and we'd won the fight. I should've been happy.

But I wasn't.

There weren't any winners in this. It was just degrees of loss.

I buttoned my shirt and began walking up towards street level, whistling the rest of the Dylan tune, and wondering what I was going to do with myself now.

Chapter 29

What I did over the next few days was try to get into good habits, cutting back on the drinking, jogging each morning, training at Savages in the afternoon, keeping busy and out of my head.

I knew I'd have to get another job pretty soon – money was running low, and with Napier in custody and McGovern's burned down, I had too much time on my hands.

But I couldn't muster the energy to go scouting around shops and pubs, handing out my patchy CV and smiling feebly. Instead, I kept myself to myself, waiting.

Since Napier's death threat had arrived with Dr Steiner, I'd tried, somewhat feebly, to persuade her to take another sojourn in Brighton, just until things had simmered down in the city and Vincent Brown was in custody. She refused, of course, cigarette in hand, her expression unyielding, insisting she wouldn't be bullied out of her own home, now or ever, and that I should know better than to make such a request. In her position, I'd probably have done the same.

Instead, she and I spent more time together in the house, where I could keep an eye on things. Lunchtimes, I cooked simple meals someone of my culinary limitations could stretch to – soups, pastas, things like that – and made brief jaunts out to leave Tupperware containers of the food in front of the charred remains of McGovern's. These offerings sat alongside the multitude of cards and flowers others had left. For all I knew, they ended up in the bin or got taken by passers-by. But it was all I could think of to do.

I saw Suzanna again on Thursday afternoon. Like before, she was clad in Paddy's old Crombie, and wore the same bleached, cried-out expression. Spotting me, she wandered over and accepted the tub of food.

I asked how she'd been, and she said, 'OK'; she asked me the same, I said 'OK' back. Then we stood there a while, not saying much.

Things with Diane were equally muted. I left her a couple of messages, and eventually she got back saying she'd been snowed under with work. I could sense the distance in her voice, a hangover from our attempt at intimacy. I blamed myself.

Evenings, Dr Steiner and I ate on the decking in her garden, watching the spring skies darken. I trimmed her bonsai trees, finished a David Attenborough boxset and persevered with my father's allotment in time for the summer heat.

Hargreaves called early Friday morning, confirming Napier had been formally charged with intent to supply Class As. The young detective sergeant was bang on – the recording from the car park meant Napier's plea for bail was refused due to his flight risk. When Mick's Bar was swept, they found schematics for several vacant flats dotted around Hackney and Tower Hamlets. Sniffer dogs found uncut drugs with a street value of at least two million beneath their laminate flooring and plasterwork. Even more incriminating, there were photos and phone messages linking Napier to two high-ranking serving Met officers, confirming he'd been receiving police intel for some time. A feather in the cap for Hargreaves, whose career was poised to do quite well out of this.

All Napier's assets were frozen, the bar impounded and he got remanded in Pentonville, pending trial. The bloke was going down for some decent time.

Hargreaves called again later that same day. This time it was to inform me that a hefty supply of pornographic material showing Tommy with various unidentified older men had also been discovered on Napier's laptop and phone. Additional footage showed Tommy with Napier himself.

Hargreaves seemed to sense my unease at hearing this, and reassured me that, as this evidence was of no benefit to the CPS in pursuing the drug charges, the videos were to be archived and eventually destroyed. Reading between the lines, it was clear what was happening – the young officer was burying the smut. I thanked him.

My mood dipped when he told me Vincent Brown hadn't been apprehended, in spite of several possible sightings. He assured me this was unprecedented, which I didn't doubt, and that it was only a matter of time until he was in custody, which I did. Until then, he said I should keep myself safe. They had plain-clothes surveillance on the Berkowitz house on the off-chance Vincent turned up there. But my role in the case was over. I told him I understood, and we let each other go.

Tommy's funeral was due to take place that weekend. To my surprise, Harriet sent me a text late on Friday saying that Saul and she would be happy to see me there. I broached the subject with Dr Steiner, expecting her to be dismissive, but she insisted it was a good idea, and grudgingly agreed to spend the day with an ex-colleague while I was out.

I hadn't worn a suit since Rosie's funeral. The blazer was snug and smelled of dust and that nameless musty scent that only time and disuse bring. There were creases in the hem and a few scuffs and stains, but with a white shirt and a shave, I think I scrubbed up all right.

It was a humanist service at a small crematorium out near Edgware. The rain from the previous week had finally relented, leaving the spring morning crisp and bright. A few minutes before ten, I was locking my bike to a lamp post and strolling up to the entrance gates to the grounds.

Saul was standing by a sycamore, greeting people. He'd lost even more weight, and the shapeless black suit he wore hung from his long frame like a gown on a hanger. Lost too was his former poise and certainty, replaced by a clumsy woodenness in his movements.

Harriet was standing a few feet to his right. She was wearing her black mac, a black skirt and smart black shoes. Aviators concealed her eyes as usual.

I wanted to stay cautious around Saul, polite but with a boundary, not giving anything away.

Why? I'm not entirely sure.

I guess I was still bothered that he'd been so easily duped by Bob Riding, and that, years later, he still wouldn't acknowledge how that whole episode had bulldozed his family. Something didn't add up. Was he in denial? Or complicit somehow? I'd probably never get to the bottom of it.

But as I wandered over to Saul and took in his stooped shoulders, forlorn expression and the vague, fishy grey colour behind his horn-rimmed glasses, any uncertainty was pushed aside by pity. Here was a broken man, a grieving father, much like me.

'Thanks for coming, Kasper,' he said, offering a hand.

'I appreciate the invite,' I said, and took it.

He was trembling. 'How are you?'

I told him I was fine.

'Have you finished your . . . *investigation*?' He tilted his head. 'About Tommy?'

Harriet tensed.

I waited a moment; then, with caution, said, 'I have.'

'And did you learn anything I should know?'

I hesitated, and saw her shake her head, the slight but unmistakable movement aimed directly at me. She and I both knew there was a great deal I could have said to Saul, but what she'd told me in the hotel room was right: the truth might kill him. And there had been enough killing.

'I learned Tommy loved you two,' I said, and waited for a reaction.

Saul merely blinked. 'Yes,' he said. 'Well, that's good to be reminded of.' He smiled and looked at the crematorium. 'Come,' he said, and guided us in.

It was a simple space. The flagstoned floor was split into two rows with enough benches for maybe a hundred mourners, but there was nothing like that number here: maybe twelve to fifteen people, tops. Plaintive violin music played from speakers in the background. No one spoke.

There were orders of service stacked by the entrance. As Saul and Harriet walked to the front pew, I held back, picked one up and looked ahead.

Tommy's coffin was mounted on a conveyor belt, topped by a framed photo. As I moved up the aisle, I took it in. It showed

Tommy, aged sixteen or thereabouts, wearing pinstripes and a trilby, performing as a gangster on a stage, a fake cigar hanging from his mouth. Leafing through the order of service, I learned the photo came from a production of *Bugsy Malone* he'd acted in during his brief stint at drama school. He looked confident, flamboyant, a little ridiculous too. I liked it.

I took a place in a middle pew on the left of the crematorium. Over the next ten minutes, thirteen others arrived: some were Saul's peers, I assumed, fellow activists and academics judging by accents and mannerisms; others were younger, Tommy's age or thereabouts, friends and acquaintances from a brief life. Among them was Jazz.

He must've been discharged from the psych hospital. His cheeks had some colour back, not spray-tan orange anymore, but real vibrancy. As he took a seat, his biceps and pectorals swelled through a neat charcoal suit.

I caught his eye, gave a nod, and was considering moving back to sit by him; but then the music stopped and we all turned.

Saul stood. With his head bowed, he stood beside the coffin containing his son. He looked at it, and at us; then he spoke.

It was a simple, unpretentious speech. He talked with frankness about the violence of Tommy's death, the cruelty of suicide and his hope that his son had been reunited with the mother he'd loved.

As I listened, I tried to stay present, to think of Tommy, and not allow my mind to reel back to Rosie.

Impossible.

I was transported to that cold late-January day. I'd done my best to write a few words, but when I stood beside my child's coffin, and I looked down at the cluster of schoolfriends, teachers, my ex-wife Carol, and then at the small – *too* small – rectangular box containing Rosie. I couldn't find the strength to speak.

Instead, Carol's withering cries tore through the silence. It's a sound that still echoes in my heart somewhere.

Saul's voice faltered, rose a semitone, and drew me back. He took a moment to compose himself. But he did not crack.

When he finished speaking, there came a heavy quiet. He returned to the front pew and sat next to Harriet. She placed a hand on his. With his other, he removed his glasses and wiped his eyes.

Debussy's *Clair de Lune* came through the speakers: Judith Berkowitz's favourite piece of music, so our orders of service revealed. She used to play it to Tommy during her pregnancy, and to help him sleep as a newborn.

The piano notes spiralled before careening down like droplets of ice; as they did, Tommy's coffin began moving on the conveyor belt, passing an altar, disappearing through a set of mauve curtains. And he was gone.

I found Harriet beneath the sycamore at the gate, smoking.

'All right?' I said.

She glanced at me and looked around. No one from the funeral was in earshot. We could speak freely.

'I'm fine, Kasper,' she said. Her voice was stiff, her manner guarded.

But when she lifted her sunglasses, her eyes painted a different picture.

'Maybe after today, you'll be able to talk to your dad,' I said.

She inhaled smoke, held it down.

'You two need each other more than ever now, Harriet.'

When some of the smoke escaped, she sucked it back, held it longer, and let it trickle from her nose.

'I don't think so,' she said.

'I can help,' I said. 'Just say the word and—'

'No, Kasper.' Her voice was firm. 'I can't do it.'

I waited a moment, and nodded.

'OK,' I said. 'Just be careful. Vincent's still out there.'

'Don't worry. There's plain-clothes police watching the house day and night.'

'Yeah,' I said. 'So I heard.'

There was more to say, and a ton of questions still unanswered, but it would've been pointless to push. The Harriet I'd spoken to in that scuzzy hotel room was gone. This woman was armoured, her protective shutters were up; she and Saul would go home that afternoon and revert back to the denial that had brought them here. And that would be that.

'Take care, Harriet,' I said. 'We got him. Don't forget that.'

Her lips thinned into a smile. 'Bye,' she said, and turned her back.

Saul was by the crematorium entrance, talking with a couple of women. I considered joining him, but held back. The funeral had stirred something in me, and I wasn't in the mood for small talk.

Instead, I wandered over to a handsome oak at the tip of a slope and turned to face the grassy grounds of the cemetery. The Debussy music still lingered in my head. As the light piano keys played out, I leaned on the bark and took in the spring blossom.

The pinks and violets from the cherry trees embraced one another. Coupled with a chilly moisture in the breeze, they created a lilt to the air. In time, autumn would claim their petals. But they weren't to know. All they had was now.

'Kasper?' a voice said behind me.

I turned.

'Good to see you, Jazz,' I said. 'How've you been?'

'Surviving. You?'

'Same.'

'Did you sort things out?'

I shrugged. 'As much as I could.'

'Nice one. Tommy would've been pleased.'

'Yeah,' I said, 'Tommy . . .'

I didn't get to finish. My throat was constricting, and whatever I'd planned to say was lost. Then I heard a groan come from me, and the strength in my legs went. Were it not for the tree I was leaning on, I would've fallen straight to the ground.

'Oh fuck,' I managed.

I tried looking at Jazz, but couldn't focus. Rosie's face was filling my mind, beautiful and consuming, and the sight overwhelmed me with sorrow. It came like a physical pain, scrunching my chest and blurring my eyes with searing tears I never knew I had.

'I'm sorry . . .' I said.

I felt Jazz's strong hands around my shoulders, holding me.

'It's OK,' he said. 'Easy.'

'Christ.' I covered my mouth.

'It's OK,' he repeated, hoisting me back up.

'No,' I said, leaning against him. 'You shouldn't be seeing this.'

'Why? You saw *me* cry.'

That caught me, and my next sob fused with a laugh.

From the corner of my eye I saw someone coming over, a woman who'd been at the funeral.

'Do you need help?' she said. 'I can call someone—'

Jazz shooed her back. 'We're fine,' he said curtly. 'My friend's just a little upset.'

'Friend?' I looked at him blearily.

'Yeah,' Jazz said, his own eyes wet. 'Friend.'

He meant it. I could tell.

'And now,' he said, 'we both need to stop moping and get on with life. Remember that thing you said at the hospital?'

I thought back to that day, Jazz lying in the bed in that bare, sterile room. 'No more feeling sorry for yourself,' I said.

'Exactly.' He grinned. 'It's not a good look for us hard-nuts.'

Chapter 30

Jazz was right. I did need to get on with life. And as I pedalled away from the funeral, with Rosie's face still floating in my consciousness, I could feel a small yet discernible change.

But another part of me knew this wasn't over, not yet. And two nights later, when my phone started vibrating in the small hours, it came as little surprise.

I'd been lost somewhere in a half-sleep. On reflex, I reached out and squinted at the handset.

Number withheld.

'Yeah?' I said.

'Kasper?' It was Harriet's voice.

I sat up, fully awake, pushed the blanket off and swung my legs across the bed. 'What is it?'

'I need you to come, Kasper. Right now. He's going to kill me . . .'

Her voice trailed off. I heard moaning, a rustling sound of movement beneath it.

'Kasper . . .' she said, further away now. She was crying. 'Oh God . . .'

Something gripped at me. This wasn't play-acting — it was real.

'Tell me where you are, Harriet,' I said. 'Come on.'

More static followed, then a harsh clap that made me pull the phone away. Finally, I heard the gravelly voice of Vincent Brown.

'Get yerself to the professor's office,' he said. 'Don't talk to no one. Don't make any calls. Leave your gun. Come quick, or else she dies. Understand, pig-fucker?' He breathed heavily down the receiver, the sound like sandpaper on my ear.

I considered threatening him with the police, but held back. They might get there quick, but not quick enough for him to cancel Harriet's ticket.

'Why're you doing this?' I said, keeping my voice refined.

'Don't stall,' he said.

'Vincent—' I said, but was cut short by a high-pitched cry from Harriet, the sort that only comes from real pain.

'Hear this?' Vincent said. 'Try and pull a fast one, I'll gut your lassie here. If you don't believe me, take a look outside your house at what's left of your friend.'

A horn blared in my head. Dr Steiner!

'Vincent, what have you—'

Before I could speak, he hung up.

Dropping the handset, I hurtled down the stairs, flung open the front door and sprung back at what met me. There, hanging by the gate at the end of Dr Steiner's porch, was Marmite. The cat was impaled on a pole that was shoved into the soil like some kind of totem. Its tip protruded through his shoulders and glistened blackly in the moonlight. The rear of his velvet coat had been flayed and hung loose around his frame like wings. His eyes were open, and his purple tongue flopped like a cut of ham. In the elongating shadows of moonlight, he looked a little like a bat.

'You sick bastard,' I whispered.

Swallowing the taste of bile, I walked to Marmite, pulled the pole from the ground and slid him from it. It was a length of lead piping, sharpened at the tip with cruel precision.

I stood there a moment, trying to think. I'd known Vincent would make a move eventually, and this was a trap, without question. But why take Harriet? And why go to Saul's office?

Calling the police was the right thing to do. I'd tell them to head to Professor Berkowitz's Bloomsbury office with their guns and hostage negotiators and let them handle it. I reached for the phone, but stopped.

I'd started this thing. Tommy's death, Paddy's, now poor Marmite's – I'd had a hand in all of them. And I needed to be the one who ended it.

Keeping the lights off, I went back into the house, hearing Dr Steiner snoring from her bedroom. I fetched a bin bag and put Marmite in it. Then I threw on my clothes and boots and unchained my bike.

The ride to Bloomsbury was quiet, the kind of quiet only people used to the staccato of cities notice. Roads were empty but for a few night buses and cabs, and the pitch-black sky was devoid of stars.

I cycled central along the canal footpaths. Homeless people were pitched in tents or on benches on the wider strips of the causeway. None seem interested in me.

About halfway to Camden, I stopped by a lock, dismounted, and found a couple of heavy stones from the sloping bank.

I put these into the bin bag containing Marmite and tossed it into the black waters.

'Sorry, mate,' I said as the bag puffed out, momentarily outlining the shape of a four-legged thing before the stones tugged him down.

Standing there, I caught sight of my reflection. The outline of my body was vague and shuddering; my eyes were lumps of coal. The image shattered when I chucked in the lead spear. I took a moment, watched the waters calm, the ripples subside, and pedalled off towards town.

I passed St Pancras, the British Library, the Renaissance Hotel, then rode further up towards Friends House and Euston. Empty stares met me from the nocturnal wanderers – alcoholics, addicts, insomniacs. No one spoke.

I was sweating by the time I arrived in the academic district near Gower Street. Looking up, I saw Saul's top-floor office. It could've been any office. There were no lights, no signs of a disturbance.

But they were up there, Vincent and Harriet. Her Skoda was parked obliquely in one of the bays a few feet up on the kerb.

I chained my bike to the railings, mounted the townhouse steps and pressed the button with *Prof B* written on it.

I pressed it again when no one answered. This time, I heard the crackle of breathing.

'Vincent?' I said.

An electric buzzer sounded and the door clicked open.

I was back in the foyer of the social science department that had all the Ps in its name. The first time I'd been here, a hip young receptionist was handing out guest badges, and the place and area held a vibrancy. Tommy had been alive then, too.

Now, it was barren, listless, unnaturally quiet. I allowed my eyes to acclimatise to the cool darkness, the perspiration on my back to chill, and thought about my next move.

Taking the lift up to the top floor would be a bad idea – if Vincent planned on jumping me, then just outside the lift was an obvious spot. I took the stairs.

As I ascended, photo portraits of academic types stared at me from the walls. They were all dressed in ceremonial suits, looking clever and austere. It wasn't long before I passed a headshot of Saul himself, looking younger, vibrant, full of optimism.

A moment later, I reached the fourth floor and stepped into the hall. I crouched slightly, ready to attack.

Saul's office was at the end of the hall, its door ajar. The lights were off, but I could hear movement inside.

The floorboards creaked as I drew close. Peeping through the gap in the door, I saw Harriet. She was kneeling in front of her father's desk. Her eyes were raw from crying. A swelling wept above her temple. Her blouse was ripped at the hem, several buttons missing. Books were spread around her on the floor like rubble.

Her face tightened as I came in, revealing myself.

'Kasper—'

'Where is he, Harriet?' I said.

Her eyes answered, flitting to the left, behind the door.

I nodded.

On cue, Vincent's voice came from the darkness. 'You gonna stand there all night?'

A flick of a switch and harsh light flooded the space.

I squinted. Then I turned.

Vincent was wearing the same Everlast tracksuit from the morning of the sting, now daubed with mud and dirt. Judging by his stubble, the stale reek of his body and the wide, zappy look in his eyes, my guess was he'd been hiding out here for days.

I looked at his hands. The left held a copy of a book called *A History of Sexuality* by Michel Foucault. In the right was his Smith & Wesson revolver.

'Evening, pig-fucker.'

I nodded.

'You alone?'

'That's what you wanted.'

'Close the door.'

I pushed it with a heel, keeping him in sight.

'Lose the coat. Pull up your shirt.'

I did.

'Turn around. Slowly.'

I did that too.

Satisfied I was unarmed, he gestured inside with the gun. 'Move.'

I stepped beside Harriet.

Vincent stood in front of us, blocking the door with his thick frame. He pointed the gun at my face.

'Any tricks, you're dead. Understand?'

'You killed my landlady's cat,' I said.

That got a smirk. 'Grabbing kitties is a speciality of mine,' he said. 'Grabbing this one was a little trickier.' He aimed the gun at Harriet, then back at me. 'There's police guards outside her house, see. I had to bide my time, wait until she left for her pretend City job. Right, bitch?'

Harriet gave a whimper and said, 'Kasper. Please—'

'Don't, Harriet,' I said. 'Let me speak to him.'

Vincent chuckled.

I considered him closely, assessing the risk. He looked crazier than before, his eyes crackling with rage. The gun was the main problem, but even if I could disarm him, I had no doubt he'd fight until one of us was dead.

'OK, Vincent,' I said. 'You've got us. Why're we here?'

'I need to talk,' he said. 'This seemed a nice quiet spot.'

'So we're talking. What about?'

'Be patient,' he said.

'What for?' I said.

'We're not all here yet.' He discarded the Foucault book and picked up another from the floor, skimming through its pages before tossing it with the others. 'How's your old man make sense of this shite, Harriet?'

'They're academic books,' I said. 'No pictures.'

'You takin' the piss?' he said, and aimed the gun at me.

'Whoa,' I said, and for a second I thought that was it. Normally, I could predict when someone was about to go for me – but there was something raw and unpredictable to Vincent. 'My apologies,' I said.

Then he laughed. It was a rough, gassy laugh, and gave off a smell like dead fish. 'Don't get cocky, boy.'

'Let Harriet go,' I said. 'Have me. You won't get anything from hurting her.'

'You might be right. But it'll make me feel a bit better.' He paused, like an idea had just popped into his head. 'So will this,' he said, and moved in again.

I tensed, leaned forward to save my nose and eyes. The butt of the gun slammed down, the impact landing with a crunch on the thick of my temple, making my vision explode. Both legs turned to rubber.

'That's for Mick,' I heard him say as I lay on the ground.

First numbness, then scorching pain and a warm stickiness oozing from my head. I tried looking and there were two Vincents, both glaring down with the same crazy grin.

'Mick was good to me,' he said. 'Made me one of his own. I was happy. And now it's over.' His voice was wavering.

Through the haze, I saw his teeth were gritted, eyes fizzing. I think he was close to crying.

'Vincent,' I said, trying to keep my voice measured, 'we can work something out—'

'Shut it!' he said. 'Tie him up, Harriet. Do it.' He reached into his pocket, pulled out a thick plastic zip tie. 'Go on, just like I showed you.' He chucked it on to the rug a few inches from my feet.

Harriet stood and picked it up. She clambered behind me. Vincent kept the gun on me the entire time. I felt her hands attach the cords, weaving them around my wrists, then locking them together.

'Make it tight,' Vincent said. 'Show me.'

'OK, OK . . .' she said.

He came round to inspect, the gun always there, ready. I winced as he pulled the zip tighter. Within seconds, the blood flow was restricted in my hands and my fingers were tingling.

'Good,' he said.

Now, I was defenceless, on my knees. I shook my body like a wet dog, the movement raining specks of blood on to the rug from the blow to my head.

Satisfied, Vincent wandered to the desk and stood in front of the window. He parted the curtains, peered out and grinned.

'Daddy's here, Harriet,' he said. 'Let's get the party started.'

Through the shock, my focus sharpened. I suddenly had a sense of where this was going.

'No,' I said. 'Vincent, you don't need to do this.'

'It's like you said the day you came to threaten Mick at his bar.' He winked at me. 'Oh, but I do.'

Seconds later, we all heard the ping of the lift doors, the echo of feet galloping up the corridor and a familiar voice outside.

'Harry? Are you in there?'

I looked at Harriet.

Vincent grinned and walked to the door, the gun pointing head height.

'Shit,' I said as Saul Berkowitz entered his office, saw the gun, and froze.

Chapter 31

Before Saul could speak, Vincent had the gun an inch from his temple.

'Don't fucking move,' he said.

Saul's whole body stiffened. He grunted, but he did not recoil.

Vincent grabbed his blazer collar, tugged him into the office and pushed him towards Harriet and me by the desk.

'Stay put,' he said. 'Try anything, I'll kill you.'

I was hunched a few feet to Saul's right, Harriet to his left. Blood was dripping from my forehead, sticking my eyelids together. I had to keep blinking to see.

'What the—' Saul said, stepping forwards. He was cut short by a backhanded slap from Vincent across his cheek that lopsided his glasses.

'I said, don't move!'

With shaking hands, Saul repositioned the glasses. He looked at Harriet, stepped to her.

'You've hurt my daughter.' He cradled her face, inspecting the cuts.

'There's plenty more where that came from if you don't do what I say, *professor*.'

Harriet whined. Her breathing came harsh and fast.

'Easy, Harry,' Saul said. He looked at me, then back at Vincent. 'Who are you?'

'Don't worry about who I am. Worry about what I'll do.'

'Just tell me what you want, and go in peace.'

'Go in peace?' Vincent said, mockingly. He wiped his nose on his palm and the palm on the wall. 'You may not be a violent man, prof. But I am. I like hurting people. I'll hurt you if you don't give me what I want. Take a guess what that is?'

'Money?'

'Figures, you're as smart as you look.'

Saul looked more bewildered than afraid. Removing a cracked wallet from his trousers, he offered it to Vincent. 'Take whatever's in there. But first, put that down.'

'Saul,' I said.

He turned to me, eyes like iron.

'He's not leaving. Put that away.'

'He's right, prof,' Vincent said. 'I'm not some mugger nicking purses off grannies. This goes a little deeper. I've got a score to settle with that man an' your daughter. Right, Harriet?'

Saul turned to her. 'Harry?' he said. 'What does he mean?'

'Dad. I'm sorry . . .' She couldn't finish.

I knew this had to come out; there was no turning back now. 'Saul, listen,' I said. 'Harriet had a drug debt to a man called Napier. He ran a pick-up bar where Tommy hung out. She subbed a load of cocaine from Napier, intending to sell it to clear off some of the debt your wife racked up. But Tommy found the stash of drugs. He panicked, thought Harriet was going the same way as his mum, and destroyed the lot.

Then Harriet told Tommy she was in trouble and why, and he realised whose drugs they were. So, he decided to try and help her.'

Saul was expressionless. There was nothing in his face, no sense that ideas flowed beneath its surface.

Except for his eyes – as what I'd said sunk in, they sharpened to bullet points.

'So what happened?' he said. 'What exactly *did* Tommy do to help?'

'He started selling himself and giving the money to Harriet,' I said. 'But when a few of his tricks got funny and refused to pay, Napier devised this honeytrap scheme, filming rich married men with Tommy, then getting Harriet to use the videos for blackmail. It worked for a while, until Tommy found it too much. That's when his problems really started showing. And then I came on the scene.' I paused, taking air. 'Tommy wanted to tell me about all this. He came close. But he couldn't. He was scared of putting you all at risk.'

Saul shook his head. 'No,' he said. 'No, no, this is wrong.'

'Dad,' Harriet said, 'please—'

'Shh!' Saul said, and made a cutting gesture with his hand. His eyes were back on me. 'So where's this Napier now?'

'Out of business,' I said. 'Last week, we nabbed him in a police sting. He's behind bars. This man here used to work for him.' I gestured at Vincent with a nod.

Saul's mouth opened, then closed.

'Dad?' Harriet said.

'Is this true, Harry?' He spoke without looking at her.

'I was trying to help the family. Mum left so much debt—'

'What about your job?'

'I lost it.'

'How?'

'I got sacked.'

'When?' Saul said, aghast.

'Last year.'

'Last year! Why didn't you tell me?'

'I wanted to handle it myself . . .' She reached for Saul's hand. When he butted her away, she fell silent.

'You should've said something.' He spoke quietly, but his words simmered with anger.

'Come on, Dad. How could I? Everything would've come out if I had. You've been living in a bubble for years, unable to face the truth.'

'Unable!' he shouted. 'I did everything I could!'

She shook her head. 'I'm sorry . . .'

I saw something in Saul's eyes that I hadn't seen before. Rage.

Harriet stared emptily.

'Tommy wanted to help, Saul,' I said. 'He felt guilty for flushing the drugs, and indebted to Harriet.'

Saul turned back to me. 'Why was he indebted to Harry?'

'Because *she* told the truth about Bob Riding, the abuse.'

The look Saul gave almost pushed me back with its force. 'Don't mention that man's name in this office.'

Vincent cackled.

Saul shook his head. 'So that's how Tommy helped?' he said, to all of us. 'By letting himself be meat-marketed?'

'Aye,' Vincent said. 'It was a nice little earner, too, right up until your daft boy got funny ideas and squashed himself under that train.'

A surge of emotion seemed to rock Saul. He reached for the desk, planting his hand between the paperweight and the framed photo of his wife and children. There was something unravelling in him, tearing through the foundations of his veneer.

Vincent stepped forward. 'So, prof,' he said, 'now you know the truth. You've lost your son. I've lost my boss. I need cash. And I'm not the kind of man who can go down the job centre to sign on.'

'I've already told you,' Saul said through his teeth, 'whatever I have is yours.' He removed his glasses and rubbed his eyes.

'That's generous, but I need more than a few bits of loose change.'

'Haven't you been listening? We don't have much money.'

'Not quite true.'

Saul looked up. 'Meaning?'

'Tommy's money.'

'What?'

'Harriet told me about the mum's life insurance. Quite a bit of cash, so I gather. Now Tommy's gone, that money could use a new home.'

Slowly, assiduously, Saul said, 'I've just laid Tommy to rest. That money's in a trust fund. I can't just go to a cashpoint and withdraw it.'

'Aye,' Vincent said, tapping the gun against his thigh, 'but you could pull some strings. Make a few calls. Right?'

Silence followed.

'And what if I say no?'

'Then I'll shoot you dead.'

'Do that, and you'll leave empty-handed.'

Vincent hesitated. He looked at the gun, and pointed it back at my face. The black tip filled my vision once more.

'All right, then I'll kill this wanker right here, and leave his blood and DNA on your clever wee books. Police will think you done it. Picture it. Ex-copper who chatted up your son, found with his brains splattered in your office. That's murder, mate. Bye bye, Harriet. Bye bye, professor.'

The barrel tip dashed across my temple.

'Enough, Vincent—' I said.

'I thought I told you to shut it!' he said, and caught me with the butt again, this time totally off-guard, a cruel hook to the right cheek.

I hit the floor, my whole body wrenching. An atonal screech filled my ears and my wrists strained against the zip tie. Twisting my torso, I forced myself back up to my knees. The office was spinning.

'No!' Saul said. 'You're lying. None of this is true!'

'Need proof, do you?'

'Proof? What are you talking about?'

Vincent shook his head. He unzipped his tracksuit pocket and pulled out a Samsung smartphone. I recognised it immediately. It was Napier's.

Saul's Adam's apple distended, rising and falling as he swallowed. 'What is this?'

'Quiet,' Vincent said, and pushed buttons on the screen before holding it aloft. 'Mick dropped his phone in the car park. Lucky for me, I grabbed it before the police could.' He was grinning again, enjoying himself.

Muffled voices emitted from the phone, and for a moment, I didn't know what we were seeing. Then I heard the pleas from Tommy and Harriet's shouting, and understood.

It was the video Napier had shown me, filmed a few hours before Tommy took himself to the underground station and threw himself in front of Emmanuel's train.

'No, Vincent,' I said. 'Don't do this. There's no point . . .'

But I was powerless.

'Watch, prof,' Vincent said. 'Watch and learn.'

I couldn't bear it a second time, but even with my eyes shut, the sound was enough. Tommy's cries tore into the office and everything spilled out – Uncle Bob, their drug-addled mother, Tommy's misguided attempts to help Harriet, all the years of pain and trauma kept buried; lastly, Tommy confessing to stealing the cocaine from her car, and the thwack of her slapping him again and again.

My pain fizzled into anger. What if I could launch an attack on Vincent? From this range, charging low with a well-placed bite, I could reach his neck and sever some of his important pipes before he shot me.

Then what? Bleed out on the carpet, and leave Saul and Harriet to face the consequences?

No. If I was to strike, I needed to be certain.

In the video, Tommy was telling Harriet what he needed to do. We all knew what that meant. Then he left her alone in that room. A few more seconds, and it ended.

I looked at Saul. He was rigid. A film had fallen over his eyes.

But when he spoke, there was a change. Any fear had drained from his voice.

'You're a monster,' he said to a smiling Vincent. 'And my family have dealt with monsters before.'

Harriet collapsed on to her knees, covering her face. Saul ignored her.

'And I won't give in to your demands. Now get out of my office.'

Vincent's smile fell apart. He dropped the smartphone, grabbed a handful of Harriet's hair and wrenched her up.

'Tell your dad to pay me,' he growled. 'Do it, bitch!'

'Dad!'

'I want my money!' he pointed the gun at Saul, leaving an opening.

Something snapped.

I drove forward. Shock registered on Vincent's face, a shock that helped me get through his hands to sink my teeth into his neck.

Hot citric blood, a stench of testosterone, the rank taste of sweat and stubbly skin. He dropped Harriet and fought with the strength of a drowning man as I parried and bit deeper.

I had him hurt, but his pain had sparked a cataclysmic fury, and suddenly he was lifting me from the floor. Up and over he threw me, and I landed hard on Saul's desk, the impact cracking something in my shoulder. Nerves screamed beneath the skin. My world became a flash of electric pain and I fell to the ground.

I tried to get up again, but nothing was working, everything shook.

'Dad!' Harriet said. 'Dad, stop him!'

Above me was the shape of Vincent. He was trembling. Blood seeped from his neck.

I tried speaking, but my words weren't coming out. I couldn't even push myself up on to my knees. All I could do was stare.

Slowly, Vincent raised the gun and pointed it at my face.

'Time to die, Kasper,' he said.

So this is how it ends, I thought. I closed my eyes.

But instead of a shot, there was a dry thud.

I looked.

Vincent was standing. But only just.

He was bent double, the gun hanging precariously from

his right hand, the left clutching his scalp. A syrupy patch was growing between the fingers. Blood.

Behind him, Saul was holding the engraved paperweight from his desk, his fingers splayed around its surface like it was a rugby ball. He raised it above his head and smashed it into the base of Vincent's skull a second time.

'Don't, Saul . . .' I managed, but something had already detached in his eyes, and in that moment, I saw someone else standing in front of me. This man had taken life before.

The third blow was devastating, like a breezeblock to a flowerpot. The desk cascaded under Vincent's collapsing body and his gun clattered to the floor.

Saul kneeled down. He kept hammering the paperweight, up then down.

I watched as he descended into the realms of violence few men know, and I realised then – too late – how I'd misjudged him. He wasn't blind or a sap: he was a father in pain, a father who'd failed, and a father who'd do anything to assuage his guilt.

When the sight became too much I turned away. The sound was enough. Wet smashes and animal grunts echoed around the room. Harriet tried shouting something, but it was lost.

I couldn't tell how long it went on for. Eventually, the intervals between blows grew wider, until they stopped completely. All that was left was Saul's heaving breaths and Harriet's sobbing.

Chapter 32

I opened my eyes and saw nothing. Something felt very wrong.

Rolling over, I arced my chin down, and realised what it was. My right collarbone looked like it was broken. It hurt like hell.

As I propped myself up on to one knee, the floor became a swirling mass of shapes. My eyelids were sticking again. I forced myself to focus.

Saul was standing to the right of his upturned desk. His legs were shoulder-width apart, bent slightly. His hands were red, clawing thin air, and blood covered his blazer, shirt, trousers and shoes.

Harriet was crouched by the desk, hugging her knees, trembling. Her eyes and mouth formed a trio of black circles.

They were both staring at the same thing – the body lying on the Persian rug.

Vincent was sprawled on his back, one hand over his chest, the other by his side. Blood gullied from his skull, colouring his cheeks and brow, his hair and ears, even his eyes. His lips were parted and stretched thin, a grotesque death mask, and the teeth that jutted up in his mouth were red tombstones.

The sight turned something. My guts began to expunge, my mouth to fill, and I vomited bile in three loud hacks. I saw Saul come to my aid. Then he hesitated, reeling back as he registered the blood on his hands.

He looked at Harriet. 'Help him,' he said. 'Untie his wrists.'

She got on to her knees and began crawling towards me, fishing out a pair of scissors from the desk on the way. I felt her fumbling, trying to cut though the plastic. Finally, my hands fell free. Pain screeched through my right side, my bust collarbone its epicentre. I dashed forward, resting my left hand on the upturned desk.

'Kasper!' Saul said. 'You need an ambulance.'

'No,' I said through gritted teeth, 'just give me your belt for now.'

He removed the canvas belt from his chinos, and I bound it around my shoulder in a makeshift sling. 'Hold this,' I said, giving him one end, bracing as I pulled the other taut.

The pain peaked and I ground my teeth together, panting through it. Slowly, it began to ebb. I made a tight knot and bound it; then I looked at Saul.

'What have I done?' he said, and held up his hands.

'What any decent man would've,' I said.

He reached into his breast pocket, came out with a handkerchief and began scrubbing his fingers frantically.

'Is he dead?' Harriet said.

'He's dead,' I said.

'I killed him,' Saul said.

Harriet stood back. 'Dad?'

He kept on with the handkerchief.

'What happens now?'

'Call the police.'

'Dad, please—'

'If you won't, then I'll do it.' He dropped the handkerchief and pulled out an ancient Nokia from his chinos.

'It was self-defence—'

'No, it wasn't, Harry.' His voice had gained some composure. 'I wanted him to die.'

'Just like you wanted Bob Riding to die?' I said.

Saul nodded.

A silence fell in the office.

Harriet's sharp intake of breath disrupted it. I glanced at her. She looked more puzzled than shocked.

'Your father killed Bob,' I told her, and then turned to Saul. 'Didn't you?'

'Yes,' he said, 'I did.'

'But I thought . . .' Harriet said. 'We thought—'

'You and Tommy thought your mother murdered Bob, because I let you think that. I'm a coward.'

She stared.

'Judith finally traced him to California. She told me where he was, and I flew out. I pretended I'd gone to a two-day conference. Nobody doubted it. I went to the address and waited until dark. He came out and went to unlock a hire car. I went at him with a hammer, Harry. I lost count of the number of times I hit him. Then I threw his body from a tall cliff and left him on the rock face. And I'd do it again.' He looked at his daughter. 'Our family was poisoned by that man. Tonight, it ends. I must turn myself in and accept the blame for the pain I've caused.'

Harriet turned her gaze back to Vincent's corpse. 'But he would've hurt us. Just like Bob did.'

'That's not the point, Harry. No one deserves what I did.'

'He did,' I said.

Saul turned to me.

'I only wish *I'd* killed him,' I said.

'Don't say that, Kasper.'

'But it's true. He'd have rinsed you for everything he could get. Call the police now, chances are you'll get sent away for doing society a service.'

'Please, Dad,' Harriet said. 'I need you . . .'

He was staring at his phone. 'I don't know,' he said. 'I don't know . . .'

Harriet glanced at me. 'Can you help us, Kasper?'

I wasn't sure. We had the small problem of a stiffening corpse to get rid of, and not a lot of time in which to do it.

Several beats passed. Then an idea landed.

'There might be a way,' I said. 'But we need to be quick.'

The dialling tone sounded. Three rings and Emmanuel answered, sounding awake.

'Kasper. Hey, man.'

'Can't sleep, Mani?'

'You know how it is.'

I heard a murmur, a woman saying something in the background.

'You ready to do good on that offer you made?' I said.

'Wait a sec,' he said, a subtle change to his voice. There was a rustle of fabric, words exchanged with the woman, then footsteps on floorboards and a door opening and closing. 'Right,' he said. 'What's up?'

'It's big. And I don't want you to know the full story. The less I tell you, the better. But I need you to know that if you do this thing, it'll help Tommy's family.'

The shock from my injuries was beginning to take effect. I was shivery, my head was a wreck, and I had to focus hard to keep things from crumbling.

'OK,' Emmanuel said. 'I'm listening.'

I began. Saul and Harriet merely stared. But as I went through my plan with Emmanuel, their eyes expanded in unison.

When I'd finished, Emmanuel gave several loud swallows, and coughed sharply. For a second, I thought I'd lost him, that this was a mistake.

'You're saying this'll help out that boy's family?' he said.

'Yeah.'

'You sure, Kasper?'

'Yeah.'

'All right, I'll do it.'

'Good,' I said. 'Then here's what I need.'

Five minutes later, we were loading Vincent's body diagonally into Harriet's Skoda.

The gun, Napier's phone, and everything else incriminating from the office went into the boot. I slammed it shut and stood beside Saul.

Fresh air chilled the sweat on my face. The makeshift sling was helping with the pain a little, but a cold was seeping inwards, and what little I could see was punctuated with puffy floaters. A couple more hours, I was passing out.

'First bit done,' I said, catching my breath.

'I don't know if I can do this, Kasper.'

I turned to him. 'There're men out there who've done plenty worse, Saul. They're getting on with things just fine.'

He looked away. 'When did you guess? That it was me who killed Bob. Not Judith.'

'I started wondering when Harriet said how you'd shut yourself off from it all. You're a smart man. It didn't seem possible that you were that blinkered. I guessed you had something to hide. Then when I saw what you were capable of tonight, it became obvious what that thing was.'

Saul went back to looking at his hands. They were still marred with coppery-red stains. From somewhere close came the rumbling hydraulics of bin vans.

'Judith's anger came outward, in destructive fury. Mine was concealed, and burned like a cancer. But we were both inconsolable, suffering with rage. A man posturing as a friend hurt our children. Can you imagine it? She told me she'd tracked him down, but was too weak to go herself. I had no choice but to take her place and do what was needed.'

Slowly, he turned and looked at the car. I followed his gaze. Harriet was in the driving seat, her face hooded behind her aviators.

'Harry is Bob's daughter,' he said.

The breath caught in my throat. 'What?'

He nodded. 'I raised her as my own. But unconsciously, I treated her differently. I was always harder, expecting that bit more. She's inherited Bob's strength, his cunning. I suspect that's why Judith asked her to resolve the debts, and not me. She knew Harry possessed the right set of skills.'

'Does Harriet know?' I said.

'Judith and I never told her. But deep down, I'm sure she's guessed. I suspect that's why she went to such lengths to keep all this from spilling out. Her own biological father sexually abused her – it's so awful. The truth is sometimes too awful to say aloud, isn't it?'

In my dazed state, it took me a while to process this. But

when I looked at Harriet again, I could see it: the same sharp chin, pale complexion and deep-set eyes as the man called Uncle Bob whose photo I'd found under Tommy's bed.

'She's a tough young woman,' I said. 'She's made mistakes, but you should be proud of her.'

'Yes,' Saul said. 'You're right.'

'What about Tommy? Was he Bob's child too?'

'Oh no,' Saul said, looking at me. 'Tommy was mine. Can't you tell? He and I are alike. We may come across as confident. But in truth, we're dependent. Needy. And weak.'

'Tommy wasn't weak,' I said. 'Neither are you.'

'Oh, I am. I've never been able to accept the truth, not until the damage has been done. After I killed Bob, and Judith passed, I should've sold the house, moved Tommy and Harry away from those wretched memories, and got us all into some family therapy programme. But to do that would be like an admission of my failures to protect them. So we stayed. I told people my wife died of cancer, and I retreated into work, buried in phoney self-righteousness. It was all to convince myself that I wasn't a disgraceful father and a cold-blooded killer. Yet under my nose, Harry got involved in all this mess. And Tommy . . .' He trailed off.

I flinched at a car horn, a siren, the hum of traffic. The clock was ticking, and we hadn't long.

Saul seemed oblivious. He looked back at me and gave a plaintive smile. 'Remember when we first met? Up there in that office, and I asked you to help Tommy?'

'Yes.'

'I think a part of me hoped you'd dig all this up. It needed to come out, the lies and denial, and I sensed a man like you – strong and uncompromised – was the kind to do it.'

'I'm plenty compromised,' I said, 'but I thought that's what you wanted, in the end.'

'I just never realised what it would cost me.'

'You've made your fair share of mistakes, Saul, but when it came to it, you did what you needed to do, and punished the men who hurt your kids. I just wish I'd had someone to go after for my daughter.'

He cocked his head. 'Daughter? You told me you had no children.'

'I haven't. Not anymore.'

In as few words as possible, I told him.

'Tommy found out about Rosie and copied her suicide. I think he wanted all this to come out too, and knew because of my past that I'd keep at it till the end.'

'My God,' Saul said.

'I'm sorry. I should've told you all this the day he died, but I didn't. I guess I was afraid. If anyone's been weak or held things back, it's me.'

Afterwards, there came the inevitable silence.

In that moment, I knew I was looking at a man like me, burdened with an invisible wound. Over time, it would internalise and harden, but it would never heal; and it would be with him until his final days, haunting his dreams, infecting his mind when he was awake.

'I suppose we have something in common, then,' Saul said. 'Don't we, Kasper?'

'Yes,' I said.

'It's unnatural, isn't it? Parents like us, outliving our kids.'

When sober, my father had been a man of few words, which made those he did say all the more resonant. He once told me, if in doubt, it was best to say nothing.

So that's what I did.

The floaters were filling my vision, and my hands were trembling. We needed to act pronto, otherwise I mightn't have the strength to do what we had to.

I made eye contact with Harriet in the car. She nodded.

I looked at Saul. He nodded too.

'Come on,' I said. 'Let's finish this.'

Chapter 33

It took till the weekend for Diane to catch up with me, as I knew she eventually would.

I was padding down the banks of my father's allotment. The mid-afternoon sunlight was hidden behind a dense hovering cloud, as if uncertain where it wanted to go. From behind the recreation grounds, Paradise Towers Estate loomed, casting a shadow over the wet, uneven soil.

'Hey, Kas?'

I turned, saw her strolling up the grassy verge, and liked what I saw. I pushed the shovel into the earth and rested my good arm on the hilt.

She was dressed off-duty – silk blouse, denim coat, tight blue jeans cut close around her hips. On her feet were blue All-Stars, and on her face just the right amount of make-up. She was carrying a square cardboard box in both hands. Several holes were in the lid.

'Your landlady Dr Steiner told me you'd be here. You're a hard man to find.'

She came up close, stopped, rested the box on the soil and put a hand to my swollen face, touching the temple where the gash had scabbed over. Then she looked down at my right arm, held perpendicular to my chest in a foam sling.

'Battle scars?'

I nodded.

'If I asked what happened, would you tell me?'

'Best not to know,' I answered.

Smiling, she stood on tiptoe and kissed my cheek. She smelled of perfume and coconut cream and her breath was warm and sweet.

'Why you been avoiding my calls, big man?'

I looked back at the earth. 'I didn't want to freak you out with how I look.'

'I've seen you worse. That the only reason?'

I shrugged. 'I suppose I needed to be alone for a while. I'm sorry.'

'Don't be sorry. Aren't we past apologies?'

'You're right.'

'Will you be OK?'

'My collarbone and nose are bust. Got stitches in my shoulder and cheek. No permanent damage, though.'

She nodded. 'I was worried.'

'Thanks for worrying.'

From the cardboard box came a high-pitched yelp, followed by a scrambling noise like small feet.

'I'm guessing that's not a cake in there?'

'Nah,' she said. '*That's* a surprise.'

Behind her, the sky was darkening. Dusk clouds had begun to join at the horizon.

'Tell me what happened, Kas,' she said. 'I'm asking you to.'

I looked away. 'I can't, Diane. I'm not police anymore, but you are. It's best you don't hear it.'

'I thought you'd come up with some crap like that. I'm pretty pissed off with you.'

The box shook again. This time, a high bark came from within it that caused a crow to caw from one of the hawthorns nearby.

'OK,' Diane said. 'Let me tell you what *I* know. Five days back, transport police reported a body on the tracks. It was a mess. Unidentifiable. Middle-aged male found at Upper Holloway, of all places. Presumed suicide. Presumed because there's no CCTV, so no way to tell what happened. Weird, eh? Of all the places to do it, the guy chose a spot without cameras. All we've got is the train driver's account. Trouble is, this driver never realised he hit anything. So we've got sod-all but a mashed-up corpse.'

My pulse was beating, and the hairs on my neck had started to bristle. Diane was studying me with the fixed unblinking eyes of the shrewd police investigator. There was no bullshitting her.

'Why're you telling me this?' I said. I knew the answer, but also that we had to go through the motions.

'I'm getting to that. See, the autopsy reports came back day before yesterday. Fingerprints revealed this dead duck was none other than your man, Vincent Brown.'

'Oh. Him.'

'Yeah. Him. Looks like poor Vinnie got overcome with grief and put his head under a train. Strange, don't you think? I didn't have him down as the suicidal type. How about you?'

The corners of her mouth curved upward. It wasn't a smile, more the recognition of something implicit.

Not waiting for an answer, she said, 'Stranger still is what I learned when I tried speaking to the train driver. See, I wasn't happy with this suicide story. So I called him this morning. Guess what? He's none other than your other man, Emmanuel Meads. Recognise the name? Course you do. He's the driver of the train that killed Tommy Berkowitz. The same guy who'd been haranguing me for your number. Doesn't that seem an incredible coincidence?'

'Incredible,' I said.

Now she was smiling, but her eyes weren't. 'Cut the crap, big man,' she said. 'This has you written all over it.'

I let the shovel fall to the banks and my arm hang easy. 'What do you want me to say, Diane?'

She breathed noisily through her nose. 'I could lose my job,' she said. 'I could go to prison if it came out I buried this.'

'But you're not burying anything. That's the whole point. As far as you're aware, it's another suicide. Open-shut, right?'

'Fuck you,' she said, and turned her face to profile. A tear rolled down her cheek and plopped to the soil. She rubbed her eyes with the balls of her hands. 'You know, I thought it might've worked out between us this time. Stupid, right? I thought maybe enough time might've passed for us to give things another go.'

I changed footing. The ground beneath my boots squelched. 'I wish it were true, Diane,' I said. 'Christ, I do.'

An insistent breeze was catching the awning of the hut, making it rattle. Rain was coming again, the first droplets light on my nose and brow.

Carefully, I reached for Diane, pulling her under the shelter with me. I wiped away her tears.

'Don't cry, baby,' I said.

She moved close and we hugged. Time stood still and all we had was each other, the closeness of our bodies, the shared knowledge that the passing of time wasn't enough.

I've no idea how long we stayed this way, but by the time we let each other go, a steady drizzle had settled in.

Stepping back, looking up, she said, 'You think we can still be friends?'

'Always.'

She gave another smile. 'OK then.'

Bending down, she lifted the box and offered it to me.

'What've we here?'

'A gift.' She opened the lid. 'Murphy gave birth. Thought you could give this little one to Dr Steiner. She mentioned something about losing her cat, and I haven't got the space.'

I peered inside. Scrunched up in a foetal curl there was a scrawny dark-grey pup. Its skin was flaccid, limbs and ears flopping all over the place. As it wriggled, I saw it was a boy. He seemed to sense the change in light and air and scrambled upwards in the box, panting and alert. His eyes were round, a heavy brown.

'Easy, boy,' Diane said.

I gave the puppy my hand. He sniffed the skin and licked a knuckle with a hot, rough tongue. Carefully I picked him up, balancing him in my palm.

'Thank you, Diane,' I said. 'He's a champ.'

'He's got spirit all right.'

'Just how Dr Steiner likes them.'

I returned him to the box and Diane closed it and placed it by my feet.

'He likes this, and this,' she said, handing me a carton of milk and a squeaky rubber cat from her bag. 'Let me know what you call him?'

I thought for a minute. 'How about Tommy?'

Diane smiled. 'Nice.'

She pulled an umbrella from her shoulder bag and started back along the muddy banks to the exit gate. Then she stopped and turned back. I hadn't moved.

'So how's the train driver?' she called. 'You mates with this Emmanuel, or what?'

'He's all right,' I said. 'We're going for a pint next week.'

'Good,' she said. The gap in her top front teeth showed as she smiled. 'He's lucky to know you.'

Diane walked to the gates and left the way she'd come.

I stayed with her as long as I could, and when she was out of sight, I looked at the soil. Already, her tears were long absorbed. No traces.

The only sound was the patter of rain, until my thoughts were interrupted by another yelp from the box. Crouching, I withdrew the pup. He sniffed the damp air. Sitting on a stool in the doorway of the hut, with him placed in my lap, I pulled out the milk, poured some into a bowl I dug out, and he sipped it.

'Good boy,' I said.

After he'd finished, I withdrew a brown envelope from my pocket with my good hand. It had arrived two days back. I'd kept it on me ever since.

Inside were half a dozen photos of Tommy Berkowitz at different ages, from a baby up until his final year, like the ones I'd found in the shoebox under his wardrobe. Along with these, there was a cheque for five thousand pounds and a handwritten note from Saul.

I read it, hearing his voice in my head:

Kasper,
   We're indebted to you.
   Changes are to come. I'm retiring from academia and am

selling the house. After clearing Judith's debts, I plan to
volunteer in South America on a humanitarian project. It's
time to move on. Harriet is coming with me. She sends her
regards.

Please accept this money, which comes from Tommy's trust
fund. He'd have wanted you to have it, I'm sure.

Also, I thought you might like a few memories of him.
S

He was right about that. I did.

A little after five, I left the allotment and strolled through the
rain towards the High Road. I've always thought London looks
better in the rain than at any other time. It seems to wash
away the grime, levels the poverty with the pretence, reawakens
the trees and parks with a silky vibrancy, and makes the
concrete slabs, the cladding, skips, scaffolding, cracked paving
and fly-tipped litter shimmer and, from certain angles, become
something close to beautiful.

I had my North Face zipped to my chin, the hood over
my head. Tommy the pup was under my left arm, ensconced
within his box. As soon as I turned the corner that led to
Savages Boxing Club, I spotted Jazz hovering outside the
chipped wooden doors.

He was early. A hoody and sweatpants clung to his muscular
frame; nerves were etched into his expression.

I gave a whistle. He looked round, waved.

Strolling up, I said, 'Good to see you,' and, ignoring his
offer of a handshake, I gave him the box to hold.

'What happened to you?' he said, eyeing my sling and face
and considering the vibrating box, all with equal disdain.

'If I told you, Jazz,' I said, 'then I'd have to kill you.'

He laughed uncertainly. A high bark came from his cargo.

'You like dogs?'

He shrugged.

'How're you feeling?'

'Better.'

'Me too,' I said, and pushed open the doors.

Inside, the smells of chalk and sweat met us, along with the sound of gloves smacking bags. Savages stayed open late most evenings, and I had an arrangement with management to train with the kids from the flats who'd be out causing mischief otherwise.

But tonight the rain seemed to have kept most of them away. Apart from a couple of burly lads on the free weights, the only boxer there was a lean, mixed-race nineteen-year-old standing by the heavy bag. His face was beaded with sweat, defined by the same angular nose and commanding eyes his father had borne at his age.

'S'up, Kas,' Ricky said, wandering over. 'This the boy you were talkin' about?'

I nodded. 'Ricky, meet Jazz. You two are sparring tonight.'

They considered each other in that cautionary way young men do. But ten minutes later, they'd loosened up, and I was by the ropes shouting like Burgess Meredith as Ricky took it easy on an over-zealous Jazz. Tommy the pup slept in his box by my side, occasionally making doggy noises.

It felt good being there. I guess it reminded me of when I was their age, before all this grown-up crap took its toll, and I found something I could get good at. Jazz lasted twenty minutes, by which time his turquoise vest was navy with sweat and his chest heaved up and down. He touched a shaky fist with Ricky's and the two kids removed their head-guards.

'OK,' I said. 'Now you're warmed up, let's look at technique.'

With my good hand, I worked with Jazz on the bags and pads, doing combinations, tapping out rhythms. For a newbie, he wasn't bad – heavy-handed, perhaps, but the spark was there, the bite. It just needed refinement.

Ricky watched from the periphery, doing his own thing with medicine balls and skipping, until eventually he came and sat by the bench.

When Tommy the pup began stirring, I gave Ricky the box to hold on his knees. A moment later, Jazz and I turned as Ricky yelled out, 'What the fuck!'

He'd shoved the box on to the bench and was standing and grimacing at a soggy patch on his sweatpants. Tommy had pissed on him through the cardboard.

'Take it as a compliment,' I said. 'Means he likes you.'

Ricky kissed his teeth, but I saw the crack of a smile.

An hour later, I was waiting beneath the club's awning while the boys showered and changed. Tommy was sleeping inside a different box I'd dug out from the office, which I'd rested on a ledge.

My collarbone had started aching. I took a couple of codeines with a glug of water, and as I waited for the pills to kick in, I listened to the patter of rain, the puppy's breathing, and watched the skin of the night above.

At the sound of the doors, I turned. Jazz emerged with a sports bag over his shoulder.

'Same time next week?' I said.

His face said it all. 'Definitely.'

Behind him, Ricky was pointing at the box. 'Keep that thing away from me, Kas,' he said, and we all went our separate ways.

I got to Dr Steiner's around nine.

The lounge door was open and I peeked in. She was reclining in her armchair, smoking, immersed in an Iris Murdoch paperback. At the sound of my boots, she looked up.

I'd been cagey around her all week. After getting discharged from hospital, I'd told her everything that had happened, omitting the horrific details of Marmite's death, but stressing my culpability. It was my fault, and nothing would make up for his loss. As a result, I'd be leaving the house as soon as I found somewhere affordable, which I now had. That very morning, I'd paid a two-week deposit for a bedsit in Edmonton. I just needed to pack, book an Uber and get gone.

To my surprise, I heard Dr Steiner say, 'Good evening, Kasper. Come in and sit for a moment.'

Tentatively, I walked into the lounge, holding the box containing Tommy. 'Evening,' I said.

'And what have we here?' she said, looking at the box.

I rested it by her feet. 'He's from Diane. Because of Marmite . . .'

I removed the lid. The puppy's head stuck out like a periscope. He gazed at this strange new world with wide, incredulous eyes.

'Good grief,' Dr Steiner said, placing her cigarette in an ashtray and leaning down. 'What a creature.'

Delicately, she held him under his front two paws and lifted him on to her lap. He settled immediately and began sniffing her hand as she stroked his ears and brow.

'Has he got a name?'

'I was thinking of Tommy. If you like it?'

'Hello, Tommy,' Dr Steiner said. 'It's a pleasure to make your acquaintance.'

He licked his mouth.

I left them to make friends and went to the kitchen, where I poured some of the milk Diane gave me into a saucer. As I came back in, Tommy leaped down, scuttled towards me and began slurping.

'How are you, Kasper?' Dr Steiner said, a fresh smoke on the go.

'I've found a place to rent,' I said, avoiding her eyes. 'I'll just get my stuff.'

'And what do you plan to do?'

'Get settled. And look for work.'

'Back as a barman?'

I shook my head. 'McGovern's is finished. And besides, I fancy something different.'

'Returning to the police, you mean?'

Another headshake. 'It's not for me.'

'What then?'

I looked at Tommy. After devouring the milk, he'd discovered Marmite's old cushion by the lounge door. He sniffed it from different angles, trotted in a circle and curled himself into it, staring reverentially at us both from his new-found bed.

'Saul Berkowitz sent me some money,' I said.

'So?'

'It got me thinking. What if I did this kind of thing for a living?'

'What do you mean?'

'You know, working privately for people, when they need a bit of help.'

She took two deep drags, one after the other, and blew out a curl of yellowish smoke. Then she stubbed out the cigarette and removed the filter from her holder.

'Well,' she said, 'you do seem to have an aptitude for "this kind of thing", as you put it. And I suspect you're ready for a new challenge.'

I nodded.

She looked away, then back at me and smiled. 'I've been thinking too.' She paused. 'This business about you leaving.' There was hesitancy to her voice, something I'd rarely heard. 'The fact of the matter is, you're settled here, aren't you?' She paused again. 'So I've decided, you don't have to go. If you don't want to, that is. If you do, that's fine too. Really, it makes no difference to me either way.'

Emotion swelled in my throat. I didn't know what to say.

She was waiting for a response. When I didn't give one, she said, 'Well? Do you want to go, Kasper?'

'No,' I said.

'Then you should stay. And we'll say nothing more of it. Agreed?'

'Thank you, Dr Steiner,' I said. 'I'd like that.'

'So you'd better start making some money pretty sharpish. Your next rent payment is due this Friday. I'm not running a charity here.'

'Understood.'

'Now tell me, how does one begin with a new vocation like the one you're planning?'

I started laughing. 'I have no idea.'

A little later, Dr Steiner retired to her bedroom. I considered having a Bushmills, but wasn't in the mood just then, and instead brewed some tea. Mug in hand, I walked over to Tommy. He made a dog noise as I put a hand to his brow, then carried on snoring as I made my way to the back of the house.

I slid open the conservatory doors and stepped on to the patio. The air was fresh and smelled of the day's rain and freshly cut lawns; above me, wispy clouds were floating past a bleached crescent moon. As I watched them, I let the past few weeks play out in my mind.

I'd meant what I said to Saul – I wished it had been me who'd killed Vincent, not him. But maybe it was good that he did it. Killing might bring some retribution for Tommy's loss.

Whereas with Rosie, that door will always hang open. To this day, I still had no idea why she did it. She just did.

Christ, I missed her. Five years on, and it hurt more than ever.

And along with her, I missed the man I could've been, and the life I might've had, if she'd just fucking lived.

As if on cue, my phone started vibrating. I rested my mug on a windowsill and pulled it from my pocket.

It was a text from Suzanna, Paddy's daughter. It read:

Hi Kasper,

How are you?

Aunt Sharon and me are going through Dad's things. Would you like to come over and help us? Be nice to see you.

X

My chest tightened. Before I could think myself out of it, I typed back:

OK.

Thirty seconds later, another landed. She'd messaged me a smiley-face thing, like the ones Tommy used.

Feeling strangely subdued, I returned the phone to my pocket and had a rummage around. Amidst keys and loose change, there was a silky metal object. After Diane's visit that afternoon, I'd taken it from the allotment hut, not entirely sure of the reason.

Now I knew.

It was the sole bullet from my Beretta. I pulled it out, and held it aloft between thumb and forefinger. It looked harmless, a strange, anodyne thing, shiny and smooth. How many times had it been locked and loaded, inches from my temple, ready to explode?

I swung my arm back and lobbed the bullet far and high, aiming for the moon. I sensed more than saw it arc somewhere, maybe heading into one of the neighbouring gardens. I half expected a crash of glass or a burglar alarm to go off like in some bad comedy film. Instead, there was a swish of leaves.

It was gone.

Acknowledgements

Thanks to –

My agent, Gordon Wise, plus Curtis Brown's Niall Harman, Lisa Babalis, Anna Davis, Jack Hadley, Katie Smart, Charlotte Mendelson and all the crew from our three-month course; then there's the writers, Tony Parsons, Jake Arnott, Andrew Taylor, Mark Billingham and Amer Anwar, to name a few; trusted beta readers Scott Maynard, Jo Malone, Liz Prinz, Niamh Ni Longain and Megan Davis; Dea Parkin at Fiction Feedback, Aliya Gulamani from Unbound, copy-editor Jill Cole and for her proof-reading skills, Tara O'Sullivan; Aki Shiltz and co. at TLC, and all the wonderful people at Spread the Word, Ruth, Bobby, and my fellow LWA authors from the 2019 cohort; Allison Arekion, Helen Middup, Jose Michel, Nigel Yard, David Hamilton and everyone else I've worked with at Camden and Islington NHS Foundation Trust, in particular the CDAT and Camden AMHP teams, you guys rock; more recently, there's Jack Butler at Wildfire, for his belief; lastly, to my parents, partner and son, for all you've done and continue to do.